Praise for
Blackbird Whistling

"The writing, both witty and deeply introspective, invites readers to reflect on life's twists and turns. Amidst the backdrop of a transformative motivational seminar and the stark beauty of Duluth's landscapes, the story explores family secrets, the pain of past decisions, and the liberating power of second chances. This book isn't just a story; it's an invitation to embrace change, find strength in vulnerability, and celebrate the courage it takes to rewrite one's destiny."

—Shavaun Scott, author of *Nightbird*

"In *Blackbird Whistling*, Dian Greenwood weaves a masterful story of intergenerational trauma and the unforeseen terrain of renewal. Marta Bufford, a successful divorce attorney, seeks peace at a meditation retreat after her spouse cheats on her. But instead she discovers much more about the truth. When her granddaughter Jennifer arrives with her own secrets, their trek together—from the frosty beaches of Lake Superior to the sun-baked cemeteries of North Dakota—becomes a marvelous study of how we inherit both our ancestors' strength and their unfinished business. Greenwood deftly mixes the past and the present to highlight how the stories we tell ourselves may trap us and how the ones we expose can set us free. This novel is a wise, compassionate tale about women finding their way back to themselves and to each other.."

—MM Desch, author of *Tangled Darkness*

"Dian Greenwood takes readers on a rollicking ride with generations of strong women who try to find their rightful place in an often confusing and uncharitable world, as seen through the lens of today's challenges and yesterday's hardships."

—Nancy Townsley, author of *Sunshine Girl*

"Blackbirds are often seen as symbols of transformation and renewal—all of which await Marta in *Blackbird Whistling*, Dian Greenwood's poignant and powerful novel. At the apex of midlife, yet caught in a pending divorce, Marta retreats to a meditation center in search of solace. What begins as a quiet escape becomes an unexpected road trip with her granddaughter—back to North Dakota where Marta was born and home to her immigrant ancestors. Told with vivid imagery and emerging insight, Marta's journey reveals generational secrets along the matrilineal line, unearthing family histories that echo the familiar desire of women to claim their voice and agency."

—Judy Reeves, author of *When Your Heart Says Go*

BLACKBIRD WHISTLING

BLACKBIRD WHISTLING

DIAN GREENWOOD

Travelers Moon Press
Portland, Oregon

Printed in the United States

ISBN 9798989510337

1 2 3 4 5 6 7 8 9 10

To Grace & Madison

There is the beauty of the moment
And of the moment gone
I do not know which to prefer . . . .

from "Thirteen Ways of Looking at a Blackbird"
by Wallace Stevens

Part I

Chapter One

Sunday, June 9, 2002

RIGHT TO LIFE SIGNS TOWER over the highway at predictable five-mile intervals. Some show deformed fetuses encased in blackened wombs. In others they hang lifeless from photoshopped nooses. I glance up, then quickly look away. There's a racing in my chest that isn't supposed to be there. I know I'm not in California where these signs wouldn't exist. Frustrated and angry, I miss the red and blue lights behind me until the officer has practically climbed onto my rear bumper.

Dammit. I pull over to the gravel shoulder. My hands shake while I fiddle with the glove box latch. My wallet with my driver's license lies buried inside the chaos of my purse. My fingers brush against the egg sack, Oma's Easter egg. Part of the agenda for this trip. Finally I find the car rental papers and clutch them in my hand with my license. Of course I look younger in the photo. A short pixie cut, rimless glasses, my narrow face with Daddy's high cheekbones. Mom's straight nose. My only other speeding ticket? Thirty years ago, driving the girls to Yosemite on an ill-conceived vacation.

The officer, with gray hair cut close to the scalp and wearing trademark aviators, stares down at me. If he had a hat, he left it in his car. "You must be in a heck of a hurry," he says. "Eighty-five in a sixty-five-mile zone."

From two feet away, I smell cigarettes. My eyes on his hands hanging on to his hips. His fingers are long; the gray hair that is absent on his head fans across the tops of his knuckles. The nails cut close. If I keep my eyes there, I won't obsess about what this is going to cost.

"Sorry, Officer," I say. "I've had some bad luck getting to Duluth. You know, June lightning storms in Denver."

I hold my pink wallet in my lap and shove my driver's license, along with the car rental papers, through the top four inches of the driver's side window. The doors remain on automatic lock. You can't trust anyone these days.

"Don't go anywhere," he says.

Damn. Nothing but the flat Minnesota landscape falling away from the highway in all directions. The blue sky, expansive and yawning along with the blackbirds on telephone lines leave me feeling more alone than I could have imagined. Oma warned me that this feathered fowl is a mixed omen. I pull out my cell phone. Three voicemails from Stan, probably anxious about the divorce settlement now that he's received my counteroffer. Another from my secretary, Joanne: "Jason's demanding discovery, and all the depositions fell through for next week." Another from Jennifer, number-one granddaughter in Madison: "Have a surprise for you, Oma."

My finger holds the off button until my phone goes dark. Can't I run away just once? And those flashing lights, that cop, why is he taking so long?

I can't help seeing Stan pace in front of the fireplace. That visual has been an obsession the last two months, ever since we were having drinks in the living room, my stocking feet on the coffee table. I should have known something was wrong. Stan had been moping for days, reluctant to make plans for our fortieth wedding anniversary. I kept thinking he was bored in retirement now that his glory days were over.

"That young activist you met at the gun show? Do you remember her?" he asked.

"Not really," I said.

"Long black hair, curly," he said. "I introduced you."

"All I remember is we had no business being there with all those gun activists overtaking the parking lot." I picked up my drink, the Scotch slow to do its job. "I barely remember her, Stan."

He sat on the edge of the hassock in front of me. An intensity constricted his face, the freckles now blending with age spots and his eyes growing smaller all the time. "She's my friend," he said. "Actually, she's more than my friend."

The deadweight in my stomach shouldn't have been a surprise. "Your lover?"

One of those moments when there are no words. Not *what the hell are you saying?* and not *when did this happen?* I'd grown used to his dalliances with younger women, but this was different. The timing was shocking considering I was in the middle of my biggest-ever trial.

"I'm flying to Reno at the end of the week." He hesitated and his voice dropped until I could hardly hear him. "I'll get a quiet divorce there. All you have to do is sign the papers."

Before I knew what happened, my drink was in the air and in his face, running down his Hawaiian shirt and onto his neatly pressed trousers. My voice was hoarse and shook with disbelief. "After nearly forty years of marriage, this is your idea of a surprise party?" My feet on the floor, I was up and off the sofa while he sat dripping with my Scotch. "How convenient! Everything carefully planned and never a word to me before now. What kind of coward are you? Besides, who the hell do you think you're talking to? Or have you forgotten you're married to one of the best divorce attorneys on the West Coast?"

He wiped at the Scotch under his eyes and dripping off his chin. "You're never home. We stopped fucking years ago. You don't need me to escort you to the symphony or to cocktail parties. You should feel relieved."

To quote my best friend, Nancy, this was the five-minute conversation forever memorialized.

I laughed. Really laughed. It wasn't the kindest or most appropriate response. I didn't care. I am who I am. Smart and powerful and tough. This soap opera happens to other people.

The look on Stan's face reminded me of a disappointed child. The sad eyes, the hanging-down mouth. He thought he'd finally gotten to me.

"Is this a guy thing?" I asked. "About sex after sixty? About needing to prove you're still your own man?"

He let his head drop. A familiar gesture. He'd given up so many times before.

"Do you have any idea what you're getting yourself into if you go through with this? Or is this some goddamn midlife crisis happening too late? You need to get over yourself, Stan. You'll never come out of this without significant scar tissue."

"I'm tired of waiting around for you," he said. He was sputtering now and, finally, mad. Maybe the reality was sinking in for him. Not for me. My heart had fallen into my toes. And shaking my head didn't seem to clear what I'd just heard. Then, the zinger: "For your information, Rita is pregnant . . . with my child." Red in the face, his blood pressure already elevated, his lips bubbled like the little boy he once was. All I remember is that my shoes were still under the coffee table when I left the room. Big emotional scenes are never my friend. Not even the possibility of vengeance erased the uproar inside me.

If Nancy hadn't promised that this seminar leader and Duluth would deliver me from my recently decayed marriage, I wouldn't be here now. All these weeks later, I'm still shocked that Stan finally tipped me over. I thought I was insulated against sorrow.

The cop feeds my license and rental papers along with the yellow ticket through the cracked-open window. "San Diego," he says. "Haven't been there since the navy." He laughs, making the coffee or cigarette stains on his teeth more apparent. "That was a few years ago."

I paste on a smile, glad for my sunglasses.

He stands beside the car door, his hip cocked at an angle. "Have to give you something, lady," he says. "Eighty-five costs an easy three hundred, so I took it down to seventy-five. Half the other ticket."

"Thanks, Officer," I say. "Appreciate it."

I turn over the ignition and the headlights flip on. I wait for the officer to walk back to his patrol car and turn off his flashers. He makes an abrupt U-turn, gunning his car in the opposite direction.

I'm pissed. The trip has already cost me two days of the seminar and the added expense of sleeping in Denver's last available room, as bad as the Bates Motel. Orange shag carpet and a broken dead bolt. The parking lot was nothing but construction trucks. The guy next door was busy humping someone; I could hear the bed banging against the wall. Across the courtyard the Marguerite Café played brass horns and guitars until the bar closed at two. Not one friendly woman in sight, not any woman for that matter. Yes, I'm tired. Frustrated. I can stay mad, or I can do what Oma would do. *Be grateful for the small things*, she'd say. I say those words out loud, just to hear them. I only have fifty-eight miles to go. The sun is shining, the car is comfortable, and I can write off the entire seminar. If it's a complete bust, I'll fly to Madison and spend the week with my granddaughter, Jennifer. She'll be glad to see me.

WITH CLEAR VISIBILITY AHEAD, THE highway is dotted with signs to lakes I can't see and stands of trees shielding back road towns hardened by winters that go on too long. The Dakotas where I grew up those first years are never far from memory. Here, there are just enough similarities. When I pull into Duluth the houses, the hills, and the main downtown might as well be indentured servants bowing to the cold, unmerciful gray of Lake Superior. Farther north, storm clouds are turning black with the threat of heavy rain. Another bad omen.

At the Union Hotel the doorman gathers my luggage and car keys. He leads the way to the elevator. On the sixth floor he swings open the door of 616. Inside, the floor-to-ceiling windows are visible through long, filmy drapes, which blow back into the room from the same icy wind that tunnels through the hotel lobby. Everything in the room is neat and white, the way Oma and Mom would have loved. The room service menu has been strategically placed on the small table beside a comfy chair. I spot the coffeepot and open the refrigerator to a fully stocked bar. I'm immediately sorry I missed last night.

By the time I shower and change and have lunch sent to my room, it's two o'clock with enough time for a nap before the late-afternoon gathering at the university president's house. Swaddled in the hotel's terry robe, I pull the comforter around my feet and turn the table lamp on low.

When I wake from inside my cocoon, two hours have passed. I sit up, nearly panicked. For a moment I don't know where I am. Neither do I recall the ham sandwich or the tall local beer until I see the empty plate and glass on the small table. Four o'clock. The afternoon party at the university president's house started an hour ago. Damn! I pride myself on never being late.

What to wear, how to find the place, take a cab or should I drive? Too many decisions when I'd prefer to lie in my robe and wait for room service to deliver an evening salad, maybe a piece of fish, and the liter of wine I ordered from the doorman. There's the refrigerator, glasses, a corkscrew. Everything I need is right here.

Chapter Two

I'VE WORN THE WRONG SHOES for the long gravel driveway. Ahead of me and surrounded by eight-foot shrubs rises a white two-story Cape Cod with a double front door painted the green of Irish clover. I'd have suggested tomato red, but it's not my door. First I raise the brass knocker, a lion's mouth open and ready for the kill. When no one comes, I try the door; it's unlocked.

Beyond the entryway, folks—probably from Minnesota, their skin the color of long Northern winters—mingle in an open living room with floral sofas. There are folded quilts draped across the arms. The coziness seems consistent with the long, low coffee table that's seen better days. Glancing toward the sofas, I notice open bottles of wine set up on a dining room sideboard. Another table is crowded with near-empty salad and buffet dishes.

"I'm Emily Blunt, the president's wife," says a white-haired woman who approaches from inside the crowd. She takes my hands in hers. "Are you the missing participant?"

"Got caught in travel mishaps," I say.

Emily is a tall and elegant woman with a warm, steady gaze, her sea-green eyes matching her cottage-comfortable home. The warmth of her fingers and the way she holds my hands feels like they are being lifted in prayer, the way Oma used to hold my hands. It's like Oma is here today, cheering me on and saying, *You can start over again; I did it.* She meant learning to drive in 1946 so she could sell her kuchen at a local restaurant.

Emily slowly drops my hands. "You likely haven't met Roland yet. He's the seminar leader."

We pass the wine bar, but there's no chance to stop and fill a glass. She leads me toward a thin, ancient man, his skin dark and wrinkled. A kind of déjà vu swirls in my memory, some inkling that I've met him before. Maybe Nancy showed me a photo, but that was of a much younger man. This man is so small he seems weighed down by his full white hair. He sits on the far end of a sofa. Folks my daughters' and granddaughters' ages are gathered around his feet on large cushions.

Emily bends down close to his ear. "Roland," I hear her say. "This is your missing student. She just arrived."

I note Roland's intense focus on the long-haired young woman in front of him. The slow withdrawal of his attention is an apology itself. His gaze turns upward toward me as if I'm the only person in the room. "Glad you made it."

I bend at the waist and take the hand he offers, his ringed fingers mere bones with only a soft and very thin skin protecting them. His glance, steady and unflinching, makes me uncomfortable. I start to pull my hand back, but he doesn't let go.

My stomach aches with disappointment. I'd hoped for someone younger and more attractive like in Nancy's photo or the one on the internet. Yet his calm manner eases my immediate discomfort. When he smiles, the deep wrinkles and heavy eyelids reduce his eyes to mere slits. "Your place has been empty."

A flush warms my face.

"You thought you wouldn't be missed?" he says. His eyes water when he speaks. "Only seventy-four have found their seats in the auditorium; now there are seventy-five. Finally we are complete."

"I'm sorry if I kept you waiting."

"We start where we are," he says.

People around us stare, some smile. "Thank you," I say, though I'm not sure what I'm thanking him for.

He squeezes my fingers. "What do I call you?" he asks.

I withdraw my hand. "Marta," I say.

I RETREAT TO THE MAKESHIFT bar with its array of wine bottles and pour myself a glass of Chablis. *He will change how you see your life*, Nancy had said. *See*, an interesting word choice. She went on to say that it's time to angle my view in a different direction and reclaim the dreams of the twentysomething woman I was when we were both in college. To find again the woman who dreamed of bicycling through Europe, who had her heart set on living in Manhattan. Now Nancy's telling me it's time to return to poetry and drama, maybe act in a local play. In other words, take back all of who I once was.

On the sun porch I find a wicker chair in the corner. Few have come out here, likely because of the chill. The late-afternoon light seems so gray this far north, yet a single sunray slants across the grass. Children play croquet and squeal each time they manage to get the ball through a hoop or lose their ball in the hydrangeas. The white wine, sweeter than I like, warms the jitters of being a stranger among strangers. It's a surprising response I don't understand. I'm usually the first to extend my hand and introduce myself. This sudden shyness is peculiar for someone used to holding a courtroom in absolute silence during an argument. At least the wine soothes the strange discomfort. I feel more like myself.

"Emily said I might find you here."

The man's close-cropped gray hair reminds me of a runner or bicyclist, though he's too meaty for either. My eye measures him at six feet or six-one. He motions for me to remain seated. "She said you'd finally found us."

He extends a muscular hand. "I'm Gilbert Russell. From California just like you. Long Beach."

He could be my age or ten years younger. His well-tanned skin indicates someone who likes the outdoors. "How did *you* find your way to Lake Superior?" I ask.

"Originally through friends."

Why I feel self-conscious, I'm not sure. Maybe it's my covered chest in a room filled with young cleavage. Or the heavy turquoise necklace at my throat, a dead giveaway for women my age. My laugh sounds strangely nervous, forced. "My friend Nancy Dillon neglected to tell me about summers in Duluth."

"I understand you're staying at the Union Hotel," he says. "I think we're the only ones there."

"Where are the others staying?" I ask.

"Here on campus in the dorms."

"Thank heavens I was spared that," I laugh. "I don't know about you, but I'm quite happy at the hotel."

He keeps looking over his shoulder as though he's expecting someone. He turns again in my direction. His gray eyes. My attention there. An awkwardness that isn't mine.

"Would you care for a glass of wine?" I ask.

"No thanks," he says. "I've had enough soda water to float away."

An uncomfortable silence follows. "I assume you've been here from the beginning," I say. "What did I miss?"

He pulls at his ear. A part of the lobe is missing, as though it was cut off at an odd angle. "I'm part of the staff. I sometimes coteach with Roland."

"Oh," I say. "He's charming. How old is he?"

"He's ninety-two and quite healthy."

"Today, folks live into their early hundreds," I say. "Work, like retirement, doesn't have to start and stop with a certain number." I need to eat or get out of here before I have another glass of wine.

Gilbert tips his head in a way that could be a salute to my seemingly wise comment, or it could be the bored response of a know-it-all. I notice his right earlobe again. A slight half-moon remains where a flap of skin should hang down. "I don't think life ever stops, do you?" he asks.

I'm still trying to take that in when he says, "Excuse me."

He leaves me to talk to a young woman, blond with large hoop earrings. I suddenly feel old and less attractive compared to these young people. How ridiculous! Here I am, a successful attorney in her early sixties, obsessing over cleavage and long blond hair when I should be questioning what happened to my longtime marriage. Would I return to Stan if given the chance? I'm less sure now that I'm this far away. I know myself well enough that I'd never forgive him if that counts for anything. I will not let Stan's shenanigans or being scared about what comes next get in the way of having this week to myself. And who the hell is this Long Beach guy who made such an aborted effort to be nice?

Gilbert returns to where I'm sitting. His easy smile has disappeared while his attention, once generous, has gone somewhere else too. "I'm sorry to rush off. It's been a long day."

What was pleasant on first meeting is now annoying. "Right," I say, my tone droll. "See you tomorrow."

I drain what's left in my wineglass and return to the buffet table. I scoop what salad is left, the remnants of what was once a small sandwich, and some fruit onto a paper plate. I return to the quiet porch where I focus on the kids and their croquet game. The sky has turned to slate, a color matching the cold breeze disturbing what could have been a pleasant afternoon under other circumstances.

I devour the meager leftovers and down another glass of too-sweet wine before calling the number on the card the cabbie gave me.

When I stand to leave, I realize I should have anticipated that Emily would be vigilant about movement toward the front door. "You're not leaving already?" she asks.

"I am. Thank you for the afternoon," I say. If my snarky tone leaks out and betrays me, I can blame it on being tired. "I need to say goodbye to the man in charge. Roland."

I pivot in the direction of the old man, surprised he didn't leave with his first lieutenant. No longer surrounded by his followers, he's busy talking to a young woman. I overhear him say, "All that matters is the breath. The outbreath in particular. We're always preparing for that final moment."

The seminar leader notices me standing at a respectful distance. His eyes meet mine, and he smiles the half smile I saw when we met. "See you in the morning," I say.

He again reaches for my hands, this time caressing the fingers with his own bony ones, his index finger running over the top of the wedding band I haven't yet removed. When he releases my hand, he bows his head. Puts his hands together in namaste. "Until then."

Purse over my shoulder, I head toward the front door. This wasn't the gathering I had hoped for. A strange pair of men. So far I'm failing to grasp what Nancy saw in them. *He'll change the way you see your life.* Like a mantra, it keeps ringing in my mind. For now, what's important is the hotel's terry cloth robe and a room service menu. Surely the doorman has delivered the wine I ordered.

Chapter Three

Hope your time away helps. Stan. The note nestles inside the basket of fruit and bottle of champagne that crowds the table in my room. Helps with what? In all our years of marriage, he's never sent a gift to my hotel. Why now when he's renounced *us*?

I place the champagne in the refrigerator and reach for the cold bottle of Kendall-Jackson I ordered. I pour a glass of wine. Finally I can relax.

Those early years when Stan worked summers in a fire tower for the US Forest Service, I often sneaked a picnic supper up those insane stairs where he lived atop the tall steel structure. One night thunder echoed too close, and lightning struck all around us, hitting the tower. I'd swear that's the night Kelsey was conceived. The lightning probably explains why she's so fiery and has an ever-difficult personality.

A second glass of wine. I lie back against the pillows, struck by another memory. Those first ballet lessons when I was seven. The awkwardness and out-of-body feeling when I tried to bend into a plié, then hold it. Not unlike my experience this evening at the university president's home. I recall that then I could hardly stand in fourth position. I always waited with dread for Miss Nelson's voice or her firm hand against my back or leg, always redirecting me. I worried that I'd never perform the graceful leaps of advanced students who streaked across the practice room. In the same way my pink shoes and tights never made me a ballerina, Duluth probably isn't going to give me a new life.

I'm jolted out of my reverie when the hotel phone rings.

"Oma?"

"Jennifer. I didn't expect to hear from you so soon."

"I'm downstairs in the hotel lobby."

Damn lumps in my throat. "What are you doing here?"

"Thought you'd be happy I saved you the trip to Madison. Instead, I came to stay with you in Duluth."

Before I can stop myself, I say, "But I just got here."

"What do you mean, you just got here?"

"I was stranded in Denver for nearly two days."

"Wow," she says. Then, without a breath, "Think I can bunk with you?"

"Bunk with me?"

"Yeah. Summer break. I've got three nights off from my summer job, including tonight."

This isn't happening. I've just endured the worst travel nightmare and managed the obligatory appearance by going to the president's party. Now Jennifer, even if she is my darling granddaughter, wants to "bunk with me"?

"I'm used to sharing, Oma. I live in a dorm, remember?"

Of course it's no big deal. Most young people fly through their lives from one impulse to the next, no destination too sacred or remote as long as it satisfies the appetite. Didn't I do that?

"Just to warn you, I have a terrible headache and have already taken a sleeping pill," I say. "I hope you're ready for lights out and some extra shut-eye. We can catch up tomorrow."

"No problem," she says. "I have a book with me."

No problem. My tattooed, multiple-earringed granddaughter with spiky pink hair who chose University of Wisconsin–Madison over Amherst. In truth, I haven't quite forgiven her for choosing fun over academics, for not following my advice and going to Amherst, where I wish I'd gone. Instead, I did my prelaw at San Jose State, more convenient for the mother of a two-year-old and a husband just starting his law practice. That was just the beginning of putting my own dreams on hold. And, clearly, the seething resentment since that afternoon with Stan two months ago.

The rest of the wine goes down too fast. I take the glass into the bathroom where I rinse and carefully wrap it in one of the clean hand towels. I place it in the drawer with my underwear. Why I'm self-conscious about drinking alone puzzles me. Maybe wine has moved too quickly from being a social lubricant to becoming an anxiety intervention.

The minute I open the door, I see my granddaughter in an oversized jean jacket, the standing collar outlining her pink hair. Add tattered jeans and boots: the costume of someone who rides her bicycle to and from class every day with a backpack permanently fixed to her back. She is definitely more prepared for the weather than I am.

"Isn't it lucky we could both be in Duluth?" Jennifer asks.

I caress the shoulders of my unexpected guest and don't miss the patchouli oil or marijuana in my granddaughter's partly pink hair. "Yes, it is lucky."

Jennifer lowers her backpack. "Look at this," she says. She throws her arms wide. "Wow, this room! You're going first class, Oma."

"Glad you approve."

"That bed's big enough for both of us," she says. "Holy shit, is it ever."

"I was just about to take a bath."

"You don't have any wine or anything, do you?" Jennifer asks. "Since when are you drinking?"

"They usually let me drink at home. I'm old enough."

"Nineteen and away from home for the first time isn't exactly grown-up."

"At nineteen, Oma, you were talking about getting married and were practically pregnant."

Practically. If she only knew. I unwrap the wineglass I just put away and offer it, half-full, to Jennifer.

"Too bad Granddad didn't come with you. He'd have loved it here in the brisk air. Or would it be bad for his emphysema?"

"Not good," I say. "Now, if you'll excuse me, I'm going to take a bath. The remote is on the nightstand."

Jennifer touches my gown-draped arm. Tears cloud her eyes. "I hope this is okay, Oma."

I drop my gown on the chair and pull my granddaughter toward me. "Why these tears?"

Her eyes, the deep blue of her father's, meet mine. I pull her closer, feeling the cold of her coat, the smell of lake wind in her hair.

She squeezes me tighter, and I'm aware for the first time that I haven't been hugged in a long time. We hold each other for a long minute. When I back away, she smiles like she's embarrassed. I climb onto the bed. "Tell me what's going on."

Jennifer's cheeks flush. She blinks nervously. "Promise you won't tell Mom?"

"Is there some kind of trouble?"

"Not trouble exactly," she says. She bites her lower lip, her perfectly straightened teeth a testament to the kind of parental care I never knew.

"To start, I flunked advanced algebra first semester."

"And?"

"I got pregnant."

Jennifer's words explode. Then silence. Shallow breathing.

"And?"

"I had an abortion."

I can't say anything with my breath caught halfway in my throat. I recall a similar long-ago conversation with my own mother, long after the fact, and I wonder if I'm wearing Mom's look of horror. Her disappointment.

"Are you mad at me?"

"No, of course not. Why would I be mad at you?" I take a deep breath. "Maybe sad for you."

"Because I'm a disappointment?" Jennifer asks.

I reach behind her shoulders and pull her against my terry robe, marveling that I can be so calm. I stare toward the closed drapes, our feet, mine and Jennifer's, covered by the white coverlet. In front of me is the memory of my own half-drugged self, groping one step at a time out of that awful clinic. Aunt Ada held my arm, cursing under her breath.

"Are you disappointed in yourself?" I ask.

She shakes her head back and forth, stifling a sob. "I guess what I want is for you to . . ." She hesitates. Tears layer inside her blue eyes.

"Forgive you?"

She turns away. The sob deep in her throat finally arrives, and an outpouring of tears falls on my white robe.

I pull her tighter. "Of course I forgive you," I say. "Why wouldn't I?"

I take her hand in mine, feeling the wetness on her fingers. We are silent for what seems a long time. "You aren't the first woman in our family who had to make that decision."

"Who, Oma?"

I turn to face her, the knot in my throat too big. A particular heat behind my eyes. I make myself look at her. "I was nineteen, your age."

"Oh, no," she says, her eyes wide, her lashes wet. "Was it Granddad?"

"No, it wasn't Granddad."

The silence of *oh my God* and a knot stuck in my throat threatens to unravel my long-held secret and bypass the numbness I've carried all these years. Everything I never talked about, not to Stan, not to my daughters. The irony of traveling to Tijuana, my back against the white leather upholstery in Aunt Ada's baby blue T-Bird. The so-called nursing home. A doctor who wouldn't make eye contact, his white coat flapping around his legs, his air of business as usual. Aunt Ada held the white envelope before she passed it to him. Afterward, there were strange smells of alcohol and burnt hair. Burnt blood. They were like a halo around me.

"Oma, I'm so sorry." Jennifer's voice breaks, new tears shine on her cheeks. Am I now the one who needs forgiveness?

When she puts her arms around my shoulders, I think I will break in two. The tears and the shame so long in hiding. But I hold on. What started so innocent, so young. A mattress in his parents' basement, the sun on his back and in my eyes. All that *want* needing an escape, a release. Six months later, he lay dead inside a wet rice paddy in Vietnam.

"Can we forgive ourselves?" I finally say.

She shakes her head in affirmation. "We have to."

We're quiet for a long time. She leans in front of my face. "Did he know?"

"No," I say. "He didn't have a chance."

"Did you love him a lot?"

I say nothing at first. "More than I knew," I finally say. "First love and so young, just nineteen, the same as you. He was so eager to sign up as a military advisor in Vietnam, despite my protests and the unspoken fear that he'd never come back. We had such great hopes. How could we know it would end with him dead?"

"What did Great-Grandma say?"

Indeed, what did Irene, my mother, say? Aunt Ada brought me not to the front door but to the kitchen the next morning. Dad was already gone, the way Aunt Ada and I planned it. Mom sat on the living room sofa with her usual after-breakfast coffee and cigarette, watching *Queen for a Day* on the TV.

"Look what the cat dragged in," Mom said. "Why are you so pale?"

She lifted her chin and looked at Aunt Ada more than at me, the old accusatory lines around her narrow chin. "Are you sick?"

"She didn't sleep well," was all Aunt Ada said. "Probably food poisoning. Chinese Wok, you know how dicey that place can be. Think she needs to sleep in her own bed. She'll be good as gold in the morning."

"Well, you look like hell," Mom said. "Better get upstairs. Coffee, Ada?"

Jennifer's hand is warm on my arm, surrounded as we now are, cuddled by pillows and the white coverlet where we lie together on the bed. "She didn't say anything, Jennifer. Truth is, I didn't tell her until years later."

"Why not? Why didn't you tell her?"

"Maybe the same reason you don't want to tell your mom."

I lean forward when she wraps her arms around me. The volcano of emotion threatening to spill forces me to look at the drapes, now quiet with the windows closed.

The sadness I thought was long forgotten has ripened with Stan's leaving. That last time I saw Robert, his duffle bag was slung over his shoulder, his army cap slightly crooked, and the wide smile that always revealed a slight gap between his two front teeth remains. A final blown kiss. His tall back when he walked away.

This silence with Jennifer seems so private and shared at the same time. It seems to go on for a long, long time. When I move to get up from the bed, Jennifer picks up the remote. She doesn't turn on the TV. She just hangs on to the remote. "Oma," she says, "I'm so sorry."

"I am too."

Finally I stand and take a step toward the bathroom. "By the way, what happened when you told your boyfriend?"

Jennifer's face reddens. Her blue eyes change. She stares at the ceiling.

"Well?"

"He isn't a boyfriend," she says. "Not exactly."

"Who is he?"

She picks at a hangnail on her left hand, her nails painted deep purple and not quite as bitten down as in the past. "You have to promise not to tell Mom."

"I can promise that *if* you're honest with me."

"He's my history professor."

"Your what?"

"See, I knew that you wouldn't want to hear it." She jumps off the bed. "I expect disapproval from Mom, but I hoped you'd be different."

"How old is he?"

The silver studs that create a half circle up and down her ears, and the one in her lip, betray her youth. Even more, her innocence.

"Jennifer, that's awful. Is he married?"

Jennifer starts to walk away from the bed. "You promised you wouldn't tell Mom," she says.

Jennifer's arm is tense and solid when I grab hold, the sinewy muscle of a woman at the beginning of her life, someone who knows weights and upper-body machines.

"I wouldn't think of it," I say. I let go of her arm. Without looking at me, Jennifer disappears into the bathroom. She closes and locks the door.

Chapter Four

Monday, June 10

WHEN I WAKE THE NEXT morning, Jennifer lays curled in a ball facing the window away from me. I climb out of bed and tiptoe toward the bathroom. I gather the clothes I laid aside last night and lock the bathroom door. The fan's white noise masks my movements. Having whisked the coffeepot into the bathroom last night, I've just poured my coffee and am bent over the commode to shave my legs when a harsh rap sounds against the door.

"I have to pee."

I throw open the door.

"Sorry, Granny."

"You know I hate that word."

"Granny?" Jennifer rubs her eyes.

Setting aside my shaver, I gather my coffeepot and cup. I'm fuming when I set them on the desk, then return to the bathroom to retrieve my cell phone. Jennifer, her hair spiking on its own, stands watching me, a puzzled or hurt expression on her face.

Once I sit at the desk I grab my cell phone. I'm annoyed beyond words. A college professor plus Stan with his damned messages. Three more, in fact. Hasn't Stan said enough? He's the one who walked out and left me to tell the goddam story. He can damn well read the email I sent him. Here it is, seven forty-five and I don't have directions to the university. Forget breakfast. What the hell is keeping that girl?

Jennifer emerges looking refreshed, her hair wet with new spikes and her face scrubbed clean. "Hope you don't mind, but I used some of your face cream."

"Jennifer, I do mind."

Her eyes widen.

I haven't used this tone since she was a young girl. I soften my voice. "You know why I'm here."

"You're attending a seminar."

"Yes. Two days of which are gone because I couldn't get out of Denver. Point being, I'm disappointed and I'm frustrated." Before she can respond, I raise my hand. "This room was supposed to be a retreat of sorts. That said, I'm thrilled you're here. And you're right. You're saving me a trip to Madison. But right now I need to finish my coffee and dress. Then I'm going downstairs to the front desk to ask about a room you can have to yourself."

"You're just like my mother."

"What's that supposed to mean?"

"You only want me around when it's convenient for you."

I'm stunned. Speechless for a minute or two. "I'm so sorry you feel that way."

Weren't those Stan's words? Is that what my daughters Kelsey and Tara think? They were still in grade school when my practice shifted into high gear. "I hope that isn't true."

"Of course it's true. That's why I wanted to go to school as far away from San Diego as I could get." She turns away. "Now I can't even count on you."

"That's not fair and you know it," I say. "Turn around and look at me."

When Jennifer turns, I'm surprised by her red face. The tears waiting to spill.

I reach out to take her shoulders, but she backs away.

"I'm sorry. You couldn't have known why I came here. And now I've hurt your feelings. You're no doubt still recovering from the procedure." For some reason, I can't say *abortion*. Couldn't say it then, can't say it now.

Jennifer closes her eyes and, again, turns away from me.

"We shared our secrets last night," I say to her back. "In many ways, we're not that different. Wouldn't you agree?"

She turns, her eyes still closed. She nods when she opens them.

"We're here. We'll have plenty of time together. You said it yourself," I say.

Though she steps away, she doesn't break eye contact. "I'd actually prefer staying at the youth hostel near campus."

"Fine. Suit yourself."

Now who's pouting?

"Maybe it's better if we have separate spaces," Jennifer says. "We can always hang out in the evening."

I look down at my feet, more confused than when I came to Duluth. The ongoing ripples of shock over Stan, then the surprise of Jennifer showing up after that weird experience at the president's house. It's clear that my big reaction over her professor lover is the problem. I open my arms and reach toward my granddaughter. "Come here."

She hesitates for a moment, the hurt still alive in her red cheeks.

I hold Jennifer close. "I didn't mean to make you feel unwelcome."

"It's okay, Oma. You weren't expecting me."

"Clearly, there are a lot of things I didn't expect. We'll talk about that later."

She smiles sheepishly. "We can still have dinner or popcorn and movies in your room and maybe we'll even have dinner out," she says. "I can tell you all about Duluth."

Something has happened that's let the air out of our being together. I'm left with the awful feeling that my sharp reactions and quick tongue have once again robbed me of a connection I want and need.

"I'm sorry I didn't ask this before, but are you going to be okay? I mean, did you have a follow-up with a doctor?"

"Don't worry, Oma. It's going to be alright."

I'll have to believe that. I take her hands for reassurance as much as anything. This time, she doesn't look away. "I only want what's best for you."

She smiles. "I know."

There's only the briefest eye contact before I look at my watch. "I have to get ready."

When I emerge from the bathroom, Jennifer has left with all her things. Good. I just wish I hadn't been so ambivalent. It's unlike me, wanting her here and not wanting her here. Then, to have it end on that note.

THE MINUTE I SEE THE doorman's gray uniform, I realize I've forgotten the seminar packet of information in my room. However, when I turn toward the elevator, the door swings open. Gilbert and the ancient teacher, Roland, stand before me.

"Are you coming to this morning's seminar?" Gilbert asks.

"I am." I hold the elevator door. "But I'm on my way back upstairs to get the packet since I don't know where I'm going."

"You don't need the packet," Roland says. "Come with us; we'll take you right there."

I release the elevator door with its infernal buzzing. "I hate to impose."

Gilbert shakes his head. "No imposition," he says. "Roland

and I will have a chance to get to know you better." His smile comes easily this morning. I can't help but wonder why.

Roland's eyes above his half smile appear to penetrate my thoughts. When I pivot away from the elevator to follow the two men, I notice Jennifer down the hallway, two heads shorter than the tall, gray-haired fellow who has his hands on her shoulders. Who leans down to kiss her. Not a daughterly or granddaughterly kiss but the kiss of a man who possesses a woman.

I stare in disbelief. My heart pounds with the kind of heartsickness you read about in bad novels. My granddaughter. This older man. Maybe married. Jennifer's absolute innocence. The abortion.

Gilbert touches my arm. "You know that young woman?"

"She's my granddaughter."

Both Gilbert and Roland stop and turn toward where Jennifer stands inside the older man's arms. "Would you like to invite her to the seminar?" Roland asks.

"Thank you," I say. "I think she has other plans."

"Looks like she does," Gilbert says.

Maybe he has young people in his household who prefer paths and directions he doesn't like or understand. I settle against the butterscotch-colored leather back seat cushion of an older Volvo while Gilbert helps Roland into the front seat. I need to get my mind on the seminar and stop obsessing about a relationship I know nothing about but seems utterly wrong. Hopefully Jennifer didn't see me. Maybe she'll call or text this evening. But the ache in my chest won't stop no matter where I direct my gaze. The doorman. The morning's gray sky. The cold wind that won't let go. Jennifer's face. Those red cheeks and tear-filled blue eyes less than an hour ago.

My hungry stomach churns. No breakfast and now I forgot the energy bar as well.

In the car, Gilbert looks over his shoulder and catches my eye. "Let Roland tell you about the first days," he says.

I lean forward toward the center console as far as my seat belt allows. At least I can pretend I'm here in this car, in this moment.

"We begin each day with ten minutes of meditation," Roland says. "Do you meditate, Mrs. Bufford?"

"Please call me Marta," I say. "Yes, I've had some experience meditating." Not to my liking, especially after Nancy talked me into an eight-week course at an ashram across town. I quickly tired of the so-called guru who needed to prove himself cool by throwing around four-letter words including the f-bomb.

"It's an easy practice," Roland says. "Just think of a sentence you particularly like. It can be from a prayer, a poem, something that inspires you. Anything that evokes the sense of a higher order. Or, as the traditionalists do, you can just watch your breath."

After spending over five-thousand dollars—counting the seminar, hotels, and misguided air travel—I've come this far so I can recall some obscure line from God knows what in order to meditate?

"Let's take 'easy come, easy go.' That's a good place to start," Roland says. "Close your eyes and I'll guide you."

"Okay," I say. I lean back against the worn leather. But when I close my eyes, I'm jumpy and nervous.

"Slowly, begin to say 'easy come, easy go' to yourself, repeating the phrase as you breathe. 'Easy come' on the inbreath, 'easy go' on the outbreath. I will use the same phrase and meditate with you. We'll do this for five minutes."

I try to concentrate, but I keep seeing Jennifer and that tall, bearded man in the hotel lobby. The thought that Jennifer might have planned this whole thing long before I came to Duluth saddens me. At least I didn't give her my room key. I'd never forgive her if she took that cradle robber up there.

I force myself, using my law practice tricks, to rid myself of that image. *Easy come, easy go.* Two groups of words, one group advancing, the other retreating. But as soon as I say *easy go*, Stan's face looks at me through my wedding veil. His blue eyes pleading and so full of hope. My smile, tears in my eyes. I was so young, so afraid. I was only twenty-two. I couldn't get the thought of my ex-boyfriend Robert's military funeral out of my head. Even behind my smile as I faced Stan, I could still hear the sound of military taps. I wanted to—had to—believe this marriage to Stan was meant to be. That Stan would change my sadness into joy I didn't yet feel. That our life together would blot the past and a new baby would change everything.

I open my eyes and see several four-story brick buildings that stand out on broad lawns among the rolling hills of the university campus.

"How are you doing back there?" Roland asks.

"Not too well," I say.

"Good," he says.

I lean forward. "Why *good*?"

Gilbert swings into a parking space marked Restricted.

Roland stares ahead. "If it doesn't go well in the beginning, it's easier to feel successful next time. You've already experienced the worst of it."

Chapter Five

GILBERT OPENS THE BACK DOOR and takes my hand. His long, slender fingers are firm and confident as he helps me out of the back seat. I'm trying to remember the last time a man treated me with such courtesy. He's probably gay. Maybe he's Roland's lover.

There's hardly anyone walking the sidewalks or hanging out on the green lawns that spread between the fifties-style brick buildings. Almost a dozen similar buildings scatter across what appears to be acres of green lawn. Retro, many people would call it. The air is sunny but cold, the wind off the lake still reaching this far inland from the shore.

Inside the fluorescent-lighted hallway, magenta and lime and sapphire-blue posters campaign for study groups and Greek rush while obscuring the otherwise gray walls. Elevators wait unceremoniously on one side of the enormous passageway.

"We're going in the back way," Gilbert says.

When we exit the elevator, a crowd is waiting. Immediately those who see Roland gather around him, and Gilbert moves ahead, clearing the way by extending his long arm while his other hand grips Roland's arm. "Let's just get him into the auditorium," Gilbert says to no one in particular. He glances over his shoulder. "Follow me, Marta."

Who is this guy? I feel myself getting annoyed. One moment this man fulfills the old-fashioned word *gallant*, and the next he shouts orders with a sergeant's precision. I can't help but wonder if that's who I am when I'm in my office and my poor paralegal is attempting to help me prepare for trial.

I walk closely behind Roland, respecting his pace. His cane reaches out in front of him as he steps forward with one foot then the other. He nods at the folks pressing around us with his usual half smile. I remind myself there's no reason to be angry with him.

As we near the double doors, two large men dressed in black open one door wide enough for our small party of three to enter. Gilbert nods to the mustached member of the pair. "Would you please bring me a seminar packet?" he asks. He nods in my direction. Once we're through the door, each participant behind us is stopped and checked for a photo ID and to have their purses and backpacks searched. Not me. I'm with the top brass.

The semi-dark lecture hall holds about a hundred seats in a half-moon circle. Those few inside wait in near silence, perhaps meditating already. The group's size doesn't surprise me as much as the number of folks under thirty. The rows of seats graduate upward until they end below a windowed projection booth. On the stage, a comfy beige leather chair sits on a small Oriental rug beside a table with a lamp, water pitcher, and a single glass. The lectern, standing behind the chair and to the side, has been draped with an embroidered Asian or East Indian cloth, the red threads shining under the single spotlight. Gilbert walks Roland to the chair. He arranges a pillow for Roland before setting his cane aside.

Without warning, the screen behind the single chair is backlit, revealing giant photographs of Roland projected against the walls. Roland with dark hair, Roland with two black Labradors. Roland graying. Roland sitting alone on a giant cushion surrounded by bronze statues. At an ashram, most likely. Roland with someone who appears to be an East Indian dignitary. Roland in front of the Taj Mahal.

"Marta, why don't you sit in the front row with me," Gilbert says. His eyes are intense with a sense of duty.

I simply want to disappear, to become as anonymous as possible. Jennifer's tearful face is still in front of me—the smudged mascara, the rawness of our new connection. Then she left so abruptly. How would I have known that detestable man might have something to do with why she came? That it likely has nothing to do with me. The sting of that thought sits behind my eyes.

Trapped in my seat, I remove my reading glasses and a tissue from my purse. A silk pouch buried inside reminds me that I've come with purpose. I place cough drops in my skirt pocket, then slip my finger under the new envelope's flap and pull out the assorted pages. From practice, I know a distraction can shut out the commotion around me. But not necessarily the snarl of my own emotions.

Yet how gracious that these men spontaneously invited Jennifer to the seminar. Maybe I've been too hasty in judging her, in assuming she has other plans with her fatherly lover. When I was her age, I would have counted myself lucky to attend a seminar like this. Anything that diverted me from the culturally acceptable pattern of Sunday dinners followed by Monday laundry and Tuesday ironing, then Wednesday grocery shopping—Oma's destiny as well as my mother's.

I page through the full-color program and land on a section called Promises. According to the printed statement, I will leave the week's seminar with clarity of purpose and a plan as well as a commitment that manifests that purpose. Last I will accomplish the first three steps in bringing the plan into reality. I smile as I flip back to the first page and read, "The Purpose: to impel participants forward toward an endeavor or goal to which one commits one's energy and resources for the purpose of service, the result of which will bring one's mind, body, and soul into alignment."

The language reflects the sixties, which carried over into the seventies, a time that nearly cost me my marriage to Stan. All that nonsense about open marriages and our overenthusiasm with the concept. Stan was only too happy to participate, yet I could never get over my ambivalence and discomfort at having an open affair with Nancy's then-husband. In the end it only took two months for the charm of Wednesday afternoons at the Holiday Inn— followed by hurried appointments, a dinner to cook, and children to retrieve—to wear off like a pile of hastily discarded clothes. Romance is simply that: romance.

The houselights dim until only the table lamp onstage and the backlights remain. Roland, a much older and smaller man than in the photos projected onto the screens behind him, sinks deeper into his chair. Gilbert adjusts the mic now pinned to Roland's sport coat and edges away to the side. He soon takes his seat beside me. The room becomes quiet.

"Good morning." Roland puts his hands together. The lamp illuminates his face, his white hair, the furrows in his cheeks, while he sits backlit by the giant photographs behind him. He closes his eyes and, while sitting, bows his head to the audience. "Namaste," he says, first to one side, then center, and finally the other side. The audience seems to wrap itself around him in response to his greeting, mimicking the prayer fold, as does Gilbert beside me. After another silence Roland says, "We will now begin our ten-minute meditation." He hesitates for a few seconds. "If this proves challenging, sit quietly and watch your breath. Do not resist your thoughts. Without judgment, allow those thoughts to come into your mind and then, gently, let them return to the stillness inside you. I will ring a chime to end the meditation. Please continue to sit in silence afterward."

The silence makes me edgy, as though a foreign object's been inserted under my skin. A silenced notification from Jennifer's phone lights my cell phone screen. I quickly turn the phone face down. When a call vibration breaks through, I'm really nervous. I can't really look at the phone with Gilbert beside me. There's something so still about his face. Then a tickle seizes my throat and I cough. Other people cough. A sob breaks the quiet several rows behind me. Someone sneezes; another clears their throat. My eyelids begin to dance against my eyeballs. How can I keep my word to Jennifer by not telling Kelsey, her mother? Kelsey would never forgive me. Irene, my own mother, wouldn't have forgiven me either if I'd confessed at the time. This is now my secret and Jennifer's, and I don't like secrets.

The chime rings. I jerk against Gilbert's arm. He gives no indication he's been jostled; his eyes are open and focused toward the front.

Silence. "Now, what I love most," Roland says.

His voice comes from another world and wouldn't be audible except for the small microphone attached to his sport coat. "I want to hear the miracles that have happened since yesterday," he says. "Please go to the mics and share in one sentence or a few words any out-of-the-ordinary experience or event that happened since we last met."

People line up at each of the four mics placed in the aisles. Gilbert nudges me and whispers. "If he calls on you, and he will, say whatever comes to mind."

"Why me?"

He puts his hand on my arm. "Newcomers are always chosen first."

I'm still recovering from Gilbert's hand on my arm, the slight pressure, when Roland says, "Mrs. Bufford?" I'm embarrassed. Without standing, I blurt the first words that come into my head: "I hope the seminar will change my life, especially since my husband's about to become a father with another woman." How humiliating! Where did that come from?

Roland nods.

Other participants speak from various mics.

"My boss called."

"My girlfriend apologized."

"My manuscript was accepted."

"The pain in my right eye subsided."

Only the first person at each microphone is able to speak before Roland nods to end the responses. Others continue to stand.

"How many of you were able to right a wrong?" he asks.

Those who stand second in line, most of the lines fifteen deep, take the microphones.

"I apologized to my father."

"I sent a check to my creditor."

"I prayed about my grudge."

The testimonials aren't noteworthy, just human, mostly meaningless in the everyday world. However, in this auditorium and with this particular group, they take on significance.

"Please sit down now," Roland instructs. "We will meditate again for fifteen minutes. This time, however, we'll do a walking meditation to the chant, 'Let go; let spirit rise.' The room is large and there are many of you here. Move slowly and be mindful of others. For your safety, we will turn up the lights enough to see. When I ring the chime, walk back to your seat."

I glance down at the folder, my purse, the small packet of Kleenex crowding my lap. No way am I milling with all these people. Just ignore Gilbert, who is nodding for me to follow him. He probably thinks he's being helpful. Faking a bad knee or back is out of the question. I've already climbed in and out of the back seat of Gilbert's car like the able-bodied person I am.

Gilbert rises from his seat. I wait until he's several steps into the meditation. Though I don't want to, I stand and walk behind him with two others between us, his height always in sight. He turns right and follows the others ahead of him, climbing the steps toward the higher seats, head down, one foot at a time. The soft landing of feet against tile is the only sound as the participants shuffle along. At first I don't hear the murmuring voices. When I do, the sound confuses me until I realize people are chanting. The room fills with what sounds like loud humming. Along the aisles and up the stairs into the highest bank of seats, along the back aisle and then down the other side, everyone chants. Whenever I dare glance at Roland, a certain quiet surrounds him. With eyes closed and lips moving, he too is immersed in the singsong of the chant.

The walking, more like shuffling, continues for fifteen minutes. The cell phone I've slipped into my skirt pocket vibrates in a long, dull rhythm against my thigh, vibration after vibration. With Gilbert ahead of me and Roland onstage, I imagine that they would know if any one of these seventy-five people slipped away or stepped out of line. I keep walking.

DESCENDING THE STAIRS UNDER THE muted light for what must be the fifth or sixth time, I almost trip. I've been too much inside my head recalling a time when I sat on the ground around a campfire in the Wasatch Mountains. I'd insisted on taking my daughters to visit Oma's grave in North Dakota. I was then forty-five and filled with sorrow that I'd never said goodbye. Oma died with only her cousin beside her in the Myra farmhouse where she first lived as a young girl. I can still feel the grassy stubble under my hips as I sat in that campground, my legs crossed, my cowboy boots gouging each other. The quiet around us seemed held by the crackling fire and the wind through the pines. It was at that campfire that Kelsey asked, "Why are you so quiet, Mama?" How do you explain to a twenty-three-year-old girl that you seem to have missed an important beat in life and now you are stuck with an unexplainable longing? The same quiet half-light seems to fill the auditorium where I now take one step at a time.

As quickly as it began, the chanting walk ends with me in front of my seat. The meditation makes me wonder if I'm looking again for a mentor in Roland the same way I did years ago in Oma and then Aunt Ada. Or am I looking for validation because my husband just left me for the classic younger woman. What am I looking for and why was I so easily persuaded by Nancy?

The questions stay with me through my lunch walk and the afternoon session. Another suggestion from Roland to find and act from a higher self follows me into the five o'clock hour. I grab my things and shove them into my purse, not waiting for Roland and Gilbert but rather opting for a cab back to the hotel. A glass of wine is all I can think about even as I wonder what the hell I got myself into. Higher self, what is that supposed to mean? How is that supposed to help me find clarity? I retreat to my hotel room and order take-out Chinese from the concierge. Finally a glass of wine, the only thing that makes the evening worthwhile.

Alcohol's subtle lift permeates my arms and legs and eases my brain toward rest. I place my glasses on the nightstand and stretch along the length of the bed, pulling the spread over my feet. My arms and legs, now warmed by the blanket, allow tension to drain from my back. With a quiet evening ahead, I'm more happy than lonely.

I close my eyes while the drone of the low volume on the TV quiets my rumbling stomach. For the moment all is well. With nothing more to do but wait for my delivery, I can almost pretend I've been lying here all day. That half-awake, half-asleep bubble I've been longing for. There and then gone when my cell phone rings. My automatic response in this dulled state is to pick up the phone.

"I was beginning to wonder if you were alive," he says.

"Nice greeting, Stan. I didn't think you cared."

"You do this, Marta. Never check in. Never let me know where the hell you are or what you're doing. I end up sitting around wondering if we're even on the same planet."

What I hear under his scolding words is a backhanded care that leaks out no matter the circumstances. When you've known someone as intimately as we've known each other, when you've allowed someone to take up residence in your heart, it doesn't end as easily as a snap of fingers or the signing of divorce papers.

"I'm sure you have other concerns foremost in your mind," I say.

"Forget about me. There are papers you need to sign."

"I'm sure they can wait until I'm back. Besides, I'm on vacation, and Jennifer's here."

"That's a surprise," he says.

"Quite a surprise." I laugh. *More than you'll ever know*, but I don't say that. "You must still be in Reno."

"I am. But there can be no divorce without your signature."

"Send them to the hotel. I'm interested in what you drew up. And Stan . . ." I hesitate, the lump in my throat unexpected. "I'm sorry this is where we ended up."

Silence on the other end of the phone. A long minute that feels like more. "Jennifer should have come to California and spent time with both of us."

I say nothing. An impending divorce. Separate living quarters. What would he do or say to Jennifer considering the circumstances? Become the irate grandfather and scold her? Call Kelsey? There's an outside chance he'd pass it off as youth and circumstances, the same way he's passed off his own affairs. In many ways I don't know this man I've been married to for nearly forty years.

"Right," I say. "Especially since both of us are no longer the both of us."

Stan has long practiced the magic of pausing, of saying nothing. Finally he says, "Is the seminar worth the fuss of getting there?"

"Amazed you're interested," I say. "It's only my first real day. I'll know more tomorrow."

"I'm going to send you the papers today so you can look them over and sign," he says.

Silence.

"Well, it's good to hear your voice, honey," he says. "To know you got there."

Honey? Where did *honey* come from? Habit? A slip of the tongue? Did he forget that he knocked me off my feet when he announced he'd already taken an apartment in downtown San Diego? Forget that eight weeks in Reno can't go by fast enough for him. After all, his girlfriend Rita is thirty-six and pregnant, and he isn't getting any younger. Does he call her *honey* too?

Dinner arrives and I curl up on the bed, wrapped inside the cozy terry cloth robe. Nancy's parting gift, Pema Chödrön's *When Things Fall Apart* sits open beside me. But not even a second glass of wine eases the grinding in my stomach.

Chapter Six

Tuesday, June 11

I WAKE WITH A START as the alarm buzzes at six-thirty. I've been asleep for nearly eleven hours. This is my second day in the hotel, and what's not to love about room service? Coffee with toast, a soft-boiled egg. Orange juice. An energy bar for lunch. Unlike yesterday, whatever happens today, I'm ready. Stan can send *honey* whatever he wants.

When I check my cell phone, Jennifer's voicemail from yesterday is foremost on the screen. "Staying with a friend. Will call this evening." No call came.

My return message: "Missed you. Thought you were going to call. Maybe we can have dinner tomorrow."

I drive myself to campus thinking I'll be early but I arrive at eight forty-five. Other conferences lock their doors after a certain length of time. How embarrassing if I can't get in. Or is it? A good excuse to return to the hotel, except now I want to be in the seminar.

I approach the front door which, as I suspected, is locked. However, inside is a woman who also seems lost. She opens the door and lets me in. "The Roland Cosgrove seminar?" I ask.

"We're late," she says.

From the way the woman is bent forward and the intensity around her mouth, she appears as anxious as I am.

"Do you know where we're going?"

"Third floor," she says. "Maybe it won't look as bad if we go in together." The woman's smile provides a bridge of solidarity I need right now.

In her mid-forties, she's on the stocky side. Around five-feet-seven, slightly taller than me, her brown hair curls to the point of frizz. She limps ahead of me in a way that indicates more birth defect than accident. I slow my pace though my watch indicates we are now a full fifteen minutes late. The first meditation will be over, and people will be lined up to talk about their so-called miracles.

"I'm Audrey," the woman says as we huff down the hall toward one of yesterday's bouncer types who guards the double doors. The large fellow stands with his arms crossed. He appears bored and suspicious at the same time, but he comes to attention when we approach. Fortunately I remembered to wear my name badge around my neck. He glances quickly at my badge, then toward Audrey, who wears no badge. His jaw tightens.

"I'm Audrey Bloomington," she says. "*Duluth News Tribune.* I have a pass."

She produces a press card and flashes it at him. "Roland approved."

"Take the side door," the bouncer says, forgetting to check our purses. He points down the hall toward a single door into the auditorium. "I'd let you in here, but there's too much light from the hallway."

We nod and walk less hurriedly toward the other door. We enter from the back of the auditorium, higher up and toward the top tier of seats. Lucky for us, there are empty seats in that section, which allow us to slip in closer to the aisle. Easier to escape the others for lunch. A good walk would be a better use of my time. Hopefully the day will be warmer.

Audrey squeezes my arm like we're accomplices who have just pulled off a prank. Her squeeze is still there when, through the speakers at the back of the room, we hear Roland announce the next meditation. I assume that like yesterday this will be a walking meditation.

"Today, I will introduce you to open-eye meditation," he says. "Though more challenging, this meditation will teach you to focus against both visual and auditory distractions, namely the chatter in your own head as well as your surroundings. Unlike yesterday, this will be a guided meditation. My fellow teacher, Gilbert, will lead. We will meditate for thirty minutes seated where you are with your eyes open."

I search the front row, but Gilbert isn't there. Perhaps he's behind us in the sound booth which, even at this elevation, remains invisible from where Audrey and I sit at the outer edge of the auditorium's half circle. Wherever he is, his tone is clear, so clear that I turn to see if he's sitting behind me. All I see is a blank wall.

Though I feel awkward, I keep my eyes open. I sink into the rise and fall of Gilbert's image of running water, a bank beside the stream, the forest, and surrounding sky. I return to Bass Lake where Robert and I went the weekend before he reported to Fort Lewis, Washington. Inside the rustic cabin tent, both of us lay on the narrow bed. Robert's hand covered mine, the skin coarse from woodworking with his dad, our eyes directed toward the tent's peaked covering. We made love again and again, rocking on the thin mattress. Though we never said it, we knew we'd have to make our pleasure last a long time. To hope that lovemaking would bind every whisper and moan of a weekend we expected to repeat. The open tent flap, the lake's bluer than blue water. What we wouldn't or couldn't say.

The open-eye meditation is the most challenging for me, especially given my tendency to be distracted by anything in my line of sight. On previous mornings, I had to keep my eyes steady and focused on a small hole of light in the curtain behind Roland. That became my spot, in the same way I learned to use a visual point to repeatedly turn in ballet.

Audrey's arm brushes against mine on the connecting seat and jostles me enough to hear Gilbert guide the participants back into the room. I'm not ready to let go of Robert, his breath curling at my neck. I don't want to return to this auditorium and its near darkness.

I've treated the seminar as an invasion on my solitude, hoping to sort out my confusion and sadness. I've negated the chance to glimpse something I once knew in Robert's presence. That same calm I knew sitting at Oma's kitchen table where I watched her move between the sink and the stove. The same quiet when she stoked the fire with pieces of wood that Uncle Ivan had split. The hot kuchen on the cast-iron trivet, the smell of yeast rising from the hot pastry alongside the cookstove's burning wood. Oma's insistence on the cooling period before the butcher knife came down and divided the pie-like pastry. Waiting in her warm kitchen, I watched the sun slant through the window over the sink. In that warm room it never mattered what I was waiting for.

ROLAND ANNOUNCES A BREAK FOR a half hour and suggests the participants maintain silence. I smile and nod as Audrey moves past me to descend the stairs with others. Onstage, Roland is helped to his feet by a young aide before he totters offstage.

An unexpected hand rests on my arm. "Sorry to break your silence," Gilbert says. "Hoped you'd join me for lunch." He hesitates. "I know a quiet place."

I glance at his fingers, long and slender, a damaged thumb on his right hand. Maybe crushed at one time. The pressure of his hand on my arm. "Sure," I say too quickly. His invitation is a complete surprise.

Why me? I'd think he'd be attracted to the younger set, like the blond participant from the president's house, or any number of women. What can he want? I'm old enough to be his favorite aunt.

It's now impossible to keep my head clear and return to the silence that Roland suggested. Like the true obsessive I am, I begin to imagine all kinds of things. A winter-summer romance. Advice from someone older and perhaps wiser, though why would he need advice from me? Legal advice? Who is this mysterious man who has attached himself to the leader, the guru?

Audrey returns and an hour passes though it's hard for me to concentrate. Yet the quiet of Roland's presence onstage continues. Small talk with Audrey during a brief stand-and-stretch break. Another meditation exercise followed by a talk on letting go. Letting go of our worries and concerns but also our long-held resentments. Most of all, our expectations of others and ourselves.

My eyes and ears and body are here, but I'm not. At the same time I'm awake in a way I've never been, my mind a clean slate, a calm in my chest that feels almost foreign. And there in my mind's eye sits Stan in his Hawaiian shirt. The Scotch dripping down his chin. My own stunned reaction in that moment. Then a fury I'd never known fills my chest and threatens to explode into fists. The strange sensation of wanting to hit him, to hurt him the way I've been hurting. How can I ever let go of that when, even now, I don't want to let go? Don't want to forget the jumble of feelings rumbling inside my gut shouting anything but *let go*.

Audrey excuses herself. "Back to the office," she says. "I'm working through lunch."

Lunch. I'm barely aware of the time or her leaving until Gilbert nudges my arm. "Follow me?" I'm in a state as close to a trance as I've ever been when he leads me toward an entrance door directly below the light and sound booth. Maybe this is a needed distraction. Time will tell.

Gilbert leads me into a corridor that runs through a tunnel several yards long. Once through the building's inner door, the sun blasts the surrounding plate glass windows. I'm blind and can't see Gilbert's face for the glare, his head just an outline against sun that invades the hallway. I stop and search my purse for sunglasses. Oma's Easter egg nestled in the bottom. Gilbert stares out the window, his hands on his hips while he waits for me. Why did I accept his lunch invitation when I wanted to be alone? What would have happened if I'd stayed with the silence? I resent him for intruding, but I came along anyhow, didn't I? Am I lonely in this place I've never been? A place where I'm not in charge? If I am lonely, this is new and unfamiliar territory. Is that why I just abdicated what I wanted for myself in order to be with this man and accept his invitation?

Gilbert turns away from the window and faces me. "There's a place we can walk to."

Once I put on my sunglasses, Gilbert takes my elbow to lead me down a set of side stairs to the second floor. Before we reach the mid-sixties elevator, I remove my arm from his hand. I'm not some old woman who needs help, and I don't need this man to be gallant. I clutch my purse tighter to my side. The service elevator creaks around us, then stops at a walkway between two buildings, the entire enclosure glassed in, exposing us to the windows of the adjacent building. Gilbert never speaks; his destination and seeming certainty pull him ahead. I only see the back of his head.

We enter what appears to be a private garden surrounded by a rock wall. Inside the wall a fountain trickles through and around lava rock. Ferns and wild-looking mosses cling to the large, cratered stone. A small table with two chairs rests beside the fountain. Because of the landscaping, I suspect it would be impossible to see the patio from the walkway or even through the plate glass windows in an adjacent classroom. The chairs, wrought iron, don't look particularly comfortable.

From a paper bag Gilbert produces a cut apple, grapes inside a baggie, sliced cheese, and some crackers as well as two bottles of water. "Lunch," he says.

Did he plan this? If he did, he must have a reason. Yet the meditation has made me unusually hungry. I open my purse and retrieve the energy bar, adding my snack to the assortment.

"I wasn't expecting this," I say.

Gilbert's laugh is quiet. "Fortunately, what happens in a seminar day isn't always what we expect," he says. "At least that's my experience."

He unfolds a large paper napkin on the center of the table, careful to keep the corners pointed in a way that provides maximum coverage on an otherwise dusty glass-topped table. He spreads the food in front of us. His smile is mischievous. "Sorry, I didn't think of coffee or tea."

"You've thought of a lot." I pick up an apple slice and a piece of Havarti. Placing the cheese on the apple, I relish the taste. Hungry as I am, I'm mindful of being his guest.

I unwrap the energy bar and break it in two.

Head down, Gilbert picks at his food. I follow suit but wonder why I'm trying to be polite. I'm hungry, and Gilbert's bowed head and seeming distraction annoy me. He glances up. "Roland's taken quite a liking to you," he says.

I drop my apple slice and scramble to catch it before it falls on the cement patio. This whole thing, the lunch and the private garden, feels like part of some plan. I'm more suspicious than ever.

"He can't be romantically interested," I say, blurting the words without thinking.

Gilbert grins. "No, not like that," he says. "I hope that doesn't insult you."

My face has to be as red as Oma's borscht. I pretend to search the ground for the apple slice, though I've already shoved it under the table's brace with the toe of my shoe.

"We were wondering if you're married," he says. "That box wasn't checked on your application."

"After what I blurted out on my first day? I have to say I'm surprised. Really surprised. As though that should make a difference in my being here."

I gaze at the water curling out of the lava rock and trickling down the fountain's sides. I suddenly wish it was time to get back, though we've hardly eaten a thing. "As a matter of fact, I'm in the early stages of a divorce," I finally say. "If that's what you want to know."

Now it's his turn to stare at the water falling down the fountain's irregular face and quietly splashing beside our table. "I know what that's like."

He says nothing more. And I'm relieved that he doesn't seem to need further explanation. Besides, do I really want or care to know his story? I've already heard more than my fair share, and now I get to walk through that door myself.

Unannounced, Gilbert stands to leave. But then he lingers, his hands on his hips. "The other day you said you hoped your time in Duluth would change the way you see your life. I know that being here this time is changing me somehow."

"Even though you've done this before?" Why did I ask that question? He's assuming that I care.

"Yes. I have no idea why this time is different." He hesitates. "I apologize if I seemed forward with my question or my own personal history."

"No worries," I say. "Maybe it's time for me to be more honest with myself," I say, attempting to bring humor to the moment and obviously failing.

I EASE INTO MY SEAT next to Gilbert. Then sink into a kind of darkness, relieved to be alone inside another meditation. I'm sleepy, and having had little to eat, I'm afraid the rest of the day will be a waste of time. Glancing over my shoulder, I try to see if I can spot Audrey. For some reason I feel disloyal. The overheads dim, and the only light in the auditorium comes from the lamp beside Roland's onstage chair and the dimmed backlights.

My mind returns to Oma's table. I've just turned five years old and she's telling me the story of Russia and her life there. Without warning, she leaves the kitchen, her slippered feet heavy on the rag rug, the sound of her labored breath as she rushes up the stairs from the kitchen. When she returns, she holds an old-fashioned purse in her hands. The tarnished clasp and the embroidery or crewelwork give the purse an antique look. She opens it and inside, against a lining of purple silk, lays a diamond-and-sapphire egg the size of a child's fist.

"From Russia," she says. "Your great-great-grandpapa gave it to me on my fourteenth birthday." Her tongue clucks against the roof of her mouth. "Special," she says, "for you someday, *schatzi*. Not to be talked about with anyone else."

Once again I feel the astonishment at seeing her Easter egg for the first time, the jewels like nothing I'd ever seen before. Real jewels. Diamonds and sapphires encrusted along the hard shell of cloisonné. The elegant and precious egg that had been hidden inside her farmhouse with its wood-burning cookstove, the threadbare rugs, and the outhouse beyond the kitchen window. The ambivalence and decided discomfort in being asked to keep a secret. My stomach danced at the thought of not telling my mother or my sisters. Such a secret, especially at five years of age, caused more than a small knot in my stomach. Knowing the glittering, sparkling egg would someday be mine.

I feel Gilbert's hand on my arm, though he gazes ahead at the single light onstage. Did I jump when he woke me or, worse, groan? And why does he feel the need to protect me, to guide me? His attention annoys me, and I can't help but wonder why I continue to sit here beside him.

After two, then three, deep breaths, Roland opens his eyes. "We are ready to clear the cloud of ego," he says. "Though it's dark, it's very quiet here." He pauses until the shuffle of backpacks and purses subside and most folks have found their notebooks. "My question to you is this: Why are you here in this lifetime? What is your purpose? If you don't know what that is, please raise your hand."

Nearly every hand in the room goes up. Not mine. I'm too embarrassed.

Then, as though pulled up and away from my body by some invisible force, I slowly—reluctantly and against my will—raise my hand.

Gilbert glances in my direction. To his credit, he doesn't smile or nod or even blink his eyes. I'm relieved. Though I was never Catholic, this is the moment when, in raising my arm, I've come closest to confessing a truth I've never explored or even had thoughts about. Even when others lower their hands, my hand remains aloft. Like a kind of reckoning, a shattering of some belief I've held about myself that's probably as old as my memory of sitting in Oma's kitchen.

When I finally pull my hand back into my lap, I can't help but think about my life in business, in law, my marriage to Stan where we maneuvered like robots in our responses to each other. Where the subtle and unspoken expectations settled years ago like seasoned cement. We rarely touched. We never talked. When Stan did talk, I grew irritated with his prattle about the neighbor's cat or the failure of the garbage collector to come on time. His early retirement followed an aneurism. Afterward Stan admitted that sex scared him. He pulled away from me. No more morning kisses or long goodnight hugs, which used to be precursors to more intimacy. Instead, two years of rigorous diet and prescribed exercise became his new routine. And though his medical reports proved increasingly positive and his old vigor returned, we were never again intimate the way we had been. Before long, we no longer discussed cases. He resigned from the bar. Our lives together grew smaller. I found any excuse I could to leave town or eat dinner out with friends or colleagues. Stan forgot how to smile.

"We've arrived at the center of our exploration this week." Roland's hands lift again into a prayer fold. He waits a moment. "Now, if you will open your blank notebook to the first page." He waits for a minute or two until people settle and silence is restored. "Write, in a word or two or a sentence, the first thing that comes to mind in response to your primary purpose. Do not think! Just write."

My hand, my alert pen, the blank page. *Heart. Travel.* Two words that come to mind, unbidden.

I shield them with the shadow of my hand out of fear that Gilbert's eyes might linger on my page. However, I don't need to worry. Gilbert is focused on his own page.

Sitting in the quiet, my pen remains poised. I look down at the two words. I'm reminded of Oma's story about the desperation with which her family left Russia. The crisis at Ellis Island when my great-grandfather, Jacob, lost the family gold gambling with the crew. There seems to be an odd parallel with Stan. Yet it's not Stan I've been thinking about. Robert and Oma. Those are the faces that rise up and beg remembrance.

Heart. Travel. Heart travel. I sit quietly, surprised and puzzled by the notion.

"Now," Roland begins. "Please allow those words or that sentence to speak and tell their story by putting pen to paper and writing whatever comes to mind. It doesn't have to make sense. It doesn't have to mean anything. Let whatever comes through your pen be on the page." He takes a drink of water. "If this is too difficult, please use your nondominant hand . . . in other words, the hand you normally don't use to write. Mostly, get out of your own way."

I'm curious. A minute, two, and nothing comes. There's a heaviness in my chest, like the weight of elusive sadness that, up until now, has been hiding behind nonstop activity and my work's seemingly urgent necessities. They demand my attention at all times, it seems. My chest, my heart. *Heart pain. Heart life. Heart travel.*

I go with travel. Duluth. The freezing wind off the lake. My granddaughter, Jennifer. Her older man. *That beautiful head of gray hair, but the beard would have to go. Stop!* I'm off on a tangent when I'm supposed to be thinking of heart travel. Maybe that's it. Some longing for real companionship. The clichéd soul connection. Heart.

Dear Stan, how did we lose each other and get so lost along the way?

Chapter Seven

Entering my hotel room, I drop the notebook. The hotel phone's red message light blinks like a small fire alarm.

"How about dinner tonight?" Gilbert's voice sounds different on the phone, more resonant but without the smile. Dinner? So soon? But after room service meals and not one trip to the dining room, I could do worse. Maybe the discomfort of aloneness is winning over resentment.

Another message on my private cell number I gave to Jennifer. "Hi, Oma. It's Jennifer. My history professor Michael and I wondered if you'd join us for dinner here in the hotel this evening. Call me on my cell."

At first I'm shocked. Then angry. But maybe investigation of the cradle robber would be less obvious with Gilbert there. When I call Gilbert's room, no one answers. I leave a message saying I'll meet him in the hotel lobby at the registration desk around seven. I lay out my best slacks and a red paisley-print blouse along with a shawl to protect my shoulders against the anticipated too-cold air-conditioning.

After my shower I lie on the bed in my robe and close my eyes. "Just fifteen minutes," I say to myself.

A dream transports me back to my first class on family law. I notice Curtis, a classmate, focused on my answer sheet and I automatically drop my chest to the page. I glance directly toward him before my name rings out in the silent classroom. Professor Arthur approaches my desk, quickly snatching my answer sheet as though I'm the one cheating. I awaken with a start, forgetting where I am. A shame that isn't mine floods my chest.

When I call Gilbert again, he answers on the first ring. "I'm so sorry," I say. "I overslept. I'll be down in twenty minutes." He hangs up before I can ask him if it's okay for us to join Jennifer and her friend Michael.

I dress with urgency instead of the careful, luxurious manner I like to apply fresh makeup and arrange my clothes. When I arrive in the lobby, Gilbert is leaning on the concierge's desk and talking to one of the uniformed bellmen.

The dream lingers with a sense of disorientation and the strange feeling that I'm not prepared for the evening ahead. "I forgot to ask if you got my message about Jennifer and her friend joining us for dinner."

"I'm confused," he says. "I thought we were having dinner alone."

"I'm so sorry, Gilbert. You clearly didn't get my message."

For someone who must pride himself on his composure, the outer edges of Gilbert's smile collapse. "Not a problem," he says. But a slight flutter of his eyelids reveals his disappointment. With a firm touch, he takes my elbow and begins to guide me toward the dining room. The maître d', a short and round man who has likely been at his job for a long time, says, "There are no tables, sir, unless you want to come back in an hour. Then I might be able to accommodate you."

"No, we don't want to wait," Gilbert says.

The impatience in his voice surprises me. I step forward. "Do you have a reservation for a Dr. Michael Connolly regarding a table for four?"

The maître d' glances at me, his eyebrows raised. "In fact, I do."

"Good," I say. "We'll be joining them."

I turn back toward Gilbert. I find myself apologizing again, which I hate to do. "I did leave a message. I'm just sorry that you never heard it."

He says nothing more. He doesn't need to. The tight set of his jaw says he's not pleased. Which is fine with me. After all, this isn't exactly a date.

We follow the maître d' to the table with a reserved sign.

Once seated, I order. "A martini. Two olives, straight up, no vermouth."

The waiter turns to Gilbert. "Water is fine," Gilbert says. "Ice. A slice of lemon."

"Nothing to drink?" I ask.

"I stopped drinking alcohol some time ago. It didn't work well in assisting Roland."

The edge of discomfort I noted before we were seated inhabits my mind and roils in my stomach. A reminder that I hardly know this man. "You seem to take good care of him."

Gilbert smiles. "He's done the same for me."

I smooth the napkin on my lap. "Besides arranging the seminars and getting him there, exactly what do you do for him?"

"I'm his general manager," Gilbert says. "I arrange the schedule and locations, the transport to get there." He leans in closer. "Mostly, I make it happen."

"You participate as well."

"That's how I started." He pauses. "After my first four seminars, Roland's former manager quit for health reasons. Because I'd been an events manager and an avid follower, he asked if I'd join him."

"What about your family? Your other work?"

"This is my work."

"But you're never home."

"It won't last forever given Roland's advanced years. When Roland passes, I'll carry on where he left off, or I'll close down the seminars. He's left it up to me."

Gilbert looks behind me at the same moment I feel arms around my neck. "Oma," a voice whispers in my ear.

Yesterday, the last time I saw Jennifer, she was wearing a T-shirt and jeans. Now a more grown-up Jennifer has donned black slacks, her hair has been carefully brushed, and diamond studs replace the multiple earrings. Gilbert, now standing, sticks out his hand toward Jennifer. "I'm Gilbert," he says. "You do look like your grandmother."

Jennifer takes his hand before turning toward the graying man behind her. "This is Dr. Michael Connolly," Jennifer says. "He's here to teach a specialized history course."

The two men, nearly the same height, shake hands and gaze at each other like two people wondering if they've met before. Michael, who seems older than Gilbert, looks every bit the professor: there are leather patches on the sleeves of his tweed sport coat, and his paisley tie is slightly off-kilter.

"Michael, this is my grandmother, Oma. I mean Marta Bufford. She's from San Diego where the rest of my family lives."

He takes my hand and looks at me with an intensity—yes, even scrutiny—I should be used to. "Nice to meet you. Jennifer's told me about you."

My bullshit detector snaps into high alert. Like attorneys I've met in a courtroom, the ones I'm automatically suspicious of, the charm in his voice confirms my worst fear. I can feel a flush spread up my neck. He's practiced, yes, that's the word. Practiced and winning at the same time. I retrieve my hand. I might as well be in the middle of a poker game, teasing out what might be in his hand but holding my cards close to my chest.

Michael nods toward Gilbert then, as an afterthought, toward me. "You're both here with the motivational seminar." The way he says *motivational* holds a judgment. I don't like him any better now than I did when Jennifer first told me he was the other party to her abortion.

Michael and Jennifer take their seats across from us. "Where do you normally teach?" Gilbert asks.

Michael undoes the single button on his jacket and spreads his napkin. "Since there are no summer classes in Madison, I'm here for six weeks to teach a course on the Civil War and another course as well. Budget cuts, you know. You get work where you can." He smiles at Jennifer. "It's quite painless really, to have this young woman as my assistant. To dote on me, really."

My hands twist the napkin on my lap while fury rises in my chest. What can Jennifer possibly see in this man? He's revolting. And did Jennifer neglect to tell me he's the reason she's in Duluth? Are there more puzzle pieces? A sinking sensation lands in my gut along with the sense that I've been deceived. That the tears around the abortion weren't the final punctuation mark on the professor.

Michael pivots his body in my direction. "I've heard a great deal about your expertise as a divorce lawyer," he says. "Jennifer says you're quite a negotiator."

I attempt to smile. "A girl is expected to be proud of her grandmother."

Jennifer is innocent, yes, and she's bound to get her life experience somewhere. But why with this man? Because he's older and supposedly wiser? No doubt he'll break her heart. Thank heaven she isn't marrying him, and she's no longer carrying his child.

"Actually, I'm retiring," I say. "It's time to do something else."

I'm surprised to hear myself say those words. Is it my vain attempt to be anyone but whom he's predicted? Except for the arch in Gilbert's eyebrows, my statement sounds as matter-of-fact as I intended. For Michael, my announcement is of no consequence—strange, since he seems to be of retirement age himself.

"And you?" Michael asks Gilbert. "Are you retiring as well?"

Gilbert plays with his dinner fork, turning it over and over. "No retirement for me," he says. "I've been with Roland's seminars since I left my business ten years ago. I'm perfectly happy to stay here."

"Your business was?" Michael asks.

"The ammunition industry." Gilbert speaks as though working in ammunition is like being in the grocery business or selling automobiles, common and everyday, just another big corporation left to the imagination and subsequent opinions.

"Interesting," Michael says, suddenly attentive where before he seemed only polite. "For the Gulf War?"

Gilbert nods, a half smile on his face. "Yes, for that war."

"Sounds like a big change," Michael says.

"I wouldn't be alive otherwise," Gilbert says.

I'm immediately drawn to his earlobe, the loose flap of skin. His matter-of-factness when saying that being with Roland saved his life. From what? Public humiliation? Demonstrations? For the first time I notice a scar on his neck inside his shirt collar. Not like Oma's scar, which defined who she was and who she'd become, the spiderweb across her face nearly invisible when you'd known her for long. Her story of the unfortunate fall and resulting disfigurement from landing on the Battery Park wharf was something that was never talked about in front of her but saved for moments out of her earshot. Gilbert's scar appears to be a surgical scar about an inch and a half long near the carotid artery. Was that part of the deciding event ten years ago?

"That's a pretty dramatic move," Michael says. "From tanks and missiles—I'm making that up—to this Roland person. Must be a powerful guy."

"He is," Gilbert says. His answer is quiet, but his gaze at Michael intensifies. He's no longer the Gilbert who held my papers while I settled in for the seminar, then guided me through the opening meditation. This Gilbert is more than a match for Herr Professor.

The waiter returns with our drinks, water with lemon in front of Gilbert, the frosty stemmed martini glass in front of me. He patiently waits before taking our dinner orders.

"I never put much stock in gurus," Michael says. "They never last beyond their lifetimes."

"How do you explain Jesus or Buddha or Muhammad?" I ask.

"Touché," Michael says.

His smug tone infuriates me. Even while I wring the hand-kerchief in my lap, I remind myself that I need to look at this man through the eyes of an attorney, not the eyes of a concerned grandmother.

"You say you're teaching two courses this summer," Gilbert says. "The Civil War and what's the other one?"

Michael straightens his tie. "The other course is on World War II."

"What attracts you to those particular wars?" Gilbert asks.

"What historian doesn't love those wars?" Michael says. "Especially with the help of kiddo here. My novice admirer, I call her." He drapes his arm around Jennifer's shoulder. "She's just learning, you know, not mature enough to grasp the concepts I'm teaching. But she's trying."

Kiddo, indeed. Immature as well? I'm furious. Who the hell does he think he is? Is this how he treats all women?

Jennifer beams like the nineteen-year-old she is, her smile bright under Michael's spotlight.

I can't say a word for fear my rage, stored up from my fury with Stan, will explode and disturb an intentioned pleasant evening. Yet I'm as angry with Jennifer as I am with this so-called professor. I remind myself that Jennifer I can forgive. After all, she's the inno-cent one here. But how could she possibly fall for this tripe?

"I always loved Granddad's stories about Korea," Jennifer says. "Remember how mad you'd get, Oma?"

The flush that momentarily heats my cheeks will undoubtedly stay on my neck.

I force a smile. "That's because I've heard them too many times."

"Jennifer's told me quite a bit about your husband. He seems to have quite a history as a community organizer."

My half smile that seems to work for Roland barely masks the rage going on inside where the internal tree monkeys are on high alert and swinging to branches that aren't always there.

"Looks like our dinner is here," Gilbert says. He turns to the waiter, who sets my salad in front of me. "Looks good."

"Grandpa told me that he once collected every gun that was used in World War II except artillery. He then donated them to a gun museum. Still, he says he's proud that I'm so interested in weapons."

Again, her naivete infuriates me further. God knows Stan doesn't deserve this adulation. "You may not know, Jennifer, that your grandfather also espouses to be an anti-gun activist."

"Why didn't I know that?" she asks.

"Maybe he left that part out."

In that moment, Jennifer's dinner, a rib eye steak with French fries and a side salad, is presented in front of her. "Yum," she says. "We never get steaks in the dorm. If it wasn't for Michael, I'd practically starve to death."

"Really," I say under my breath.

The conversation ends as Michael and Jennifer bend toward their steaks. I pick at my vegetable and grilled chicken salad while Gilbert relishes his halibut.

We are hardly finished when Michael announces they have to leave to attend a lecture on aerodynamics. "You might be interested, Gilbert."

"Thanks," he says. "Not this evening."

Michael glances at me. I don't like the insinuation in his eyes, that he and Gilbert are comrades who have special arrangements with their respective partners. He just proved to be the asshole I think he is.

Jennifer kisses my cheek. "Night, Oma. I'm so glad we could all eat together. Maybe we can do it again."

I feel the strain of my half smile again. A slight nod. Otherwise I don't trust myself to say a thing.

Gilbert rises from his chair. "I'm glad to meet you, Jennifer. Michael."

"I'd like to hear more about the ammunition industry. Jennifer can arrange it." With his hand in the middle of Jennifer's back, Michael ushers her toward the restaurant entrance.

I sit, dumbfounded, with my hands knotted into fists and my heart in my throat. What would my mother say about Jennifer's fling? What would she do? Oma would take Jennifer into the women's restroom and say, *This isn't a respectable man, young lady. I want you to tell him good evening and come back to my hotel room with me.* In my mind I can see the field of blue flowers on her rayon print dress, her out-of-place old lady oxfords and knee-high support hose, an overly large German nose, and the deep, elongated scar down her cheek that fanned out like a spider's web.

I smile at the image of Oma scolding Jennifer. Maybe that's what I should have done.

Gilbert remains standing. His gaze follows the disappearing couple until they leave the entryway. Once seated again, he asks, "Was that unexpected?"

"Yes, to say the least. I'm sure you can tell I'm not thrilled about this pairing."

"I understand. Jennifer seems so . . ."

"Naive?"

He shakes his head in affirmation. A faraway look overtakes him. "I have a daughter Jennifer's age."

I laugh spontaneously. "Then you understand why I'm concerned."

For the first time, deepening lines crease the corners of his eyes, lines of vulnerability and weariness. "I do and I don't," he says. "Amy's problems have nothing to do with older men or any men for that matter, except me."

"Whatever it is, I'm sorry," I say. "I suppose in many ways, Jennifer is just a normal nineteen-year-old. Tell me about your daughter."

Gilbert looks over my head and into the distance. "Amy was born with spina bifida," he says. "She's lucky to be alive."

"Oh, I'm so sad for you, for her, and for your wife. That must be painful," I say. "Where is she?"

"Long Beach. With my sister. Alice has been with Amy since she was less than a year old." His jaw tightens, and he continues to look toward the dining room entryway. "My wife couldn't deal with an imperfect child."

Though I'm tempted to ask questions, I remain silent and hope he'll say more.

"In my own way, I'm as selfish as my wife. I blamed the economic necessity of treatment for continuing to work. But my heart was so broken for Amy—and then it broke again when my wife left me—that I was pretty desperate when I found Roland's seminars. Very desperate."

"What about your sister? Her life?"

"She was there the minute my wife left," he says. "Maybe I was too eager to accept her help without thinking about her life, her desires."

He folds his napkin and places it on the table. "How about a walk?" he says. "Maybe on campus. It's too cold at the lake. The fresh air will be a relief from all this heady stuff."

BACK IN MY ROOM, MY cell phone indicates a message. Probably Stan. I figure if I call and catch him early enough, he'll have only had his second martini and not started on a third. When he answers, I ask, "Watching the news?"

"Wrong time zone, honey." He waits for me to respond, and

when I don't, he asks, "Did you get the papers? I sent them overnight yesterday."

"I'll check the front desk."

"So Jenny is there."

"We all just had dinner."

"All?"

"Jennifer and someone from the seminar."

"Who was that?" he asks.

"One of the leaders. Listen, I have to run. I'll send you an email to let you know when the papers arrive."

"Morning's fine."

I recognize a familiar hesitation in his voice when he doesn't want to hang up or let go, like he's expecting—no, hoping—I'll say something more or different. "An email in the morning or when the papers arrive," I say. "Reno isn't going anywhere."

Before he can respond, I hang up and sit back on the bed, my hands surprisingly sweaty. I tell myself that this was only a phone call. He's not a part of my life anymore. I no longer need to care. Until now, I hadn't realized that fact. And while Jennifer is our granddaughter, it's up to him to maintain that connection. There's no easy out with me doing all the legwork. Never mind, he's made it clear he's only interested in expediting his cause and fulfilling his agenda. He doesn't give a rat's ass about me. I'm already history to him.

Chapter Eight

Jeans. Walking shoes. A jacket and baseball cap against the wind. Without Roland riding shotgun, I'm in the Volvo's front seat where the leather, worn and well broken in, feels comfortable. I fit easily into the seat's caramel-colored skin.

"You're quiet," Gilbert says. His eyes focus on the road that winds through and above the campus until we end up on a side street overlooking the dormitories and campus buildings. We're as far away from the lake as we can be. We still have an hour or two of daylight. He stops the car at an old wooden gate, beyond which stretches a gravel road into the woods.

I glance at this man in his red plaid shirt, a worn gray sweater tied around his neck, and a navy-blue baseball cap on his head. Something has shifted my opinion of him, and I'm unsure what that is. Maybe his family story at dinner. I roll down the window. An owl hoots in the distance and crickets chirp close by. Blackbirds, seemingly everywhere one goes, caw from high in the trees. "I wore two layers and my heaviest jacket; it's still cold," I say.

"I have a head start on you. Knew I needed wool. Help me remember to warn folks about the cold weather in the enrollment packet."

Lunch. Dinner. The front-row seat. Now a reminder about staying warm. I hardly know this man and his attention mystifies me. A singling out I never expected let alone asked for. Neither one of us says anything for a while. With the windows rolled down, we listen to the crickets rub their legs together to create a familiar sound. "The quiet is nice," I say finally. "There's always too much going on."

"Not just with Jennifer, I take it."

"It's hard to be young," I say. I turn toward him. "Only later do we see the mistakes we made, the bad choices."

"I can't imagine any mistakes you made."

"Let's see." I twist my finger into my cheek as if a dimple waits to receive it. "To start, I married way too young."

"Do you regret that?"

I pull my collar up as high as it will go and secure the zipper at the top. "I was naive and swept along with the cultural norm. You get married, you have children, then after they're grown and settled, you think of yourself. In the meantime you live for *his* dream." Just saying that awakens the ongoing anger that resides in my gut. "Fortunately I didn't wait to formulate my own dream. Still, while he was in law school, I stayed home with the babies and went to school at night. I didn't get started with my life until I was thirty."

"Thirty isn't that old."

"Easy for you to say." I pull my jacket closer around my neck, the chill off the lake having reached this far inland. "What about you, any mistakes or bad choices?"

"We can't change the past, of course, but if I could, if I knew then what I know now, I would have changed my direction and avoided the entire seduction and glamour of the munitions industry."

"Glamour?"

"Money, power, the kind of high that comes from working with government contracts, world powers."

"If you'd done what you're doing now instead, how would that have changed things?"

"I might have been wiser . . . more compassionate . . . maybe avoided the whole divorce business. Amy deserves more than I gave to either her or her mother."

June's chill and a quick rain have conspired to leave the air muggy. Away from the influence of the lake's icy breeze, the late-summer light through the forest ahead makes the evening feel like I'm entering another country. Standing outside the warm car, I hug my arms against my chest. Gilbert opens the wooden gate, and we step through onto a gravel road that is more path than road, the tire tracks overgrown with weeds. After he closes the gate we start walking. I cross my arms to keep my body warmth close. I'd imagined summer here in the same way I think about San Diego summers, not this unsympathetic air that feels like an arctic blast too close to the water, especially where our hotel is located. Even here, away from the lake and entering the woods, the chill sits inside my veins. I wonder if I'll ever be warm again.

Once we find our rhythm and learn to navigate the ruts, our steps fall into stride. I'm still mulling the anger I felt sitting across from Michael in the dining room. His audacity. What is it with men of a certain age? Not just Michael, who happens to be preying on my granddaughter, but my own husband. Is sex always the proving ground?

"Why did you come here, Marta?" Gilbert asks, turning sideways as we walk.

At first I'm startled by his question. Then I say the first thing that pops into my head, "Time-out."

"You can go to a resort for that. Why a meditation seminar?"

"Why did you come?"

He laughs, adjusting the bill of his ball cap. "No, no, you don't get off that easy." He stops in the road. "My intention isn't to be intrusive," he says. "I'm genuinely interested."

I hesitate for a moment, trying to catch my thoughts. "I could say that I'm looking for clarity, but that would be the easy answer. Truth is I'm mad as hell, in the middle of an unexpected divorce, and for someone as smart as I am, I don't have a clue how or why this whole divorce thing happened. That's why I said time-out. I need a new perspective. My friend Nancy said I'd find it here."

"I hope you do," he says. "My biggest fear . . . always . . . is that people come with such high expectations and end up disappointed when one seminar week doesn't solve a many-years-old problem."

"I'll remember that."

We reach a creek, and the only way across is to step on two stones midstream and take a good-sized leap to the opposite side. By now the sky ahead streaks pink and orange. "Let me go first," he says.

His long legs reach the midstream stones in one leap, and he's on the other side with a second leap as if this is everyday normal. He extends one long arm back toward where I wait. But I'm dithering about how to mimic what he just did with my shorter legs. "Come on," he says.

I take a deep breath and leap across the first water obstacle, wobbling on the two stones and afraid I'll lose my balance.

"You're halfway here," he says.

I teeter on the edge of the stones. He's grinning, maybe thinking he has one up on me. That's all the challenge I need. Trusting my legs will get me there, I leap off the rocks. I'm about to fall short of the bank when his strong hand reaches out and grabs mine. With his hand wrapped tightly around mine, he pulls me onto the bank.

"You have a definite advantage," I say.

"Are you okay?" he asks. He's still holding my hand. For a moment, Gilbert's powerful hand around mine takes me back to another time in the woods, another hand. Robert's hand was all the assurance I needed on any given day. Until it was no longer there. The awkwardness inside my chest prompts me to remove my hand from Gilbert's.

Our jeans are splashed with water, and the wind magnifies the cold on wet denim. We start ahead on the wooded trail, walking side by side. The trail winds into the darker woods where the sunset is hard-pressed to penetrate the umbrella of birch and oak trees that cluster close together. "Do you ever miss the life you left behind?" I ask.

"That seems like someone else's life," he says. "I suspect your story will someday feel the same."

"My story?"

"We all have a story. It's about our history and the work we do or did, what we own—cars, houses, kids, vacations—and what we believe about all those things. You heard Roland mention it."

"I didn't know what he meant." I'm silent, reflective for a few minutes. "I never thought about having a story."

"It's what we pin our hopes on. You'll discover yours this week or the next time you come."

Next time? The idea overwhelms me. Something I need to relegate to the category of things to think about later.

The sunset has faded across the sky and only a golden outline waits at the horizon. We've been walking for about thirty minutes, and I'm aware of our closeness, our arms touching from time to time but not really. I stop in the middle of the trail. "It's getting dark," I say. "We probably need to turn back."

"If you'd feel more comfortable," Gilbert says.

"You hesitated when you said that."

His eyes close. "A personal failure," he says. "I often stop myself too soon, before I reach the certainty that I've gone as far as I can."

"What does that have to do with staying too long in the woods?"

"We could go farther. I have a flashlight; we can't get lost if we stay on the road."

"What about the creek?"

"We'll cross the same way we crossed it before," he says. "Just a little farther up."

"But what if I don't want to go farther?"

He reaches out to take my hand. "We won't go far."

I shove my hands in my pocket. I'm mad at him for not respecting my sense of safety and at myself for not bringing the flashlight on my key ring. I never go anywhere without it.

"Do you always win?" I ask.

"Do you?"

The overhead light has blued behind the taller trees, and the moon is rising out of the forest and over those same trees, lighting the path ahead of us. Without further discussion, we keep walking into the woods. The path becomes indistinct as we move deeper into the trees.

"We're losing the moon," I say.

"We never lose the moon," he says. "Our way, yes, but not the moon."

His hand keeps brushing against mine like an invitation, but I refuse to take it. I stay close nonetheless. The trail proves uneven with small branches and tree roots not always visible in the fading light. I wish I'd picked up a walking stick.

We keep walking, silent until I can barely stand it. "Let me ask you a question," I say. "Out of nowhere and impertinent as it may be."

He says nothing, and I count that as an affirmation. "Are you afraid of dying, Gilbert? And don't turn the question on me."

"I confess I'm curious why you asked."

"Nope. You don't get to wiggle out of this one. Are you afraid of dying?"

His steps and mine crunch over dried leaves from last winter and twigs that snap. "Yes and no," he says. "In all honesty, when Amy was born there was a part of me that wished she hadn't made it, especially since Carolyn had miscarriages and one stillbirth before Amy. I've never told anyone that except you and Roland. But I don't think about death for myself. Roland, yes. We've planned for that."

We keep walking forward and I'm more anxious, my hands sweating. We need to turn around sometime soon.

"I need to amend that," he says. "Yes, I'm scared of dying. For Amy's sake."

"Amy's fair," I say.

More silence. "There are times and places we die when we're alive," I say. "That's where I've been lately. Scared to be somewhere I've never been before, scared of being alone. Of loneliness." My throat feels blocked from saying those words as though they are forbidden and too revealing.

I've said more than I intended. Maybe it's the ever-increasing darkness that gives me permission. There's no way that Gilbert can read my face. Maybe it's the unexpected arrival of Jennifer at the hotel as well as her Dr. Michael. Then there are the personal circumstances that brought me here.

"I think it's time to turn around," I say.

He stops and stretches his hand toward me. "I get scared too."

"That would mean you're human." I take his hand, and his fingers wrap around mine. Holding his hand feels awkward. But the firmness and seeming confidence are reassuring. In that moment taking another man's hand doesn't feel right. Some misguided loyalty to Stan? Is it that Gilbert's a man I hardly know? But I'm afraid to let go in the darkness and with the uneven path.

"It's your turn," Gilbert says. "Are you afraid of dying?"

I walk close to his side, my arm against his prompting a comfort in my belly that I hadn't expected. Especially now, jumping when an owl hoots or the crows flock into the taller trees, something I didn't do when we had a trace of light. "I'm mostly afraid of leaving things undone."

"Like what?"

"I'm not sure. It's a feeling that there's something I'm supposed to do. It has to do with family. I think that's the other reason I'm here."

"Maybe Jennifer showing up was no accident."

"You're probably right; I just wish it wasn't so complicated. The professor. You know what I mean."

My hand in his, my fingers finally giving in to what feels natural. Those words following us to the edge of the creek where the moon has crawled out of the trees and shines on the first stone, the opposite shore half in shadow and half in light. I release Gilbert's hand and, without real thought, leap toward the first stone just to prove I can. I miss the stone and my foot falls into the shallow stream. I laugh at my predicament, the dark night, and feel like I'm a kid again. Behind me, Gilbert can't cross until I get to the other side. Rather than risk leaping one more time, I walk through the water, splashing with my knees while my arms make wide and defiant circles as I head across.

Gilbert takes his time moving from stone to stone toward the shore, the stones now slippery where I slid off the first one. We are both laughing when Gilbert reaches me. He pulls me toward him. I want to push him away. His arms around me feel strangely wrong. The strength, the certainty, and the sense of safety in being held unleash a rush of tears. Tears that never surfaced when Stan said it was over—my trained stoicism held emotion at a distance. No tears when he told me about his girlfriend, about her pregnancy. None when he said they were getting married and he would be a new father. All that wetness, whatever I'd been hanging on to, soaks into Gilbert's jacket along with my mascara. In that moment I remember the late afternoon I watched from the car's back window and waved to Oma as Daddy drove away from her house that last time. The tears streamed down my face while I tried to stop the urge to sniffle, afraid my sisters would laugh and make fun of me. Instead, I turned toward the side window and hid my face, staring into the mercifully darkened sky with the same mixed feelings I have now.

"It's okay," he says, his arms around me, loosely holding me but holding me nonetheless.

When I pull away, my eyes focus past him and toward the gate where the slender afterglow of the moon has disappeared into the trees again. "This is what happens when I take a time-out," I say, attempting to be lighthearted.

To his credit, he says nothing.

Chapter Nine

BACK IN MY HOTEL ROOM, I run a tub of bubble bath. I quickly unseal the envelope with the divorce papers that I picked up at the front desk when Gilbert and I returned from our walk. The first order of business is into the bathtub along with popcorn or potato chips, something salty and full of fat as an after-bath treat. I can read the damned papers in the tub.

Climbing into the bubbles, I lie back against the curve of the tub and try to let go of my sadness and confusion. About Jennifer and her abortion, about Stan finding someone else, about why I'm here. It's been weeks since Stan announced he was leaving the marriage and only now am I falling apart. Am I that frozen inside? And why do I feel ashamed, like I'm the one who failed in this marriage?

The tub's hot water soaks the day's stress and frustration from my skin. I relax deeper into the sudsy water. Forget any more phone messages, likely from Stan obsessing about the financial settlement. Maybe he regrets his agreement that I should keep the house. Or Jennifer wants to know what I think of Michael. Isn't he a nice guy? Didn't I like him?

I lie back in the hot, soapy water and begin to read through the papers I've brought into the tub with me. Everything looks like it's in order until I get to the property settlement, the last paragraph. That's when I notice the addendum to the standard agreement. The bastard has reversed the agreement about the house. *He* will retain ownership and pay me half the value after appraisal. *What the hell? Does he seriously think he's going to get away with this?*

Damn him anyhow.

The wine. If only I'd thought to bring a glass to the tub. Now I want it, need it, more than ever. I should have known the papers would get to me. And there, waiting in the cold fridge, is the wine. Besides, I only had one martini at dinner. But damn, I'm throat high in bubbles and have no way to get out of the tub without leaving a mess and getting the papers wet.

I lift myself up against the side of the tub, my body a slithering mass of bubble bath soap. One dripping leg over the tub, then the other. I grab my towel from the nearby rack and lift one leg to dry off. Without warning, the other leg goes out from under me. Before I know what's happened, I'm lying naked and wet against the cold tile. I have to laugh at my own poor judgment. Then I mentally check my now-prostrate body. Legs seem to work. Arms. What was I thinking? That was so stupid. Now that I'm on this cold tile, I want the wine more than ever, dammit.

I grab a second towel and wrap it around myself. I need one of the tall wineglasses. Then the bottle of wine. With the towel tucked under each armpit, I carry both the wine bottle and the glass back into the bathroom. I set them carefully on the tile beside the bathtub where I laid the divorce papers.

Once back in the tub, I wonder how I'm going to fill that wineglass without leaning halfway out of the tub. *Damn.* I maneuver myself to my knees and lean over, removing the loosened cork from the bottle and filling the wineglass nearly to the brim. I don't want to attempt this strategy again if I can help it.

I lift the wineglass into the air, protecting the precious elixir. I had no idea how much I've anticipated that first taste, the warmth when the wine slides past my tongue and into my throat. A second sip. I've just settled into the bubbles when my cell phone rings again. *What the hell? Who keeps calling? Well, I'm not getting out of the tub.*

I settle with the papers in my other hand. I reread the addendum a second time, trying to make sense of the language. I'm far too agitated when I lift the glass to my mouth. I turn at the same time. The glass stem catches on the tub's rim. Before I can blink, the wineglass shatters against the enamel siding. Holy shit. Wine in the tub and all over the floor. Glass in the tub. My left arm bleeds down the entire length of my upper limb. It's not just bleeding. Blood seemingly gushes from a piece of broken glass sticking out of my arm. My mind can't grasp what has happened except that the divorce papers are now stained with blood.

The pain. The pain and blood, and I'm terrified to move. If I shift one way or the other, I'm sitting in glass. If I try to get on my knees, I'm kneeling in glass. *Shit, shit, shit.* I'm in the bathroom. Alone. No phone. I need to get these divorce papers somewhere safe. The floor's the only place to toss them. But I don't dare bend over. I toss them onto the floor, as far away from the water as they'll go. But the floor is wet with wine and water from my previous fall. Now, the divorce papers are bloody and wet as well.

I raise my left arm above the tub's rim. Someone else is going to have to remove the glass that's sticking out of that cut; it can't be me. I'll throw up everywhere. I'm already feeling woozy from the shooting pain that radiates the length of my arm. *My God, what have I done? What can I do?* Slow as I can, I lean forward and trip the drain with my right hand while the blood drips from my left arm onto the white bubbles. I have to get out of here or I'm going to be sick.

The water slowly eases out of the tub while I keep my cut arm above the water even though I don't want to see the blood. Oh, great. Now there's nothing but soap bubbles. And the throbbing is getting worse. I need someone, anyone, to take that piece of glass out of my arm. But how?

I feel along the tub's bottom and, sure enough, there's glass scattered on my left side. I don't dare lean in that direction. I feel along the right side of the tub, but that side faces the wall. That doesn't help me at all. Still, there's an urgency to get up and out of the tub. *Get out and get help, in that order. Call the desk. Call 911. Call somebody for God's sake!*

Don't panic. Go slow. Maybe if I scoot forward toward the drain, it won't be so bad. But now I can't stop the pain, and I can't stop the tears. I'm afraid to move my left arm. I don't want to see the glass sticking out. Slowly I lift my butt. *Don't scoot. Easy, easy. An inch at a time. Don't look at the arm.* But I can't help it, the blood runs in a crooked river from the cut to my elbow. Not a sliver of glass but a big piece. How big, I'm not sure. *Just creep toward the drain where it's hopefully safe. Now grab on to the grab bar . . . thank God there is one. Pull. Harder. With everything you have in that right arm. When halfway up, step back with your right foot to balance yourself. Good, you're almost there. All you have to do is stand and grab a towel. Hold it under your arm. Watch the floor. There's shattered glass everywhere, even on the mat. Be careful. Slowly throw down another towel. Smart woman. Walk on that. Get out of this bathroom hellhole. Call the desk. Yes, you need help.*

You have to ignore the pain right now. Never mind you don't have a stitch on your body.

Jennifer. I dial her number; it goes immediately to voicemail. Of course, they're at a special lecture on aerodynamics tonight. I call the front desk. "It's Marta Bufford in Room 616. I've cut my arm badly. I need medical attention."

"So sorry about that, ma'am," the voice says. They sound panicked. "I'll call 911 and send someone up."

"No sirens and no high drama, understand?"

My left arm. *Oh my God, the throbbing pain. Bleeding. What have I done?* I'm down the rabbit hole inside my now-tiny mind. Worse, when I twist or turn my arm, the unrelenting pain shoots into my shoulder. There's nothing to do but wait. I'm helpless. Alone. *Damn, damn, damn. What was I thinking? Keep the towel under your elbow. Last thing you need is blood all over the white comforter; the towels are bad enough.* I need to pick up those divorce papers. My God, they're wet and bloody. If I can just make it to the bed and lean against it, maybe I can slip my nightgown over my head with my right hand.

I can just see Oma cluck her tongue against the roof of her mouth while looking down her long nose at me. The awful scar across her cheek, her misshapen and swollen lip. Though she would never say, *Just like your father, your grandfather*, I still would never want her to see me like this, naked and broken, all for a glass of wine.

Though dizzy, I lift and hold my left arm, desperate to find a position where the pain doesn't radiate in waves and the blood doesn't drip past the towel. I sit on the desk chair, the heat of tears behind my eyes. Tears. That's the last thing I want. Rather, I need to get myself under control and covered before anyone comes. I try to move as little as possible when I lift my nightgown out of the underwear drawer. Always, my eyes carefully focus away from the glass sticking out of my arm. *Don't give in to pain, no matter what.*

How am I going to get the nightgown over my head? I stand in front of the mirror and carefully, oh so carefully, slip the night-gown over the wounded arm first, creating a tent above the glass. As delicately as I can, I lift the nightgown and ease it until it's under my arm. Lowering that arm, I slip the nightgown over my head and my other arm. *Oh my God.* The effort makes me nauseous. I want to do anything but throw up. My lowered arm continues to throb with the stabbing pain that activates all the nerves in my shoulder.

What would Roland do? He'd say, *Breathe. In and out, longer on the outbreath.*

I focus on my breath even while I'm aware that my night-gown is too thin and see-through. The fabric was designed for hot summer nights and not Duluth's June winter. I don't want anyone to see me like this, a mid-sixty-year-old woman naked and without anything to camouflage what needs to stay hidden.

Buck up, girl. Just get to the closet for your robe. I inch along, holding my arm close to my body as though I can keep it safe or at least keep it from bumping into anything.

It seems impossible, this slow walk across the room, the nausea making it hard to leave the safety of the bed's edge, the chest of drawers. The closet remains a good six steps away.

The first wave of vertigo cripples any forward movement. *They have to be here soon. Damn and double damn.*

"Relax," I say aloud. Staring at the bedside clock is no help. It's 10:55. Ten, then fifteen minutes. Why was I so bent on that glass of wine? It was the damned divorce papers, that's what. But why do I always think I need wine to get through an evening or to reward myself after a difficult day? Why can't I be satisfied with a cup of coffee or tea? Wine, always my first choice. Now a curse.

There's a knock on the door, and I haven't yet reached my bathrobe. Somehow I need to get to the door and let the medics in despite the swirling vertigo.

The pounding grows louder, more intense. "Hold on a damned minute," I shout, though I don't know if anyone can hear me. These doors are often so thick for fire safety that they're impervious to sound.

Now I hear voices outside the door. More pounding. I'm as good as naked in this nightgown.

"Hold on," I yell again. But the pounding intensifies and nearly muffles the sound of what must be a passkey as someone tries to get into the room. No luck. That's when I notice the door guard—a simple, two-pronged, U-shaped piece of brass fitting over a brass finger meant to prohibit entry—is engaged. "I'm almost there," I shout. Closer to the door now, I inch along the wall.

The door opens without warning. I'm nearly knocked over by the impact. The door guard, now ripped from the wall, hangs alongside the open screw holes that held the guard in place. An alarmed hotel employee, someone who clearly works out, is startled by what he's just done. Two white-shirted medics, a gal and a guy with red sleeve patches, haul in a gurney and a couple of bags likely full of equipment. "Sit here on the chair," the guy says as he pulls out the desk chair. He eases me down. "We need to stop the bleeding." He grimaces when he sees the odd shaped piece of glass sticking out of the cut.

The medics pull equipment out of their bags and slap on a blood pressure cuff. I can't close my eyes or the vertigo will win. I try to forget this is happening, even while the hotel staff member calls housekeeping to come clean up the glass and the tub. If only I could relax into being the victim of my own foolishness.

Two minutes later Gilbert enters the room wearing the same plaid shirt. "I was downstairs at the registration desk when your call for 911 came in. I got here as fast as I could," he says to no one in particular, likely surprised at the entire assembled group. "What happened?"

"Would somebody please get my robe out of the closet?" I shout, my voice desperate and nearly hysterical to my own ears.

"Who are you?" the female medic asks Gilbert.

"A friend and the seminar leader. I just left her here a half hour ago," he says. "What the heck is going on anyhow?"

"Whoever you are, you need to stay out of the way so we can do our job," she says.

"Oh, my god," he says when he seems to suddenly see the blood. But Gilbert being Gilbert, he maintains eye contact with me when he opens the robe, otherwise ignoring the medic's edict. He lifts the shoulder of the robe and drapes it behind my left arm where the male medic examines the wound. I try not to twist inside the medic's hands, but every time he gets near the cut, the pain intensifies. Like I've been shot and the bullet has gone too deep.

"We're going to get you to the hospital," he says. "They'll deal with the glass and the wound there. But first we're going to insert an IV in order to start fluids."

The female medic, hearing my panic, says, "We're going to take care of you. Just try not to move."

I suppose this is supposed to be reassuring, but it's my pain, not theirs.

I flinch. "Holy shit." I don't know how long I can stand the pain without passing out. I keep staring at the blood oozing down my arm, the protruding glass like it's stuck in someone else's arm, but their pain is now mine. Pain like I've never felt before, not in childbirth, not at the dentist's, not any other time I can recall. "It hurts like hell!"

The room phone begins to ring and ring and ring. I'm nearly undone already. "Someone, please answer the damned phone!" I'm screaming now. Who is this person with my voice?

The female medic—named Sarah, according to her name tag—brings me water from the bathroom. I notice she has to step around the hotel maid. "Here," she says. "Just a few sips."

Gilbert, who has been standing behind me, doesn't remove his hand resting on my right shoulder except to readjust the robe. His thoughtfulness brings back the heat behind my eyes.

I do and don't want to see the medic insert the needle. Don't want to see her adjust the IV bag, the whole time staying away from the inch-long sliver of glass sticking out of my arm. I will my eyes to stay open and pray for the nausea to pass. I can no longer watch what the medic is doing. The pain doesn't stop and neither does my fear.

In a moment of sanity, I focus on the divorce papers that now lie wet and bloody on the desk. The maid must have picked them up and laid them there. *Damn, what was I thinking? How could I have been so stupid? What happened to the smart woman I'm supposed to be? The smart woman I like to think I am. Where the hell did she go?*

"Is there ice in the refrigerator?" Sarah asks.

I'm suddenly attentive. The minute the door opens, the bottle of champagne lying sideways will fall and crash onto the tile.

"Best to get the ice down the hall from the ice machine," the hotel employee says.

I'm relieved. Am I afraid someone will think I'm an alcoholic? Why wouldn't they? A bottle on the bathroom floor and another in the fridge? Isn't that what Kelsey asked the last time she was home? *Are you an alcoholic, Mom?* It's true that Stan and I are daily drinkers, and we've both been drinking more since the divorce drama began. That doesn't mean we're alcoholics, for God's sake.

A HALF HOUR LATER I'M lying half-awake on a gurney hearing squeaky shoes against hospital linoleum. The scraping wheels of another gurney outside my curtained cubicle tell me I'm in an emergency room. "She's sixty-three years old," I hear someone say. "Needs an EKG." The sheetlike curtain surrounding me allows light beneath and over the top. On the other side of the flimsy barrier, someone moans while the ever-loud hospital staff exchange jokes. Except for the moaner, I'm mercifully alone.

I can finally relax. Until I hear Gilbert's voice. "I'm from the seminar," he says. "Responsible for keeping her safe."

A staff member peeks around the blue curtain and either doesn't see me shake my head no or isn't buying it. "She's good."

Gilbert draws back the curtain and sticks his head inside. "How do you feel?"

"Better," I say. "It still hurts like hell."

"Good to see your feisty self," he says.

"Thanks a whole hell of a lot."

His smile this time is anything but the meditation half smile. "What can I get you?" he asks.

"One thing," I say. "You can stop being so damned nice."

Gilbert, with his basset hound eyes, gazes down at me, at my heavily bandaged arm, and is speechless for the first time since I met him.

"I can't imagine how I'll drive a car."

He shakes his head. "You won't be driving as long as you're on medication."

AFTER A LATE WHITE BREAD sandwich of ham and cheese and a fruit cup, a white-coated woman throws back the curtain. "You look perky," she says. "That was a nasty cut. Lucky for you the medics got there as fast as they did. You have a half dozen stitches in that arm. By the way, I'm Dr. Stevens."

Oma. Her face in front of me. *Young lady*, she says. *You have to eat all your borscht before you can have kuchen.* The apron over her cumbersome bosom, the steamy windows, and the smell of rising bread. Oma, who never gave up. Not her beliefs, her perseverance, or the family she lived for. That small house in town. Her garden, Uncle Ivan's pigeons, the outhouse. Why I'm thinking about that right now, I don't know.

"The bandage will keep you safe until the swelling goes down. We'll then fit you with a less intrusive bandage." She scoots around Gilbert. "Good thing you have your husband here."

"Doctor, this man is my friend, not my husband."

"Thank you for correcting me," she says.

Her youth reminds me of Kelsey, my most critical daughter who tends to see the cup half-empty. The brown hair in a short cut, her focus on what's in front of her, a certain brusqueness I attribute to today's young professional women. This doctor has Kelsey's same wry humor.

While Dr. Stevens charts on the computer, I turn to Gilbert. "I've made up my mind."

He steps closer until he's beside the gurney. "What's that?"

"I can't bear the idea of going back to the restlessness and confusion I brought with me. I'd like to finish what I came for—the seminar. Can you help me with that?"

"Of course," he says. "What do you need?"

Though his words are affirming, he sounds cautious. He's already witnessed my determination in the woods. Likely saw the wine bottle and the mess in the bathroom. Yet he moves closer to the bed. Behind him, the doctor stands with her arms crossed as she witnesses our exchange.

I turn toward the doctor. "With this deep cut, can I complete the weeklong seminar I came for?"

"Of course," she says. "Looks like you have lots of help."

My throat has gone dry and I'm having to tug the words up through my windpipe and force them onto my tongue. It doesn't help to have this doctor looking on. "What do you think, Gilbert? It's asking a lot."

He says nothing for a minute. Then he smiles in the same teasing way I saw in the woods when he challenged me to cross the creek and later, when he didn't want to turn back. "We can always give you a voucher for another time."

I gaze down at the bandage that now defines my arm only to once again experience the embarrassment and shame I felt lying on the bathroom tile, asking myself why the wine always seems so necessary. "No, it has to be now."

Chapter Ten

Wednesday, June 12

THE NEXT MORNING THE PAIN continues to burn through doses of painkillers, which I'm instructed to take with food. Dressing takes longer than usual because of the bulky bandage on my arm. Raising my arm to slip through even a short-sleeved blouse proves painful, which means I have to plan to dress thirty minutes after taking a pain pill. My only cardigan is a white cashmere I've saved for a special night out. The fashion disasters multiply. My gold-and-navy shawl clashes with most of my shirts. Poor planning and now all these lessons in humility.

I pull the sweater over one arm and drape it on the shoulder of the other, securing my small purse over my head and good shoulder. I gather up the now-dry divorce papers and shove them in the desk drawer. Before leaving, I open the fridge. Both bottles are still there. Once I return and I'm lying on the bed, I can surely have a glass of wine. No chance of me breaking another glass as long as I stay out of the bathtub.

When the elevator door opens, Gilbert stands before me, his white open-necked golf shirt and graying chest hair the first things I see. "I was getting concerned so I came up," he says. "Did you have breakfast?"

"My faithful energy bar," I say. "Maybe this is the day to have a real lunch."

"I'll help you to the car," he says. "Already thought of lunch. We have sandwiches from the kitchen."

"Audrey was expecting me for lunch today. Would you kindly tell her what happened so I don't have to repeat the whole sordid, embarrassing mess?"

Gilbert nods. "Will do," he says.

"ALL MEDITATION THIS MORNING WILL be open eye," Roland announces. The same single lamp brightens the same pitcher of water and glass, and the same small mic is clipped to his tweed jacket. His cane now rests against the vacant podium. The participants are quiet and waiting, eager for him to begin. "You are practiced now, so we will meditate for thirty minutes. Therefore, I'm asking that you simply watch your breath. I want you to inhale on the count of four, hold your breath for a seven count, and then exhale for a count of seven. As I've said before, the exhalation should be longer than the inhalation. You can then begin to feel the stillness that waits inside you."

Gilbert returns to our seats with a soft pillow he found backstage. "Lean forward; I'll put this behind you."

Though I know he's trying to be helpful, I'm becoming annoyed at his oversolicitousness. "You're too kind and thoughtful," I say.

He doesn't hear my sarcasm or he's ignoring it. Didn't I ask him to stop being so nice? "Did you talk to my new friend, Audrey? She asked and I agreed that she could interview me as part of reporting on the seminar."

Gilbert looks around the seminar room at the participants. "I did tell her you wouldn't be joining her for lunch," he says. "Why does she want to write about the seminar?" I hear defensiveness in his tone.

"Because, according to her, this is the most interesting thing happening in Duluth this week," I say. My voice has that droll edge that I usually save for cross examination of a hostile witness. Now, it's just one more thing I need to let go of.

Unlike other mornings, I'm surprised by how much I relax into the exercise. Maybe it's the painkillers. This is especially unusual since the open-eye meditation continues to be the most challenging for me. On previous mornings, I had to keep my eyes steady and focused on a small hole of light in the curtain behind Roland. I relax into my breath, relieved for the silence, for the spot in the curtain.

My mind flips to Aunt Ada. Her face when she opened the front door. "Marta?" she asked, more surprise than question. Then she saw my tears. "Come in, come in," she said. I never had to say much to Aunt Ada. She dyed her hair red into her sixties, and her second husband was more fictional than real. A salesman, she always said by way of explanation. That was supposed to account for why he was gone so much and never present for Mom's Sunday dinners.

I sat on the sofa, Aunt Ada across from me, her hands around mine. I don't think I said more than two sentences. "We'll take care of it," she said. "Just leave it to me." Though neither one of us said so, we both knew we wouldn't tell Mom. What was the point of upsetting her? Mom had covered for Aunt Ada all those years ago when Oma suspected Aunt Ada was pregnant. Now was a payback of sorts. The five one-hundred-dollar bills courtesy of the invisible husband, the white leather seats of her T-Bird. The sunny afternoon down I-5 to the Mexican border. Robert's plane had barely landed in Saigon.

The old sadness has been buried for so long, I'd forgotten it was there.

A loud sigh, mine, breaks my reverie. *Stuck.* That's the word that comes to mind. If it wasn't for Aunt Ada, I'd have been forever stuck at nineteen. Abortion, both the seeming savior and a rite of passage in our family. My breath. I need to get my mind back on my breath.

Gilbert glances over and begins to reach for my hand. I nod my head no. Return to my spot on the curtain where the small beam of light leaks through from backstage. First inhale. Then exhale. The hole of light. The darkened room.

"What happened to you in meditation this morning?" Gilbert asks.

He has led me back to the private patio, a paper bag in his hand. At least I remembered to bring my sun hat. The same wrought iron table where I shared his snack the day before. Roland, having excused himself at lunch, retreated backstage to a room where he would quietly eat his sandwich and rest.

I adjust my elbow. A twitch of momentary searing pain runs up my arm. I try to appreciate the sun's warmth, but it barely compensates for a bad night's sleep. After the first bite of my tuna sandwich, I take the pain pill. Doctor's orders: stay ahead of the pain.

"In answer to your question, Gilbert, I remembered an incident from a long time ago. Something I'd rather forget. An old love, you could say."

"We all have those."

"Some are harder to forget than others. You know, especially those first loves."

He says nothing for a minute, his face toward the lava rock beneath the fountain. "Sometimes the first and the last."

I remove my sunglasses, and for the first time, our eyes meet. I will myself not to look away.

"We all have ghosts," he says. He scrunches the used sandwich paper and tosses it into the paper bag. "You wouldn't have liked me much before I met Roland."

I remain silent for a minute or two, wondering how much I

want to know about this man. At the same time, I'm intrigued. "Why are you telling me this?"

"Maybe I want you to like me." He glances away when he says that. "Sometimes I don't like myself." He hesitates. "I keep remembering the night I walked in the door after working late, and the hallway was dark, the bedroom lights turned off," he says. "The only light in the house came from Amy's nursery, where a hired nurse dozed in a chair. The note on the bedroom dresser said, 'It's your turn.'"

I say nothing for several seconds. Finally, I ask, "Was it your turn?"

He continues to gaze toward the fountain, its quiet gurgle the only sound. "It was my turn. I just wasn't ready."

"I understand the shock. But it seems from your own report that all you were doing was running away."

He continues to stare into the fountain. He says nothing.

I'm quiet except for a quickening in my chest. I can't speak until my voice assumes a neutral tone. "I can understand why you feel guilty. I know that feeling."

When he doesn't say anything, I pull my purse over my shoulder. "Why aren't you with Amy now?"

He starts to stand. "Guess it's time to go back."

RIGHT AFTER THE MIDAFTERNOON BREAK, Roland announces, "Your assignment for this evening is to list your top five priorities. Do that before supper." There's a dramatic pause. "After supper I want you to list the five places where you devote most of your time and energy. Following that, I'd like you to write two paragraphs about the difference between the two lists."

After days of meditation, this assignment, simple as it sounds, proves the most challenging. I already know that my two lists won't match. I could easily do the second one, but the first list will be a challenge. Writing the comparison is unimaginable.

I'm relieved when Gilbert takes me to the car first before returning to get Roland. I haven't been alone all day except during meditation, and I couldn't keep my mind focused after lunch. The discomfort in my arm lingers after Roland's return to the car and our drive past the campus buildings and dorms, past the university president's house where Emily lives with her homey and lived-in furniture, her graciousness.

Gilbert stops at a pharmacy. "Will just be a minute. Need to pick up a couple of prescriptions for Roland."

He's barely closed the car door when Roland turns toward the back seat. "You were very quiet today."

"Maybe I'm more introverted than I thought, Roland."

"There are worse ways to be in the world."

I smile, taking the hand he extends into the back seat. Purple blotches like ink stains cover the back of his hand, the bones seeming more prominent than the first time I met him. His eyes remain bright but distant at the same time. In that moment Oma's fat hand comes to mind. How I would have loved to hold her hand like I now hold Roland's. The moment that is a world beyond the present. Here and then gone.

He remains turned toward me. "Was the first exercise helpful to you?" he asked. "The words, the sentence. Whatever came to mind?" He smiles and the wrinkles around his mouth disappear momentarily.

"Let's just say it was a surprise."

"That's what it's meant to be," he says. "Just looking into your eyes, I can see something has changed."

"Something did change," I say. I'm unsure whether I want to say the words or not. They feel like that moment when a baby emerges from the birth canal and you see what you've been incubating inside your belly for the first time.

"If I was to guess," he continues. "The image that comes to mind is the bear with a heart line. Do you know that image? It's Zuni." His hand squeezes mine where he still holds on.

"Funny you say that. I have a necklace with that figure embedded in agate and turquoise. A gift from my husband when I graduated from law school."

"There you have it," he says. "That bear will guide you if you trust him. Can you do that?"

Before I can answer, Gilbert opens the car door with a white paper sack in hand. Roland releases my hand and turns back to the front, glancing quickly at Gilbert.

"Were you two getting into trouble while I was gone?" Gilbert asks. He gazes at me in the rearview mirror, his lightheartedness such a strange turn from his usual seriousness.

"All the trouble we could manage," I say. When I turn to gaze out the window, the image of that particular necklace I haven't worn for too long comes to mind. A pendant with a red heart line inside a turquoise bear. How did Roland know?

Chapter Eleven

Back in my room, I pick up my cell phone. "Jennifer? I need a favor."

"Anything, Oma."

I smile. "I had a little accident last night," I say. "Before you panic, I'm fine. Just cut my arm doing something foolish, and now I have a bandaged arm."

"Did you see the doctor? Did someone help you? Oma, I'm so sorry I didn't call back."

"I'm fine," I say. "But I need a sweatshirt that zips in front. I just can't seem to stay warm. Do you think you could get that for me?"

Jennifer hesitates. "I promised Michael I'd copy a manuscript for him before supper."

"Is he going to work on it before dinner?"

Jennifer pauses again. "No."

"Then would you check the gift shop downstairs? If they don't have them, you can take my car downtown."

"I'll do the best I can."

I put a cool washcloth against my face. The medication was making me sleepy. In the mirror I notice gray creeping into the hair around my face, the dye now fading in its fourth week. In another week I'll be in trouble. What the hell. I now have a good excuse to let it go. Besides, who am I trying to impress? I study the crow's feet around my eyes, the marionette lines half-mooning my mouth and digging into my cheeks. A sweatshirt and no makeup? I won't know who I am.

A knock on the door catches me mid-reverie. "Hold on," I say.

Jennifer, out of breath and huffing, stands in front of me with a red shopping bag. Roxanne's, the hotel shop's label, glitters in silver letters. "I got a medium for more room, will that work?"

"Perfect. What do I owe you?" I ask.

"I told them to put it on your hotel bill. I hope that was okay, Oma."

We both stop at the sound of a siren directly outside the window, the whine startling both of us. The siren ends in the driveway below with the pulse of flashing red lights reflected against the half-closed drapes.

"Hope it's nothing serious," I say.

"At least it isn't you," Jennifer says. "Call if you need anything else." Her forehead frowns like it did a few minutes ago when she came into the room with the sweatshirt. "After dinner though." Then she's gone, her pink blond hair a flash when she closes the door.

Shrouded in the terry robe, I'm ready to rest. But something is missing. How will I maneuver a bottle of wine and a glass to the bed? Better to call the front desk and order a glass of red from the bar.

"Later," I say aloud. I lie on the bed and close my eyes. Drift into that liminal space where dreams reside. I'm disturbed when my cell phone rings.

"Roland has collapsed," Gilbert says. "We're at the local hospital."

I sit up to get a better hold of the phone. "Was that the siren I heard a while ago?"

"Yes. As soon as we returned, he was pale and nearly incoherent." He clears his throat. "I'll stay in touch," he says. "If it's not too late when I get back, I'll call. Needless to say, I'll be taking over tomorrow."

"I'm assuming you've done that before."

"Once, when he suffered heatstroke in Phoenix. That was four years ago."

I'm stunned. First my arm. Now this. But my arm is nothing compared to Roland's health. He's fragile. He needs help to the stage, and he requires a long midday nap so he can go on with the afternoon. Gilbert's probably on alert at all times.

It's not just Roland. After a certain age, we're all fragile in ways we can't see. I don't know what's going on in my body unless I have a pain or some breakdown that lets me know things aren't right. Stan takes what seem like a hundred pills each day just to keep his body in good enough shape to keep going at a close-to-usual pace, enough to father a child at least. This badly cut arm is the result of my own foolishness. Trying to get a glass of wine into the tub, for Pete's sake. What was I thinking? Of course, no one besides myself and the hotel staff will ever know. Except for Gilbert. Yet Roland can't function without Gilbert or someone watching over him. This ER visit must be about more than aging.

I try to lie down again, but I'm too wound up.

"Are you afraid of dying?" I once asked Oma. I must have been four or five at the time. It seemed like a natural question following so much death when Mom and Aunt Ada lived with all us kids in the little house on Myra's First Street during the war. I knew I could ask Oma that question. I trusted her more than anyone. After all, wasn't she the one who always said I was her *schatzi*, her special angel, that we would always be together, no matter what? Even then I could touch her arm at the kitchen table when we were alone and tell her how scared I was of Daddy, that funny smell on him when he'd been to the tavern or when he seemed too happy.

That day, she was leaning over the rolling pin and pushing the dough on a floured board she'd set on top of the oilcloth-covered table. Her long, braided hair was pulled back in a knot, her apron tight across her bosom. Her glasses kept sliding down her nose from the sweat on her face. "What a strange question for a little girl," she said.

I thought I'd done something wrong until she lowered her head and smiled at me, the same smile that always distorted her face where the scar cut deep beside her nose. "No, I'm not afraid of dying," she said. She pulled back on the rolling pin, then rolled it forward until the dough was even thinner.

I kept my eyes on the dough and her hands, so strong and efficient with her long, tapered fingers.

"I have the Lord, Marta. He's always with me, and he'll be there when I pass on as well. Just like he's there with you."

I must have had a quizzical look on my face. "What does that mean, Oma?"

She looked up from her rolling pin, the dough now thin enough for her to fill and roll before cutting the cinnamon rolls I'd been waiting for.

"The Lord is in my heart. Same as he's in yours."

My elbow on the table, I pondered how the Lord could be in the picture over the church entrance and also in her heart. In mine. "Like you said Grandpa Albert is? In heaven with the Lord?"

She winced. "Yes, like Grandpa Albert." She brushed her hands over the breadboard.

She never talked about Grandpa Albert. Years later, I wondered if she even liked him.

She wiped her forehead with the back of her arm. "No need to be afraid, Marta. The Lord will protect you the same way he's protecting me."

Even as she said the words, my eyes teared up and that fist I sometimes felt in my throat grew bigger. How would I know if the Lord was with me? I was too afraid to ask.

"Will you be with Uncle Philip too?" I asked.

"Yes, with him too," she said. I remember she turned away. "The Lord will make it right," she said.

The question I wanted to ask that day was *how do you know the Lord is there?* Daddy said there was no God. No Lord. Otherwise, why had all his friends died in the war? Why had Uncle Ozzie been killed? At my young age I didn't understand anything Daddy said. Even now I don't understand Oma's statement that the Lord will make it right, that the Lord will keep us safe. What did that mean? Here I am, past sixty years old, married to the same man for nearly forty years. But where was the Lord that day on Harbor Island two months ago when I walked into Seascape for a late business lunch and saw Stan with a young activist, sitting side by side, gazing toward downtown San Diego. Stan held her hand, not the way a friend would hold someone's hand but more like a lover. Sunlight fell across their table and illuminated his mother's diamond ring on the young woman's finger, the same diamond he said he was saving for Jennifer, our granddaughter. He must have had a miraculous cure because, despite the aneurism that ended our intimate life, the same woman I saw then now carries his child.

I SIT PROPPED AGAINST THE pillows, ready for the anticipated shitstorm when the phone connects. I press Stan's number into my phone. In the mirror opposite the bed, Duluth is splashed in sparkling silver letters against the fuchsia background of my sweatshirt. "The papers arrived," I say. Businesslike, short to the point of curt.

"Good to hear from you," he says. He coughs into the phone, and it takes a while for his cough to subside.

"Did you sign?" he asks.

Silence for a minute. What's there to say when you're down to dividing the assets?

"No. What the hell did you expect? You reversed our agreement on the house. What were you thinking? We agreed that I would retain the house and pay you half."

"I changed my mind." He says this slowly, almost inaudibly.

"What do you mean you changed your mind?"

"I have my reasons."

"Don't be coy with me, Stan. We agreed about the house. You can start your new life somewhere else. That's my house."

"You'll be living alone, and you won't need all of that room."

"And you will? Oh, I forgot. You're having a baby."

He says nothing, but I hear the slight wheeze of his emphysema as he breathes close to the phone.

"I can't talk to you unless you agree to our original understanding on the house. I won't sign the papers until then."

I hang up. I'm fuming. Of course he won't find anything as nice as the house we live in. He lived in. Look at all I've done to the house, never mind its accumulated value. To hell with him. He can damn well agree to what we discussed. Then he can get on with his happy fucking life.

THE BEDSIDE CLOCK SAYS SIX o'clock. Without the wine to distract me, I'm hungry. I scoot off the bed and pick up the room service menu, perusing the dinner selections. I've just settled on a steak and a baked potato when there's a knock on my door.

Jennifer rushes past me sobbing. She throws herself on the bed.

"Now, now, it can't be that bad," I say. I cross to the bed and lift my bandaged arm and elbow away from her while I scoot close. Jennifer's hair is coarse beneath my hand, my fingers working through the tangles. Her jean jacket makes it impossible to feel her body, though my right hand rises and falls with sobs that seem to come up from her toes. "Now, now," I repeat. The girl lying on the bed is the same one who, just a few years ago, insisted on beating me at Fish and Monopoly.

When Jennifer finally turns her head, I see mascara smears on the white coverlet. I reach for the box of tissues on the nightstand and hand it to her. "Take a minute, then tell me what happened."

"Michael fired me!"

"How could he possibly fire you? For doing what he asked?"

"He says I copied the wrong manuscript. It's his memoir. He accused me of reading it since it took me a while to get it back to him. He didn't even give me a chance to explain I was running an errand for you, Oma," she says. "He's furious."

"That's completely unreasonable, Jennifer."

She continues to lie on the coverlet. Her mascara has disappeared into the tissues and comforter. When she finally lifts her head, the redness in her cheeks begins to fade and her breathing starts to calm. "He's done this before," she says. "When I told him that I was pregnant."

I stroke my granddaughter's arm, both to comfort her and steady the fury pushing against my breath. I don't trust myself to say anything. "You'll bunk with me tonight."

Her eyes brighten. "Could I?"

"Of course," I say. "It won't be easy . . . with this." I point down at my crooked elbow, my bandaged lower arm.

"We'll manage," Jennifer says. She begins to sit up. "I don't know what I'd have done if you weren't here."

"Hopefully you would have called me or a friend."

"I've been so ashamed, Oma. About the abortion." She rushes on. "I don't want Daddy to ever know."

"Come here."

Jennifer scoots closer until I can put my one arm around her and pull her against my body where her warmth feels good against my own. "We need each other," I say.

When Gilbert calls, it's ten-ten. Jennifer and I have shared the steak dinner, a glass of red wine apiece, and carrot cake.

"Comfort food," I explain when I replace the chrome bell over the remains of our meal. "How is Roland?" I ask Gilbert.

"Resting," Gilbert says. "I'm just now back in the hotel and on my way to bed."

"Jennifer's with me tonight. I'm sure she can take me to the seminar in the morning."

"You know I'd be happy to take you."

"You have enough to do," I say. "I've called room service and ordered sandwiches for tomorrow. Cheddar and ham. A dill pickle?"

After I hang up the phone I sit quietly against my pillows for several minutes.

Jennifer leans in front of me. "Oma, is Duluth what you hoped it would be?"

Her question takes me back to a fantasy that's been brewing all afternoon. A house like the university president's. The sun porch. Afternoon sun streaming through paned windows. The purple clouds of an impending storm gathering on the horizon. A teapot covered in a patchwork cozy sitting on the coffee table. Crumbs on a plate where cookies have been.

"Yes," I say. "A different landscape has a way of letting you know you're alive."

Jennifer is quiet. "Like the Dakotas once did?"

I'm thoughtful for a moment, my eyes glazed and staring at the white drapes opposite the bed. "I haven't been there in years."

"We should go. See if your house is still there. You could tell me more stories about what it was like when you were a girl."

"In the meantime we need to get some sleep, young lady. I think we've had enough drama today."

Chapter Twelve

Thursday, June 13

THE NEW DAY FINDS ME up early with unexpected energy forcing me upright and eager to get into the bathroom. I even look forward to the new sweat suit, my pride having left me in the aftermath of the broken glass and the deep cut. Though I'm concerned about Roland, my only other thought is to get to the seminar on time.

Once I've made my coffee in the bathroom, I walk around to Jennifer's side of the bed and shake her. "It's time, Jennifer."

While she's in the bathroom, I sit at the desk and write out the homework I neglected to complete last night. By the time Jennifer emerges, I'm dressed and ready for makeup and a second cup of coffee.

WHEN WE PULL INTO THE parking lot, Audrey waves from across the sidewalk. Her camera hangs heavy around her neck and she's wearing a small backpack. Her press badge bounces off the camera as she walks in our direction.

"Missed being here the last day or so," she says to me. "Had other stories to cover before I could work on the article of my choice . . . the seminar."

I hold up my arm. "As you can see, it's been eventful."

Audrey turns to Jennifer. "I can take your grandmother into the building. Looks like she has lunch. We're set."

At first Jennifer appears puzzled, her eyebrows arched and her mouth in the shape of an O. She doesn't know this somewhat odd-looking woman. However, I greeted Audrey so warmly that she must be okay.

"The car and the day are yours, Jennifer," I say. "We go until four. Maybe four fifteen."

"You don't even have to return," Audrey says. "I'll get her back home."

"That's even better," I say to Jennifer. "Now you're free to have the adventure you want." As an afterthought, "Don't let anyone ruin it for you."

Jennifer smiles and starts the car engine.

"I wondered what happened to you when you were sitting down front again after lunch," Audrey says. "Figured you were old friends with the leaders."

"Staying in the same hotel is all," I say.

"What happened to your arm?" she asks.

Still embarrassed and exhausted from my partial explanations for what happened, I say, "An accident in the hotel. No big deal. I asked Gilbert to let you know. You must not have come to the seminar yesterday afternoon."

"Right. An assignment overdue." Audrey scrutinizes my arm. "The bandage looks like a big deal," she says. "Looks like you'll be wearing that thing for the rest of the week."

"Something like that."

When we reach the double doors, she says, "You brought lunch."

I pull the bag close to my waist with an awkwardness that wasn't there before. "Bringing their lunch was the only thing I could do to help the leaders today."

Audrey raises her eyebrows. "What's happened to the leaders?"

"Roland's at the hospital. Probably exhausted. It's been quite a schedule for me too. Then this." I look down at my arm.

We enter the darkened seminar space through a door opposite the stage where Gilbert, unlike Roland, sits on a high stool under a dimmed overhead light instead of in the atmospheric dark we're used to. I do a double take at his dark-rimmed glasses. He looks over the top of them and smiles down at us as Audrey walks with me to my now-familiar place in the front row. I indicate the seat beside me.

"I see you made it okay," he says.

His mic, on and loud, startles him. Everyone already seated in the room laughs, including me and Audrey. Maybe embarrassed, Gilbert turns his attention to the sheaf of papers in front of him.

Audrey seems more than happy to take Gilbert's seat. Her camera still hangs around her neck, and a notebook rests in her lap. "Are you just doing interviews or are you also writing an article on the seminar?" I ask Audrey.

"Some of both," she says. She keeps her eyes straight ahead. "I asked for the assignment for selfish reasons. Thought I might get something out of it."

"That sounds smart."

"Glad someone sees it that way. Don't know if my boss does." When she laughs, I'm aware of her whitened teeth under the bright lights.

"Where are you from originally?" I ask.

She grins. "San Francisco."

"That was a big change coming here."

"Duluth has the kind of quiet I needed after working for the *Examiner*. Too much drama. This is manageable even if it's a little boring. Which is why what happens at the university always piques my curiosity."

"This place is way out of my comfort zone," I say.

She rests her hand on my bad arm and I wince, jerking my arm away.

"Sorry about that," she says. Then she asks, "Where's Roland?"

"Good morning," Gilbert says from the stage. "As you can see, I'm pinch-hitting for Roland who is taking a day off for needed rest." Gilbert waits while everyone oohs and aahs their disappointment, along with an escaped "oh, no."

"Let's start with the last assignment," he says. "I'd like to hear what you discovered about the difference between what you want for yourselves and where you spend your time." He pauses. "Please go to the mics and we'll begin our dialogue."

No greeting. No opening meditation. Did he forget that part intentionally? Unintentionally?

Individuals shuffle toward standing, maybe as confused as I am. With that brief introduction, it's obvious that Gilbert's style is more take-charge, like a corporate leader. A noticeable departure from the serenely smiling Roland. In response folks seem hesitant as they line up at the four aisle mics. Only one or two individuals stand at each microphone compared to the half dozen or more who normally wait to talk or read their lists.

The lists of what people want and where they spend their time couldn't be wider apart. The speakers acknowledge the differences and how the two lists seem completely divorced from each other. A woman laughs, "Who are these two people?" Many are as astonished as I am. Those who remain silent may have had an entirely different experience. How would I know? I've barely done the exercise, and I'm mostly shocked at the dichotomy. What I want: travel, more connection with family, and more fun. These things directly contrast with where I spend my time: work, work, and more work. There is nothing on either list that refers to Stan or our marriage.

Audrey scribbles a note or two. She nudges me. "Sorry I missed this exercise." The only word visible in her handwriting is *poetry*.

Gilbert relaxes when he introduces the two meditations for the day: open eye for twenty minutes followed by the walking meditation which I haven't done since my second day at the retreat. To my surprise—because she hasn't been here—Audrey prepares for the open-eye meditation along with everyone else. She folds her hands in her lap and keeps her eyes open.

I follow suit, quieting myself by watching my breath. In my meditative quiet I hear the sound of the screen door slamming, my feet scraping on the mudroom rug. The smell of yeast throughout the house and bread rising on Oma's kitchen counter. Oma's apron over her large bosom, gray hair pulled tight into a single braid and wrapped into a braided crown, the scar no longer visible along her nose. That click-click of her tongue against the roof of her mouth when she concentrates.

She sits across from me. Rather than milk, she offers me a half cup of tea with milk. A slice of kuchen. Like I'm one of her church ladies or Mom or Aunt Ada. A new Bible lays on the oilcloth beside Oma's hand, the closed zipper with an attached small gold cross hiding the pages.

She unzips the book. "Inside," she says fanning the pages, "pay special attention to the red passages. That's the Lord speaking."

Because I don't know what else to do, I nod. I'm only five and I haven't yet learned to read. I blow on my tea, wishing I had the courage to ask for sugar. I take the first bite of kuchen.

She shoves the book across the oilcloth. "This is for you," she says. "But you must promise me that when you learn to read, you will read it every day. Every day," she says, her voice emphasizing *every*. "The Bible now and my Easter egg later when you're a grown-up. They're the only things I have to give you. Once your mom and dad leave here, I don't know when I'll see you again."

Her voice cracks when she says *see you again*. I've never seen her this close to tears.

Her almost-tears connect me to a terrible heat that stings my eyes. "Thank you, Oma," I say, though all I hear is *I don't know when I'll see you again.*

When I refocus on the auditorium and my breath, I'm grateful to Audrey who sits quietly beside me. Grateful she doesn't attempt conversation.

"I'd like you to pair up now and share those lists with your partner," Gilbert instructs.

Audrey and I smile nervously like girls in the fifth or sixth grade caught whispering.

"I'm sorry I didn't do the exercise," Audrey says. She opens her hands to indicate frustration. "Didn't think I'd be back again."

"I'm happy to share my list, but maybe you'd like to tell me first what the exercise made you think of."

Audrey turns to face me. "Mine would be mostly about work."

"Then we have the same list." I laugh. "Sadly."

I hesitate before going further. "I noticed my husband was left off the list."

"Fortunately for me, I don't have a husband. My job would be impossible if I did."

"Touché." I lean closer to her. "What strikes me is how women raise the kids for the most part, manage the home, have a career, and then in some unpredictable moment he—whoever he is—complains that he's not at the top of her list."

"Guess that's why I'm not with someone."

"Guess that's why I'm not either."

She raises her hand and slaps mine in camaraderie.

"I remember when I was a girl, my grandmother was there if I needed her," I say. "Even then, she lived pretty much alone and did everything except work outside the house. In those days, she hauled water from the well, planted the garden, canned, and cooked the food. She sewed most of the clothes and managed her large family. She depended on my grandfather's meager dollars when he'd let go of them."

"We must have had the same grandmother. She was my oasis."

"Likewise," I say. "I learned more from her than I realized."

A hand on my shoulder. "You guys doing okay?" Gilbert asks. He looks toward Audrey for some response.

"Our lists are identical," she says. "How strange is that?"

He smiles and his face, so tight onstage, softens. "That's the not-so-secret secret," he says. "Everybody's list looks similar if not identical."

He stops to talk to a pair across the aisle before he disappears toward what must be invisible stairs that climb back onto the stage.

"The reason I asked to cover the seminar," Audrey says, glancing toward the stage, "is that I hoped I'd find an answer to a relationship dilemma. Someone who thinks we should get married."

"Do you want to marry?"

"No, but it's a deal-breaker, I'm afraid. She moved here from Chicago so we could be together all the time. I'm afraid that's not what I want."

"You're lucky to know that," I say. "I'd like to think that having a relationship doesn't mean you have to be joined at the hip."

"That's the only way she sees it," Audrey says.

"That's more like a traditional ideal versus a more free, independent lifestyle," I say. "Unfortunately, I learned that too late. At least you have a chance. It might be hard to say no, but in the long run you'll save yourself a lot of grief."

"Tradition versus two independents. I like that," Audrey says. "Can I steal it?"

"Be my guest, except you have to say it came from someone who learned the hard way."

"I'm glad you brought lunch," Gilbert says. "How's the arm?"

The awkward moment I hoped to avoid. Now, here it is. "See you after lunch," I say to Audrey. "We'll pick up where we left off."

Her dark eyes are both questioning and hurt—yes, hurt. "Sure," she says.

I have a momentary pang of regret. In many ways I'd have preferred continuing our conversation over lunch. "You know where to find me after the break."

Up until now, I've denied even friendship with Gilbert. Either he hasn't gotten the message, or I haven't given it to him clearly enough. Yet here I am, willing to have lunch with him rather than spend the time continuing a conversation with another woman.

Unlike Roland, who normally stays and chats with the attendees, Gilbert seems anxious to excuse himself from those who approach him. "Is Roland sick? Is he coming back? What happened?" Gilbert, a hand on my good elbow, slows to answer but never stops. His response is always the same: "Roland needs to rest." Then a shift of eye contact and back to the direct path down the hallway toward the elevator. He guides me through the morass of elevators and hallways and back to the private garden. Once there, Gilbert pulls a third chair away from the table in a manner that surprises me with its roughness. He then directs me toward a chair like I'm the piece of furniture that needs to be relocated.

The gurgling waterfall and the afternoon sun reflecting off the opposite windows become my focus in the presence of Gilbert's nervous energy. There's not a cloud in the sky, but everything has changed. When Gilbert finally sits, he sighs, and his exasperation assumes another presence in the small garden. "I haven't done this in too long," he says.

"Just relax," I say. "The script seems easy enough, and you've been in the seminar so many times."

"Are you getting something out of it?" he asks.

For the first time I hear a failure of confidence. "More than I bargained for," I say. "That last exercise told me more about my life than I wanted to know."

I open the paper bag, which contains the sandwiches and dill pickles, potato chips I threw in for good measure, and a couple of bottled waters. A Diet Coke to get me through the afternoon.

"Like what?" he asks. He bends over his sandwich. "Sorry, I'm famished."

"That I work too much, and as a consequence, I've missed what's important. Those I care about, including myself. I don't seem to glide below the surface of things. I proceed like an obsessed automaton going through the predictable paces my work requires. I never really question *why* or ask how my attitude affects those I care about. I never take time to reflect. That's what I'm trying to say."

He pauses and stares at the fountain. "You're describing me, especially with Carolyn." He puts his sandwich down. "I completely abandoned her even before Amy was born. When she was working everything seemed okay. After the baby came the demands of Amy's care and the evidence of our fractured relationship were too painful and overwhelming to discuss. Besides which, Carolyn was the one who gave up her career as an artistic director in marketing. I frankly never questioned my priorities or my attitude."

I stare at him in disbelief. "How many times have you asked that question about priorities and made your own comparisons?"

A sheepish embarrassment defines his smile. "Maybe my detachment has gone on longer than I thought."

"Speaking of which." I lay down my sandwich and pull my wounded arm closer to my chest. "Maybe this is your style, but I have to ask what happened this morning in the seminar? No meditation. No introduction. I don't mean to give you a hard time; I'm just curious."

He folds the paper that held his sandwich and rips open the potato chips. "For some reason, I blew it. I'm not sure what happened. I rushed ahead with needing to get started and the next thing I knew I'd completely bypassed the usual program." He caresses the side of his crushed thumb, then looks up at me. "I apologize," he says.

"Not a big deal," I say. "Just unusual considering Roland's openings."

"Maybe I'm not as sure of myself as I thought." He attempts a laugh, but it sounds forced.

"Or you're human."

New clouds in the sky sit silently above us. Gilbert and I share the potato chips. He tells me that Roland's weak heart and advanced age make it necessary for him to remain in the hospital, probably for the remainder of the seminar. He's worn out.

Gilbert reaches for my Diet Coke.

"You know that's my Coke," I say.

"My God, I'm so sorry."

I smile. "You must need it worse than I do."

"I had no idea. Here, I've only taken one sip."

"Finish it, though now you owe me one." I laugh, but I know I want to say more. "Remember the two words exercise? Mine were heart travel."

He smiles for the first time. "Maybe that's what you're doing here."

"Pardon me?"

"You said it was your friend's idea to come, but the fact that you came and you're here and you've been willing to go through the process of something you've never done before says a lot." Gilbert crumples the potato chip bag. "Outside of your husband and career dilemmas, what have you been thinking about most?"

A hummingbird lands inside a cluster of peonies. "My granddaughter, for one," I say. "And my grandmother."

The waterfall's music curls in the background while sunlight spreads across the table. I'm relaxed, and the ease of mind has enabled me to really appreciate those two people.

I'm surprised when he says, "I envy you."

"You envy me?"

"Because you have the experience of knowing a deep love for two people."

The words are out of my mouth before I can stop them. "Haven't you had that before?"

"Not in the way I see you and Jennifer, especially when you're together. She'd do anything for you, and you'd do the same for her. That's probably why you're upset about Dr. Connolly."

"Don't you have that with your daughter?"

I'm surprised I even asked the question, which seems suddenly rude and uncalled for. My stomach starts churning as though too full. It's none of my business what his affection is for his daughter. He doesn't acknowledge her except as a patient or victim, both objectifying and dismissing her. That attitude both angers and confuses me.

"I do and I don't have that with her," he says. "That's just honest."

Staring at the waterfall again, he says, "Maybe she's been such a big concern that I've treated her like a munitions project or a tour I need to arrange for Roland. A dilemma to be worked through and managed. My head revolves around logistics. I think it's gotten in the way of my heart."

For the first time I feel something less remote in him. Call it honesty or vulnerability. He no longer seems to hover at arm's length or, like this morning, an automaton going through an exercise.

"Thank you," I say.

His forehead wrinkles. "Why *thank you*?"

"You just said something that's probably true of me as well. My constant struggle with what you call logistics has shut down the connection to my feelings. No wonder Stan had to find someone else."

Gilbert gazes across the glass-topped table. He lays his hand over the top of mine. His face is serious, but his mouth is more relaxed than when we started. "Thanks," he says.

Chapter Thirteen

After Audrey drops me off at the hotel, I offer to buy her a coffee to make up for missing lunch. Audrey pulls into the hotel's horseshoe driveway and follows me into the café. We slip into the leather booth near a window in view of the curved driveway. Audry sits across from me, an aqua-colored scarf winding around her neck and tied in front. She takes off her glasses and lays them on the table. She holds her teacup in front of her.

"Sorry about that awkwardness regarding lunch," I say. "Seems I've been more occupied with Gilbert than I thought."

"I wondered about that," she says holding the menu. "I was disappointed, that's all. You know that old thing about women choosing men over other women."

I sit back against the seat cushion. Stare straight ahead. "I know what you're talking about." I then notice the warmth and sensitivity in her brown eyes. "I am sorry."

"Here's what I don't understand," Audrey says. "Though I accept that there's value in these seminars, why are they mostly led by men?"

"Maybe it was too easy to go with what my friend Nancy recommended," I say.

"I get tired of men always being in a position of authority, as though they know something I don't."

I laugh. "I wouldn't be here now if it wasn't for Nancy."

"I'm not saying I don't get something out of it," she says. "Especially from the old gentleman who was there the other day."

"Roland?" I say. "A different experience."

"Exactly my point," she says. "Corny as it sounds, he brought a lot of feeling to the sessions—for lack of a better word. Gilbert's too mechanical. Did you notice that?"

"I did."

"Roland strikes me as an old soul, born to do this kind of thing. But I'm curious about your best friend making the recommendation. You must trust her."

"I do. And Nancy trusts Roland and his presence as much as what he says. The questions he asks. He's like some kind of . . . I don't know."

"Spirit guide? Guru? Someone who knows something ordinary people don't?"

"Yes, something like that. Or something we're afraid to know."

"Why don't we have women who do this kind of thing?"

"Maybe we do. Frankly, I never thought about it until you brought it up."

"You could be one of those women, Marta."

"What about you, Audrey?"

"The questions seem too easy. Don't go deep enough. But even when I say that, I'm not sure what I mean."

"More connection?" I ask.

"Definitely. I'd create smaller groups. Have more interactions. Bring in more outside material. Poetry. Music."

I'm silent for a minute or two. "It would definitely have a different feeling."

"That's it. A different feeling. Not just this sense of call and response you got in church when you were a kid. And it doesn't have to be all words and talk. I like the meditation. It has made me remember things I thought I'd forgotten."

"Me too," I say. "My grandmother, for one."

Maybe that's what *heart travel* means. Maybe those memories that carry *heart*—like I had with Oma and now with Jennifer. How we are talking more honestly, more intimately, here in this seemingly neutral place.

"The seminars are supposed to help us find out things about ourselves that we've forgotten or never known," I say. "All week I've been thinking about how important my grandmother was in shaping my emotional life. Then to have my granddaughter show up in Duluth seems serendipitous. I don't know if we could have planned it this way."

"I keep thinking about my older sister who died in a car accident when I was in my twenties," Audrey says. "One day she was here and the next she was gone. I didn't think I'd ever get over her sudden death, yet here she is . . . talking to me in all this silence."

I reach my unrestricted hand across the table and lay it over hers.

She gazes down at my hand. For a moment emotion plays behind her eyes. Not tears but something close to them. A glaze that lets me know she's been touched in some way. We are silent for a few seconds until I lift my hand and grab the loop of my teacup.

"The same thing's happening with my oma," I say. "Between these unseen conversations and Jennifer showing up in Duluth, I have the feeling that we're three generations . . . maybe more . . . together at the same time, in the same place."

Audrey's eyes focus on her cup. "Funny how things happen. You, me, Duluth. An unlikely combo just a week ago."

"Yes, I was supposed to fly to Madison right after I finished here. Now, Jennifer and I get to be roommates in a neutral location."

Audrey smiles, her brown eyes hidden beneath her dark brows and hair. "Do you think you'll follow these guys after you get home?"

When I laugh this time, I feel like my old self, the self that isn't as serious or intense about whatever dilemma exists at the moment. "Maybe. We did an exercise with Roland that revealed for me what I came for." I explain the exercise to Audrey in brief. "The two words that came up for me were *heart travel*."

"Wow, that sounds so interesting," she says. "I'm sorry I missed the exercise."

"You can still do it."

"Maybe I'll try tonight." She looks at her watch. "Holy cow, I have an article to write." She gathers her purse and camera together, awkward as the camera is around her neck. "Pick you up in the morning about eight-fifteen?"

"Perfect," I say. "Then I can take you to lunch."

"A deal."

WHEN I OPEN THE DOOR to Room 616, I'm assaulted by the smell of booze laced with marijuana. The white comforter lies heaped on the floor and Jennifer's pink blond hair looms above her loud voice booming into her phone. She's sprawled on the bed, all the pillows bunched under her head and what looks like her dirty socks on the open sheets.

I stand open-mouthed. *Flabbergasted*, my mother would say. The mess, the smell, the cheek in taking over my beautiful room.

At first I can't move. When I do, I march to the bed. "What the hell do you think you're doing?" Without waiting for an answer, my one good arm snatches the phone out of her ear. An open-mouthed Jennifer stares back at me. Her eyes are bloodshot, and she reeks of alcohol.

"You're drunk!"

"I thought you'd be pleeshed," she says.

"How in the hell can I be pleased with this disaster, young lady? And get your dirty socks off my sheets."

"Don't get pishhy with me," she says. "I did what you wanted me to do . . ."

"I don't care what the hell you did, we need to get you out of my bed and a maid in here to clean up this mess." I throw down my notebook. The swell of tears stings my eyes. "Oh my God, Jennifer. You keep committing one disaster after another."

"Fine. Just fine," she says. She attempts to lift herself off of the bed. "I'll take my party and go where I'm appreeshiated."

"You're not leaving here, young lady. I doubt you can even stand."

"You jusht wasssh me," she says.

When she scoots to the edge of the bed, she falls back onto the sheets. "Feel shick," she says.

I stretch my good arm toward her. "You're going into the bathroom. At least if you're sick, we'll get you someplace easier to clean up."

I'm right at the edge of the bed when she bolts upright and runs to the bathroom where she upchucks into the bathtub. Holy shit. She continues to heave into the tub. In seconds the stench invades both rooms while she's on her hands and knees vomiting into the tub, the toilet a simple turn away from her.

At the risk of her being sick all over my shoes and skirt, I move behind her and guide her arms toward the toilet. The searing pain in my arm makes me even angrier. She continues to vomit for the next ten minutes. I leave her there, bent over the toilet and halfway inside it. I call housekeeping before opening the drapes and the windows.

"Now look what you've done," I say over and over. I sound like my mother. That's the kind of thing she would say. Always a predictable response from Irene, and the message clear: you can never get anything right, and you're a disappointment.

Once the cold lake air begins to blow the sheer drapes into billowing clouds and circulate in the bedroom, I open the bath-room door and stand there looking at the poor girl hugging the porcelain. I step inside and flush the toilet. She's crying hard belly sobs. She catches her breath on the inhale and then sobs all over again. "Got rid of him . . . thought you'd be pleeshhed . . ." Her tears continue to fall into the toilet until the next attack of dry heaves takes over.

I run my free hand through her matted pink hair. Massage the back of her neck. "I'm sorry you had to get drunk to do it, say it."

"I'll pay you back," she says between sobs. "For every one . . ." Her voice is once again blurred by heaves.

A knock at the door interrupts our bathroom drama. A hotel maid enters with her rubber gloves and a mop bucket full of what look like clean rags. Her other arm is filled with folded sheets and towels.

"I appreciate you coming right away," I say.

When we both turn toward the bathroom, Jennifer is curled up on the bath mat in front of the commode, passed out.

"Oh, this isn't good," I say, pointing to my bandaged arm.

The maid looks at me, her dark eyes puzzled.

"We need to move her," I say. Again, I point at my arm.

She finally understands, setting down the bucket. She places the sheets and towels on top of the desk. When she returns to the bathroom, small as she is, she pulls at the bath mat until she's moved it away from both the commode and bathtub. Jennifer remains a deadweight and unresponsive.

"Doctor?" the maid asks, her dark eyebrows raised in concern.

"No," I say. I lift my good hand and indicate drinking. "Too much."

The maid nods and smiles.

The stench of the vomit overpowers the bathroom. I hate to leave the maid in there to clean up the mess, but I open the door and retreat to the bedroom. There, for lack of anything else to do, I strip the sheets off the bed with my good arm, pulling where I can and saving the pillowcases for the maid. When I've finished stripping the bed, I leave a fifty-dollar bill on top of the sheets and grab my notebook from beneath the pile.

I stick my head into the bathroom where the maid bends over the tub with her rags. Jennifer lies off to the side, completely passed out. "I'm going downstairs for a cup of tea," I say, making a drinking motion with my good hand and arm. I lift the fifty-dollar bill off the stack of sheets and wave it at her. "For you," I say, pointing at her.

When I close the door behind me, the lake air is already turning the room cold. Jennifer may not come back to life for another couple of hours. I should have put a blanket over her.

ONCE SEATED IN THE COFFEE shop, I marvel that I didn't head to the bar for a couple glasses of wine. Isn't that what I always do at the end of a trial or after writing a difficult brief? Looking for quick relief through a drink is so automatic that I'm momentarily puzzled. Maybe it's because Jennifer's so drunk. Or something Gilbert said about his own drinking.

I open my notebook to *heart travel*. The bear with the heart line. What does this really mean?

I recall my honeymoon with Stan. Hawaii's Mauna Kea resort was new all those years ago. I can still see myself playing golf in a dress. The intimate patio dinners outside our room. The book I read at the poolside. *To Kill A Mocking Bird.* Who would read a book about a young girl and the segregated south on her honeymoon? A rented car up the mountain to the volcano where, close by, Stan and I watched the lava flow red and on fire. Like Jennifer, we had so much hope for the future and the careers we'd planned. *Heart travel.* That's what we had, what I thought we'd always have.

I sip my Earl Grey tea until it's cold. Write a one-sentence note under *heart travel* in remembrance of that honeymoon. I stare at valet parking where cars come and go. The doormen take the keys of an SUV, then a couple of sedans.

When I glance at my watch, I see it's been thirty minutes since I left the room. I sign the check and stand to leave. Gilbert's talking to the cashier. When he sees me, he walks toward me. The sun now angles across the tables; the afternoon is fading toward early evening.

"Nice surprise," he says.

I smile from habit. "Time-out," I say. "How's Roland?"

"Improving," he says. "Out of intensive care. Glad it was only for a day."

He nods toward the table in front of me. "What are you doing hanging out in the coffee shop?"

"A little mishap with Jennifer," I say. "She got drunk and sick all over my room."

He begins to laugh. "Sorry," he says. "Is she okay?"

"Passed out the last I saw."

"We all have to do it at least once."

"Didn't think you drank," I say.

"That's why." His eyes grow small inside his grin. "Sit for a minute?"

Gilbert pulls out a chair and nods at the cashier. Soon a waitress returns with his tea. Peppermint. A little too pure for me.

He lowers his head and moves closer toward the middle of the table. "Has being here helped you find the clarity you hoped for with your divorce?"

"More than I hoped," I say. I take hold of my paper napkin and tear at one edge. "Stan told me I was brutal about the settlement."

Gilbert stares out the coffee shop window toward the circular drive. The valet takes a car then circles into the invisible underground garage. "Is he right?"

I watch his glasses slide down his nose. "Probably," I say.

"Based on this week . . . what's another option?"

"I'm sure as hell not giving him the house."

My defensiveness is all wrong, and I know it. I'm silent for a few moments, my stomach the old jumble of monkeys and my bad arm hurting.

"I could have used a different tone," I say. My sigh fills the silence. "Hard to break years of standing in front of a judge and needing to sound tough."

Gilbert pulls on his right ear. "A different tone, a different way of looking at things. I think that's what you came for. I know I did." He lowers his head. "I can't tell you how many times people told me I was cruel, including Carolyn."

I have to smile. He may not be charismatic, but he's honest in a way I can hear. "That's why I came here. I ended up being maddest at myself." My voice drops and I'm almost sheepish. Without looking up, I continue, "Stan doesn't deserve my meanness."

Gilbert folds his hands in front of the tea mug, then places a hand over the mug when our server—more Jennifer's age and pretty in the way young girls are—stands waiting to refill his cup with hot water.

Something about what I just said reminds me of the first time Stan kissed me. A Rock Hudson romance at a drive-in movie. Stan's lips were chapped from the summer sun after lifeguarding. So wet and eager. I'd been waiting months for that kiss.

"I should get back," I say.

Gilbert uncrosses his legs and shoves his glasses into his shirt pocket. "Feels like we haven't finished," he says. "Maybe dinner?"

"Have to see how my patient is doing." I hesitate. "I'll give you a call in the next hour if dinner's possible."

"If not, good luck."

Chapter Fourteen

When I open the refrigerator with its minibar, I see that all the mini-bottles are gone. Jennifer's going to feel pretty trashed when she wakes up from the bathroom floor where she's still passed out. At least the wine and champagne remain untouched. I rescue my wineglass from the dresser drawer and pour myself a generous glass of Chablis, still too sweet, but it will do the job. Kick off my shoes and pick up a magazine.

After cancelling Gilbert's invitation for six o'clock, I call the dining room and order a salad, a pork chop, and a glass of red wine. A bowl of chicken soup and crackers for Jennifer. My wine supply is running low; I'll have to order another liter from that nice doorman who found me this one.

I dial Nancy. We're two friends who talk every day, so it's hard to believe I've only called her once in the last week, and that was when I was stranded in the Denver airport.

"Wondered when I was going to hear from you," she says. "When you're in town, I expect your call at five-thirty on the nose, just before you leave the office for the day. Now I've left two messages, and all I get from you are text messages saying, 'I'll call you later.' What's going on? Is Roland alright?"

"Funny you ask. He's in the hospital," I say.

"Hospital?" she asks. "Did he die?"

"According to Gilbert, he's just worn out."

Nancy is silent for a few seconds. "Sorry you only had a couple of days with him." A pause. "How does Gilbert do on his own?"

"Let's just say he doesn't have the same charisma. I think it's affecting how people respond to the questions. Roland's clearly the main event."

"What about you? Are you glad you went to Duluth?"

"Not at first. That whole debacle in Denver, plus a two-hundred-dollar speeding ticket."

"That'll stop you."

"Not the only thing. I cut my arm badly in the bathtub."

"Don't tell me how. I don't want to know."

"I broke a wineglass in the bathtub."

How could I forget that Nancy's a longtime recovering alcoholic? But the words are out of my mouth before I remember.

"Hope your arm was the only victim."

My cheeks warm with humiliation. "Pretty embarrassing, actually. Made me slow down on the wine." It sounds good although I know it's not necessarily true. Didn't I just call the bellhop for another bottle?

"A start," she says.

My drinking has been a barrier between us. She's said nothing for the past few years, and that's been a relief. But it's always there like a ghost, stalking any given lunch or dinner or hotel room away for the two of us to catch up.

"Then Jennifer got really drunk. That was a mess and a half."

Nancy laughs until she has to catch her breath. "How is she now?"

"Not sure. She's still passed out on the bathroom floor."

Still laughing, Nancy says, "Better she learns her lesson now rather than later."

The silence that follows feels awkward. She's waiting for me to say how the seminar has affected me. She knows me too well for me to hide anything, even when I bend the truth back and forth. Finally I say, "It's been good, Nancy. I'm glad I came. Thank you."

"You're welcome," she says.

"I decided I need to retire. Do something different. Legal assistance with women or something like that. Anything but what I'm doing . . . at least after my divorce is over."

"Do you think Stan was the catalyst?"

I feel my stomach clench. I don't want to give him credit. He doesn't deserve it. "Stan's definitely had something to do with it. But I think it's mostly the effect of the seminar."

"Can I assume that you're pretty set on going ahead with the divorce then?"

"Stan made sure of that," I say. "Thought I told you that his girlfriend is pregnant. If you recall, he's actually in Reno."

"Holy shit. What was he thinking? At his age. I'm surprised he could still, you know . . . after the aneurism."

"He's not thinking with his brain. That's the point. That pretty much closes the door to any thought of reconciliation. You could say I'm getting used to the idea of divorce. But can you believe he had the gall to ask for the house . . . which I straightened out right away."

"Good for you," Nancy says. Her voice is rushed, her anxiety or fury taking over. "I still can't believe he impregnated someone and then told you after the fact."

"Stan can't be faulted for being human," I say. "I suspect he was lonelier than he said or than I wanted to recognize."

"Do you want me to call him?"

"There's nothing to be done, Nancy. He's in Reno with this young woman, and he's waiting for me to sign the papers. But we're still arguing over the house."

"Don't give in, whatever you do."

"I don't intend to."

"I'm really sorry it's turned dark like this," Nancy says. "Just glad you're where you are."

"Thanks to you. It was the best decision to just step away for a while. And I have to say that Gilbert has actually become a new friend. We're staying in the same hotel."

"Well if you're calling him a friend, you're getting closer to him than I've ever been. He's always been kind of a stick figure to me."

"He is and he isn't. We'll talk about it when I get back."

"I'm so glad you called even though I'm fuming about Stan."

"Arguing with him isn't worth it, Nancy. It's what some men have to do."

"Sadly, I think you're right."

"By the way, thanks for what you didn't tell me about Duluth." I laugh. "It's colder than hell."

"I was afraid to warn you about that. Didn't think you'd go."

I hesitate, my throat suddenly tight with emotion. "I mean it. Thanks, Nancy."

"Don't wait so long to call. And if I do call Stan, I won't tell you." She laughs. "This is why girlfriends stick together."

"Indeed."

I'M SITTING AT MY DESK enjoying the meal and the evening news on the TV when Jennifer stumbles out of the bathroom, the blanket wrapped around her shoulders, her hair every which way. With eyes half-open she plops on the side of my bed.

"No, no, kitten," I say, the fork halfway to my mouth. "Your bed is behind me."

"Whyz that?" she asks. She glances at my dinner, then the roll-away bed near the closet. "Whoz that for?"

"You," I say. "While you're getting better, you can enjoy your own bed."

She looks down at the blanket wrapped around her shoulders. "Oh," she says.

"When you're more fully awake, you might want to step into the shower and wash everything, including your clothes. Then I'll send them to the laundry. A plastic bag is hanging behind the door."

She gives me a funny look. "Why?"

"Because, frankly, you stink."

I return to my pork chop and salad, the evening news. "I'd appreciate you sitting in the other chair and not against my fresh bed. Thank you," I say. My eyes remain focused on the screen in front of me.

She looks like someone who forgot where she lives. The blanket, her hair, the sag in her face. She steps away from the bed and plops into the chair. "Smells good," she says, nodding toward my food.

"I ordered chicken and rice soup for you. Soda crackers," I say. "When you've showered and your stomach is settled, I'll heat the soup in the microwave. By the way, I left Alka-Seltzer on the bathroom counter. A couple of those in a glass of water will help you feel better."

"How do you know how I feel?"

"I've been where you are a time or two myself."

She leans forward, almost doubling over. "Think I might be sick again."

"Then please get yourself into the bathroom and *over* the toilet this time, missy."

I scoot back my chair and move toward her, prepared to take her arm with my good one.

"Don't," she says. "I can get there myself."

After she enters the bathroom she shuts the door. Before long I hear the toilet flush. Afterward the shower runs for a very long time. At least she's following directions. I don't know what I'd do if she got surly with me. I can't send her home in this condition. Kelsey would accuse me of leading her down this path.

When she finally emerges from the bathroom, I've finished my dinner and set the tray outside the door. Poured myself a glass of the remaining white wine. A towel is wrapped around her hair, and she's wearing the same terry robe I've worn. At least she's clean and she no longer smells of alcohol.

She stares toward the rollaway bed, then back at my bed. At me. She drops her head. "I'm sorry, Oma. Guess I got carried away."

"You did. Knowing our family, it's not the first and it likely won't be the last time."

"Why do you say that? Mom doesn't drink. Dad either."

"Maybe your mom had enough of me and your grandfather."

"Why would she have enough of you two?"

"She grew up differently than you did." I turn toward her. "Your grandfather and I drank a lot when your mom was growing up. At some point a counselor told us we had to cut back or go to AA for the sake of our daughters."

"Wasn't Great-grandpa an alcoholic?"

"Yes. He drank and was forever changing jobs. That's what I remember most from my childhood. My sisters and I were long gone from home when Great-grandma Irene said she'd leave him if he didn't stop." I let that sink in. "That's why they moved to Palm Springs."

"I notice you don't talk about him very much, and Mom never talks about him. Was he that bad?"

I twirl the wine in my glass. "You can understand why I was so upset to find you drunk. It was like an old movie playing over again."

"I'm sorry, Oma."

"You can't keep doing this . . . drinking, I mean . . . and, frankly, neither can I."

"Guess I was celebrating . . . I called Madison and resigned from my summer job. Sent an email to Michael," she says. "Then he called and yelled at me. I hung up. Every time he called back, I didn't answer. It was hard." Her head drops toward her chest. "He's probably furious because it's too late to get anyone else."

I don't say anything for a minute. "That was a very grown-up thing to do."

"Thanks, Oma. I hope it doesn't come back on me."

"If it does, you'll handle it."

Her eyes tear up. She shakes her head to erase the tears. "A tough lesson," she says. "I need to think hard or call you before I do anything foolish like that again." Her tears streak her cheeks. "How about that soup now?"

It's ten o'clock and Jennifer's passed out on her rollaway bed when I sneak into the bathroom to finally call Stan on my cell phone. The endless blinking of the red light on the hotel phone has made me crazy. All five messages are from him. He occasionally remembers that I gave him the new cell number before I left for Duluth. "Did you read through the papers?" he asks.

"Nice greeting, Stan. Whatever happened to 'how are you?' and 'hope you're having a good time' rather than 'did you get the papers,'" I say. "You didn't treat me that rudely when we were married, why start now?"

Silence for a few seconds. "I'm sorry. Didn't mean to be . . . disrespectful."

"Thanks. And yes, I did get the papers, but the days here are long. Then Jennifer had something of a mishap."

"Is she okay? What happened? Are you alright?"

"We're both fine. In fact, she's sleeping in the other room." I hesitate before going on, and I'm not sure why. "She got pretty intoxicated today and is having a hard time recovering."

"How did that happen?"

"Disappointed in love," I say. "Something we both know more than a little bit about."

Stan remains silent. I can't help but think of what women tend to reveal to each other that men are never privy to. Heartbreak for one. Emotional earthquakes another. A female tendency to shield them or to keep our vulnerability under wraps. I'm not sure which.

"I'm sure she'll feel better in the morning. But what about you?" I ask to cover what I don't want to say, which is *what the hell do you think you're doing?*

"Just waiting for the papers," he says. "Have rented a house here, have my Nevada driver's license for insurance. But I need the divorce papers before I can proceed."

I say nothing for a few seconds. "I've read the papers, Stan. There's a logjam when it comes to the house." I sigh into the phone and no longer care if he hears my exasperation. "This delay is tedious and boring, Stan. We had an agreement, and for whatever reason, you don't want to keep it."

"I've told you that I'm more than willing to pay you half the value."

"That's not the point." The toilet stool is proving uncomfortable, and I suddenly want to lie down in my bed. "I don't want or need the money. I want my home. Until you can come around on that, you may be in Reno for no reason at all."

"So you're going to be stubborn."

"Yes, I'm going to be stubborn. Except for living in our home, you did little to make it what it is today. I understand why you want it, but it's not yours to have. Now"—I say, before he can rebut my argument—"I'm tired and I'm going to bed. I'll wait to hear from you. Good night."

I sit on the commode a minute longer wondering how long this fight can go on. At what point he'll give in. I have nothing but time on my side. Something he doesn't think he has.

Chapter Fifteen

Friday, June 14

I leave the hotel room long before the princess stirs. Jennifer can deal with her hangover by herself. She probably won't even miss my taking the car. Some of my confidence has been restored now that the pain has let up and the wound seems to be healing. That's a good sign.

Today Gilbert leads with more of an introduction. Meditation this time. Audrey never appears, though I gave her my phone number. Lunch: an energy bar and a pack of peanuts I picked up in the hotel gift shop. A small bottle of water I carry in the pocket of my light jacket, though I have to struggle to get the sleeve over my bandage. Jeans for the first time.

I escape the auditorium at the lunch break before Gilbert is finished answering individual questions. Remembering the trail into the woods where I walked with Gilbert, I figure it's not more than a half mile away from the building where the seminar is taking place. A walk will be a chance to sort my head further and think about *heart travel.*

Though the day is what I now call Duluth-cool, I walk up the campus road toward where I remember the gate leads to the gravel road into the woods. Once I'm away from the campus the day becomes quiet. My legs push me up the hill, though I'm out of breath faster than I like. The road is still some distance away. My watch says twelve-fifteen. I have thirty minutes to reach the gate and walk.

The gate, heavier than I imagined, brings to mind Gilbert in his plaid shirt pulling it open last time. I feel the sting of a sliver in my right index finger, having forgotten the gate is splintery. *Damn.* Maybe the doctor's nurse can pull it out since I can't maneuver the other hand and won't be able to extract the sliver myself.

The woods, dark under the heavy umbrella of trees, cast shadows on the path and erase the sun. The ground crunches with spring mulch from last fall's leaves and winter's long-melted snow. My new tennis shoes are again spattered with mud, but what does it matter? In fact, what does anything matter in the same way as before? It's sad to say, but my marriage is over. The thought fills my stomach with an ache I don't like. Still too much has happened between me and Stan. If nothing else, the seminar has given me that clarity. Clarity about both Stan and the need to retire from my work. Fighting for the house suddenly seems like another distraction. Then there's Jennifer. She's helped me see myself as much as the seminar has. For all our ups and downs this trip, I feel close to her. Jennifer's only sin is youth.

The creek's gurgle announces itself before I turn the bend and see the water. The rocks we crossed the other night remain dry, just above the water's ripple. Above me, high in the umbrella of trees, the crows caw at me as though laughing in anticipation of my next move. I too laugh at the way I pouted, then walked into the water. So much pride. Is that part of what's disappearing? My need to hide behind degrees and a title? I stand for a minute at the creek's edge, enjoying the sound and watching the sun fall across the path, highlighting the darker, deeper pools and distinguishing them from the sunlit shallows. I gaze up toward the overhead leaves glittering with midsummer green. Again, I hear the crows or blackbirds caw but they're not to be seen. In front of me the rocks change color beneath the water, the blues bluer, the green moss brighter.

I listen while songbirds sing in the treetops. Without warning, blackbirds flock to the ground where they've scavenged something to eat. I feel strangely half in and half out of Duluth. This landscape surrounding me reminds me of the fairy tales I loved as a child. "Hansel and Gretel" in particular. "Sleeping Beauty" and "Snow White." Like I'm standing both inside and outside of my own life. What puzzles me is how a few days can change someone so much. But isn't that what Nancy and Gilbert said? They had to experience it to believe it. Even my conversation with Audrey has added to new understanding. So much newness coming so fast, and I question whether I'm intellectually in a place where I can handle things. Instead, I'm emotionally somewhere unfamiliar and uncomfortable. This has all happened by sitting and meditating, then answering a few questions. How uncomplicated yet complex is that?

When I turn to head back, I'm almost sad. There probably won't be a next time in these particular woods. As quickly as that thought comes to me, my mind races to the fifteen minutes I have to get back to the auditorium. Then, as if the walk in the woods never happened, the magic is lost in my downhill rush.

ONCE BACK IN MY HOTEL room, I trade my tennis shoes and jeans for the terry robe and hunker down into the pillows with my notebook. *Heart travel. Heart line.* Again I'm mystified. The bed is too comfortable, and the afternoon sun warms my bare feet in the quiet that I've needed and wanted. I've barely dozed off when I hear the slide of Jennifer's hotel card. This time when she opens the door she's tentative, more careful, but she's looking more like her old self. Her pink hair sparkles and her cheeks radiate their youthful glow. She starts to pull back when she sees me on the bed.

"No, no," I say. "Come in; I'm just relaxing."

She throws her jacket onto the rollaway bed along with her small backpack. She starts to join me on the bed when she remembers her tennis shoes and bends down to remove them. She then sits gingerly beside me and proceeds to tell me about the train museum where she spent the afternoon. "You wouldn't believe how big that steam engine was, Oma. It's twice as tall as me."

"I believe you," I say. "When I was a little girl, the trains ran on the track above our house. They were giant."

"In Myra?" she asks.

I laugh. "Yes, in Myra. How do you think the farmers got their wheat to market?"

"I'd sure as hell hate to be standing in front of one of those guys when they're traveling through," she said.

I wait for a moment. "I think you know that my other grandfather Myron, Daddy Mac's father, worked for the railroad. He told me that during the Great Depression, it wasn't unusual for folks to step in front of a train or even park their car on the track in anticipation of being hit by accident. He said that the poor engineers never got over it when they hit someone."

"That's crazy," Jennifer says. "What would make someone do that?"

"Mostly despair. Desperation. Men who could no longer care for their family or had given up on life. Even as a young girl, I knew someone not much older than you who did that. She was unmarried and pregnant. Something you didn't have to experience because you live in today's world."

Jennifer remains thoughtful. Finally she says, "But to take your own life?"

"You're lucky, Jennifer. Not everyone then had, or has now, the opportunities you do. Certainly that girl didn't. Abortions were illegal, dangerous. There was and is so much shame attached to being unmarried and pregnant. I've told you my story."

"But you were in love, Oma, and the war separated you."

"Still, I was alone and pregnant when I made the decision. What else was I going to do at nineteen . . . your age?

"Were you scared?"

"I was terrified. If it hadn't been for Aunt Ada, I don't know what I would have done. I knew she was the person I could trust, and she wouldn't betray my terrible secret." I hesitate before saying, "I never thought anything like that would happen to me. Because of when it happened—a time when abortion was illegal—I was so ashamed that I didn't want anyone to know."

"I don't think I felt ashamed, Oma, only scared," she says. "This isn't unusual in my dorm or in my sorority. It was just a terrible expense I hadn't counted on." She laughs. "Fortunately Dr. Conolly paid for it."

I smile at my granddaughter, lighthearted in a way I've never been. "I certainly never wanted Oma to know. She would have dragged me to her church and asked the congregation to pray for my soul. She would have been worse than my dad, who I was always scared of. He could change moods on a dime. His tongue hung to the side of his mouth like all hell was about to break loose. Sometimes it did. Once he got into it with Oma over my dead uncle's car. He thought he should have that car to look for a job and to move his family, us, to wherever that job was. But Oma had other ideas. Said she was going to drive it herself. Something women didn't do in the forties. Made my dad mad as hell. He called her a bitch, and she told him he was going straight to hell. The next day Dad said, 'Pack your toys. We're moving away.' We never had a chance to say goodbye to our friends. Only a quick goodbye to Oma. I never forgave him for that."

After a few minutes Jennifer asks, "Did you ever spend time with her again?"

"Once a year she'd come to visit, and we dreaded it. Grandma Irene would give up cigarettes and beer, swearing me and my sisters to secrecy. My dad would get even moodier. He just stayed in the TV room when he wasn't working. But that's when Oma gave me her Easter egg."

"What Easter egg?"

"In Russia and in Christian communities everywhere, Easter eggs are symbols for new life. New beginnings. Her egg, given to her on her fourteenth birthday, is bejeweled with diamonds and sapphires, even some garnets." I hold out my hand. "It's about the size of my fist."

"You still have it?" she asks. "Can I see it?"

"Yes, you can see it, when the time is right."

"What does that mean, Oma? *When the time is right.*"

"You'll see."

She accepts my response more easily than I thought she would. I count my blessings for now.

"Did you ever really go back to Myra again?"

"A couple of times when I was older, but I was always passing through because your grandfather wanted to get to Jackson Hole, Wyoming. He liked to fish there."

"It all sounds too sad, Oma."

I stroke her hair. "Life isn't always exactly the way we want it to be. You and I both have firsthand experience with that." I smile and pull her onto the bed with me. "We have each other. That's good enough for me."

Once seated in the auditorium, Audrey touches my arm and takes the seat beside me in the front row, her press pass around her neck. "Glad we're having lunch," she says. "I know a place, nothing fancy."

We've arrived in time for the first meditation. Sitting, we close our eyes. I've become so accustomed to the routine that after only a few days, I'm relieved by the darkness and quiet. I'm almost eager to enter the meditation again. Despite the directions or form of meditation, something I can't name settles down inside me.

Today's question from Gilbert has left me, and I'm sure others, thoughtful: "How will your normal life change when you return home?"

After all that's happened getting here, in Duluth and with Stan, plus talking to Nancy, it's clear that things will never look the way they did a week ago when I was stopped for speeding. Was this change bound to come no matter what? Or did meeting new people in a different landscape prod what might have already been there? Or is it the meditation? Though my head doesn't feel as full, there's confusion about what comes next.

I'm more than grateful to leave the university when Audrey drives downtown and parks near the train museum. While she parks, I gaze around and see nothing that looks like a restaurant.

We cross the street to stand outside an old Victorian in bad repair. Many of the roof's shingles are missing, and the stairs leading up have been patched so many times they look dangerous. "Don't worry," Audrey says. "No one's fallen through yet."

Though I hardly know her, I trust Audrey.

"Mama's Kitchen serves the best burger and fries," she says. "Their chocolate shakes, topped with a mountain of whipped cream and a cherry, rival any milkshake you'll ever sip through a straw."

"What about the food coma this afternoon?"

She laughs. "It's worth the risk."

We settle at the counter and give our food order to the waitress. Outside, the clouds gathering over the lake forecast the possibility of rain. "The seminar is different now," Audrey says. "Not that I'm an expert. I was only there that one time with Roland and twice now with Gilbert. The difference has been astonishing."

"Thankfully, Gilbert put the introduction back in and, more thoughtfully, the beginning meditation," I say. "I've come to depend on it. Strangely, the meditation helps me get . . . settled."

The small restaurant is crowded and there's only one waitress. We're sitting at the counter because there's nowhere else available. A large crowd behind us laughs loudly over their food. I'm aware that our order is taking longer than I imagined. At some point I let go of the time consideration.

"Do you think Gilbert's interested in you?" Audrey asks.

"Wrong time, wrong gal," I say, though my ears are burning. "A man is not where I want to spend my time." I hesitate. "What about you? You know why I came here, and it wasn't to find a man. So, I'm curious, what brought you here?"

Audrey spreads the remaining dressing on her salad. "Frankly, Duluth's a relief after San Francisco and, before that, Chicago. You can walk the streets alone at night, go into a bar for a nightcap and not worry that some dude is going to follow you out. But I miss having like-minded friends."

"A small town wouldn't work for me, not now. Maybe not ever."

"While I was at Chicago's Art Institute, I felt like I was with my own kind. More freewheeling thinkers. Women who weren't afraid to be strong. To show it, to say what they thought."

"But not here, I take it."

"Except for the university, which is where I like to hang out. I'm always glad to talk to someone like you."

"I grew up in a small town," I say. "Went back once in my early thirties and thought I might move my family there. But two weeks changed my mind. Not the right politics. Plus, everyone in my family who'd once lived there had either died or moved away. That's what they do in the Dakotas if they aren't tied to the land. Only the hardcore stay."

My last time in Myra was the summer before Oma died. She was alone with only her church to care for her. She hadn't lived in her house for a long time. In fact, the new owner tore it down and built a more modern house with a three-car garage. After Uncle Ivan moved to the West Coast where Mom and Aunt Ada lived, Oma boarded with a Gottlieb cousin. They went to the same church, and Irma, her cousin, remained one of her best friends. Because Irma couldn't make borscht or kuchen like Oma could, Oma was more than welcome in her household.

When I got the call from Uncle Ivan saying Oma was dying, I was involved in a big trial in San Francisco. Oma had broken her hip, but worse, her heart finally gave out. It happened inside of a week. I didn't have a chance to get there in time to say goodbye, and Mom was too sick with pleurisy to go. The guilt and sadness kept me from going back after the memorial. All these years later, I'm not sure I could find her grave today. If anyone has even tended the grave since. That had been Oma's excuse for never leaving Myra and moving west. Someone needed to tend the family graves.

"I do miss certain things you find somewhere like this that you don't find in the city," I say. "The way people take care of each other. You don't find that in the San Diegos of the world unless you've been planted in a neighborhood for thirty or more years."

Audrey picks at her salad. When she isn't eating she stirs her tea. The spoon scrapes the sides of the ceramic cup until I finally say, "That spoon's driving me crazy."

"Sorry," Audrey says absently. "If you don't mind, let's do the interview now, while we eat lunch."

I'm halfway through my burger, recalling that the last burger I ate was in the Denver airport. That one tasted like cardboard that had been left out in the rain. "I don't think I've ever been inter-viewed outside of a case." I laugh and hear a wavering edge of nervousness in my voice. "Is this personal or professional?"

Audrey looks at me for a few seconds, her brown eyes holding the same intensity I saw the morning we were both late. "Let's say both."

"What do you want to know besides why I came and what I hope to get out of the week, the seminar, Duluth . . . the usual blather in these kinds of interviews?"

"Let's start there, just to get warmed up."

"I've already told you that I mostly came because my marriage is wrecked, and surprisingly, the fact of it has put me on tilt ever since. I'm afraid I'm guilty of going along with my life on what seems a predictable course, and bam, my partner decides he doesn't want to be together anymore. Like that."

"Do you mean to tell me that this man you've known all these years didn't leave breadcrumbs along the way?"

"Maybe the real issue is whether I wanted to see them or not."

"Did you?"

"He's always been a flirt. That's probably how he hooked me in the beginning. Charming. Isn't that what we say about such men? Truth is, Stan was a rebound for me. I was still trying to get over the man I loved. A man who died in Vietnam as a military consultant. I was young, bereft, and pregnant when he left. The pregnancy was easier to take care of than the lingering grief. Of course, I didn't know any of that then. Truth be told, even when I walked down the aisle with Stan a couple of years later, I'd never really put Robert behind me."

"Did Stan know about Robert?"

"Not really. I never told him. For a few years Stan filled the black hole left by Robert. The emotional dearth wasn't revealed until after our second daughter was born."

"Because you honestly didn't see it or because you were otherwise distracted?"

"Probably the latter. When Tara was born, Stan was making enough money in his law practice that we could afford childcare, and I could finally go to law school. I'd waited long enough. Getting him through school, having the family, doing what women do put me behind by six or seven years. Not counting the unresolved grief. So once I got back onto my own highway, I was hell-bent to finish and finish well."

I push a French fry around on my plate, completely satiated by the fat and carbs. "The girls were in school, and we had a nanny to pick them up and stay with them in the afternoon. Gretchen usually started supper. I was often home by dinnertime. On the surface it appeared that everything was working. But I knew somewhere inside myself that it wasn't."

Audrey pushes her plate to the side and bends over her tea, careful to leave the spoon on the plate. Her gaze is direct. "What did you hope this Roland Cosgrove, guru extraordinaire, would give you that you didn't already have? You've said your career was the central pillar . . . I looked at your website and you are who you say you are, one of the top ten divorce attorneys in California . . . so why would you need a would-be pretender who crept out of the woodwork and put together a con game for insecure folks who think they need a guide out of the swamp of their own making?"

"You have to excuse me for laughing, Audrey," I say. "You sound more like me when I'm in the courtroom or leveling with one of my weepy clients before she understands she's been asleep most of her marriage while Sir Galahad has been diddling the secretary, or babysitter, or fill in the blank. More like the me who came here five or six days ago."

"You haven't answered my question." From the square of Audrey's shoulders, her press badge practically falling into her tea, it's clear she's looking for something, and she's not going to give up until she finds it.

"Okay. A good question. I think I've gotten as much outside of the seminar as I have sitting in that lecture hall. Like talking to you. Being with Jennifer. The entire week has forced me to stop. To see things differently," I say. "Maybe more deeply." I hesitate, reluctant to take this further. "I can blame my friend Nancy."

"No, you're not the kind of person who needs to blame anyone." She smiles for the first time since we sat down. "I use the word *need* intentionally."

"Touché," I say. I glance down at my near-empty plate before meeting Audrey's eyes again. "Roland, for me, is like someone from a world vastly different than the one I live in. If he's been useful, he's slowed me down, way down. Long enough that I can get close to my feelings, frozen as they've been. Even talking to you about Robert tells me I've made progress."

"That *frozen feeling* stuff is Roland talk. I want Marta talk."

"Maybe I just needed to wake up. Who wouldn't with that glacial wind off Lake Superior? How the hell do you do it, Audrey? We're here in summer, and I'm never this cold in the coldest San Diego winter."

"That's funny when you think about it. But no squirming out of this one," she says. "Here's my real question: What if this Roland character is really a con artist, and you've been conned? What if you spent a whole lot of money on something he couldn't deliver? Wouldn't you be pissed?"

"Even if everything you're saying is true, Audrey . . . even if it was a tremendous waste of money, it wasn't."

"How so? Because I'm not completely buying this."

"What if I spent a whole lot of money to come to this icy cold place, but it ended up being that Roland wasn't the main event? What if something else showed up that I hadn't expected? Would that make it a mistake?"

"So what showed up? Gilbert?"

I'm surprised at my own loud laugh. "We're going to be late, but this is worth it," I say. "Gilbert is a decent guy. He's smart, he means well, his heart is in the right place when he can find it. No, it's not about Gilbert. It's about me and you. Your questions have been a kind of catalyst for that."

She leans farther forward and her badge lands in the middle of her tea. "You're not going to tell me that this interview is the highlight."

"No . . . what's been the highlight of the trip is that I finally see a more authentic, more human face when I look in the mirror. The arrival of my granddaughter has been part of the catalyst. No, not the seminar alone or even Duluth, although getting away to some-place so different has helped. But seeing Jennifer has been like seeing a younger, more vulnerable me. Just watching her antics reminds me of my own foolishness. Where I was blind, where I behaved like someone without real life experience. She's helped me see that the mask I've worn is just that, a mask." I smile. "She's softened my edges, so to speak. And given me back something I loved about my own grandmother."

"Doesn't sound like one of the top ten California divorce attorneys," Audrey says.

"Let me ask you a question, Audrey. A question I'm only now asking myself."

"Shoot." She reaches down and pulls her badge out of her tea.

"Don't you sometimes find yourself lonely and you don't know why? Seriously. You live alone, but even if you didn't. My point is that Jennifer has such new, innocent energy. Without artifice. Not until I stepped away on this trip did I realize how much I've been living like a Roman warrior, putting on my armor every day and heading into battle. Then when I come home, I haven't removed the armor until I've had two, three, four drinks. By then I've disappeared. Until I get up and do it all over again. But with Jennifer, life happens now. She cries and gnashes her teeth when she's hurt. Gets drunk when she can't handle how powerful she is. Each day is like a birthday party for her. That kind of spontaneous living has *never* been part of my résumé. Never."

My sigh fills the counter. Audrey smiles at me.

"We're tough, Audrey, you and I. We've had to be, maybe for all the best and worst reasons. But I want to experience something besides tough." I laugh. "Even if it takes a so-called charlatan to get me there."

Audrey looks down at her wristwatch. "Holy shit, we're an hour late for the afternoon session."

"I'm sure they were able to go on without us," I say. "Hand me the bill."

Chapter Sixteen

I've just settled back under the white comforter when Jennifer enters with a couple of paper bags and a smile I haven't seen since the day I arrived. I have to juggle my arm to sit up.

"They have a great Goodwill here," Jennifer says.

Out of one paper bag comes a red and black T-shirt and a pair of cropped pants. "Size ten. Is that right?"

I reach over to pick up the T-shirt. On the Road is blazoned across the black in red letters. The cropped khaki cargo pants have several pockets. "What am I going to do with this in Duluth?"

"It's not for Duluth."

"For California?"

"No," she says. "All night you kept saying Myra, Myra, Myra in your sleep. At first I couldn't figure out what you were saying until it dawned on me that's where you grew up early on."

"But what do the T-shirt and pants have to do with Myra?"

"Everything." She lays them out on the bed and opens the other sack. She pulls out a lightweight purple cotton sweater. White and gray cotton socks. "Now you're ready," she says.

"Ready for what?"

"Myra," she says.

She puts up her hand to ward off my protest. "I have nearly six more weeks before classes begin. I now have no job, and you have a great car that will deal with whatever we find in North Dakota. You said it yourself: you're retiring. It's time you had a few surprises in your life. I intend to help you find them."

"But . . ."

"I won't hear one word against my plan."

"I have a trial to get back to," I say. "Yes, I intend to retire, but you don't shut down a practice in a day just because you decide that's what you want to do."

Jennifer plops down in the middle of all the stuff she's piled on the bed. She sits close enough to stroke my arm. "We may never get this chance again, Oma. Never."

I sink back against the pillows, my body nearly liquid and my eyes misting because somehow, somewhere in my world, there's a Jennifer to help me step outside of my conventional life. I reach for her hand, the bones soft, the skin smooth as white ribbon, her fingers not yet lined and veined with the efforts of doing and hanging on.

I SURPRISE MYSELF WHEN I drive up, one-handed, out of the underground garage and into the evening. Saint Luke's Hospital, no longer an unknown destination. In many ways it's a relief to leave Jennifer behind. To leave the hotel. Gilbert. Ever since Gilbert told me Roland was in the hospital, I've been meaning to find him once more. What I'm going to say, I'm not sure. I just know I need to get to the hospital, to once again connect with this man who, in his own quiet and unassuming way, has touched something in me that's been too long asleep. I don't even know what to call that something. I wonder if it even matters.

Inside the sliding glass doors, the same bustle swells with the same noise I left just a few days ago. The same blue scrubs, stethoscopes around various necks, gurneys clanging down the linoleum corridors. I discover Roland in a single room, having been moved from the ICU a couple of days ago. With yellow roses in hand, I approach the door that the floor nurse indicates. It's halfway open. I'm timid when I first knock and then peek into the white room with all its tubes and trays, the box of purple gloves on the counter beside the tissues and hand sanitizer.

Roland turns toward the door. His face is even paler than the last time I saw him. The pallor somehow matches his thick white hair, which likely hasn't seen a brush since Gilbert was last here. He smiles on seeing me, an oxygen tube trailing his nose and against his nearly shrunken chest. The bruised hand with its purple blossom rests on the bedsheet. "Marta," he says. "Somehow, I knew you would come."

I ease toward the bed and, with some awkwardness, rearrange his reading glasses and a small red book that looks like meditations or prayers. I place the vase of roses in the space I've cleared on his bedside table.

"Roland," is all I say. I hold my bandaged arm against my chest and scoot an empty chair close to the bed.

"Thank you," he says, indicating the roses. "There's so much life in yellow."

I smile as I lower myself onto the chair. "How are you?" I ask, though I already know how fragile he is.

Just seeing him reminds me again of my bear-shaped pendant with the red heart line running through it. This moment feels like a punctuation mark bridging who I was driving into Duluth just days ago to who I am now, sitting on this steel chair in a hospital room I never expected to see the likes of again. Trying to pay homage to someone who helped build the bridge.

"Thank you for . . ." I start to say *for everything*, but my throat is suddenly choked with emotion.

"Maybe we should just meditate together," he says. "Five minutes. That's all."

I close my eyes as though his words are the bell signaling us to start. The intense activity vibrating behind my eyelids nearly distracts me until I settle into the words that have now become a mantra of sorts. *Heart travel. Heart line. Breathe in. Breathe out. Allow the thoughts to flow through. Remember the river. The current. What was once here is now gone.*

How long we meditate for, I'm not sure. When I open my eyes, Roland is gazing at me with contemplation. "How has the week been for you?" he asks.

I laugh to cover my sudden self-consciousness. This conversation so different from our initial meeting in the president's living room. "Changed," I say. "Something has changed."

His eyes question without words. There's the half smile I've come to respect, to depend on.

"My words in the exercise were *heart travel*," I say.

He nods but says nothing, his silence extending an invitation to continue.

"So when you told me about the bear with the heart line, it felt . . . I don't know."

"Serendipitous?"

I nod. Any words are stuck in the new and now-familiar thickening of my throat. Clearly Roland has seen something in me that I haven't been able to see myself.

"You were ever so fortunate," he says. "Most don't shift as quickly from the outside world to the inside." He muses for a moment, his watery eyes focused on the wall opposite him. "Yes, fortunate indeed."

A nurse comes from behind. I jump, her entry was so quiet. "Nighttime medication," she announces in a voice as harsh as the too-bright light after one comes out of a tunnel, a tunnel filled with wisdom and magic—yes, magic.

On cue I replace the chair at the end of the bed with my good arm. I wait impatiently while she raises the bed. She helps Roland with the medication. Still standing at a distance, I wait for her to leave.

She turns toward me. "I'm sorry, but you'll have to leave now."

The change is so abrupt that I almost stumble when I step closer to the bed. "Thank you, Roland," I say. The words are inadequate and seemingly small—for this unexpected time with him, brief as it was, and it will likely resonate in a memory of what was between us just moments ago.

He reaches toward my hand, and I extend my good hand toward his. I take his hand and, once again, feel as though his bones will crumble if I squeeze too tight. His eyes are brown and steady behind the watery glaze. Mine are too filled with tears to hold his gaze for longer than a few seconds. I turn toward the door and enter the hallway where a different world with different priorities scurries from one place to another. The busyness that goes with all of what I have called the real world.

Outside in my car I sit quietly with the engine running, the dashboard lit, and my good hand on the steering wheel. Another reminder that I'm in the same place where I began, but I'm not the same person as when I started.

"I'm glad you were able to see Roland before the seminar ends," Gilbert says. I've just settled into the passenger seat of his Volvo. He's requested that we drive together to the final session. I'm more relaxed than I would have imagined.

"Thank you," I say. "I would have never believed so much could happen in a week's time."

"For many of us," he says. His eyes focus on the now-familiar road as it winds through Duluth's hilly streets toward the campus.

"Are you sad about closing down the seminars even though Roland wants to keep going?"

"Yes and no."

"That letting go problem we talked about?" I ask.

"I'm not sure. All I know is that it's time to put Amy first. Your question to me and an honest conversation with my sister made Roland's health event the landmark moment I needed." He swings onto the campus. Once parked, he turns toward me. "I'll leave Duluth and return to Long Beach. Take up what it means to be a dad to my daughter. All thanks to you. In a strange way to Roland as well."

His face tightens with a wave of emotion that is there and then gone. He hurries to say, "And you, a road trip with your granddaughter."

I can't help but smile. "Maybe I need to go backward in order to go forward."

"It looks like we're both going to find out if that's true." He opens the car door with the same heavy squeak I've become accustomed to. I scoot closer to the door on my side and maneuver my arm against my chest. He walks to my side of the car, offering his hand. I accept and grasp his hand, once again surprised by someone who thinks his way in and out of life situations. Leaning into him, I pull myself up and away from the seat.

We stand facing each other, his six feet to my five feet six. When he puts his hands on my shoulders, he leans down and kisses my cheek. A gentle kiss, the kiss of a friend in welcome or departure. In understanding. The sun rests warm on our shoulders while behind us horns honk as others drive past in search of parking spaces in the student lot.

"Thanks, Marta," he says. "I'm not sure I could have let go of this without you."

We stand like that for another minute, the sun shining down with what feels like the first real warmth this week. Gilbert's hands are warm on my shoulders. We keep looking at each other. We aren't who we thought we were in the beginning. Those people are gone. Those people went in other directions, like we will do shortly, walking back through the side doors to the elevator where the same two men will inspect backpacks and check for name tags. I will sit where I've sat all week, my arm against my chest unlike the beginning.

Inside the darkened lecture hall, there's the bustle of folks finding their seats, the rattle of papers and backpacks, water bottles banging on the floor. Seated in the front row, I have no notebook and no pen. I'm here to listen and meditate.

"Good morning," Gilbert says from the stage.

Likely much to everyone's surprise, he's now sitting in Roland's chair, the lamp shining beside him, the microphone pinned to his sport coat, his eyes fixed on us, the participants. His hands are loosely folded on his lap. He's relaxed in a way we haven't seen since he began to lead the seminar.

"Thank you for allowing me to be with you this week." He nods by lowering his head in a sign of respect. "I know that you've been disappointed that Roland wasn't able to return." He waits for the murmurs and the ensuing silence. "Today we will begin with a twenty-minute open-eye meditation seated where you are."

He rings the small meditation bell, and the room falls silent.

This is not the same Gilbert who walked with me in the woods or sat across from me at dinner or drove the Volvo to the college and back to the hotel. Or the same Gilbert across from me in the small garden by the waterfall. At tea in the hotel café.

Today, meditation is quiet for me. No jangling brain with a thousand thoughts and strategies for this or that. Just a quiet I can't explain, even to myself. As though all is taken care of, and I just need to sit here. *Heart travel* is now the plan as Jennifer and I prepare for our road trip back to Oma's Myra. She offered to get the car checked and gassed up for the trip. She also took charge of the suitcases and snacks. I can let go.

During the lunch break, Gilbert disappears before anyone can approach him with a question. I'm puzzled and, yes, disappointed. While I brought an energy bar and bottled water, I want something more substantial, like a real sandwich.

I leave the darkened auditorium and follow some of the participants to the basement level I didn't know existed. Along the wall of a kind of cafeteria, vending machines entice the participants who have gathered to make their selections. I stand in line, realizing that except for the two leaders and Audrey, I never really spoke to anyone else who was here this week.

I lift my credit card to buy a ham and cheese sandwich when someone touches my elbow. "I'm ahead of you," Audrey says with a smile and a lightness she doesn't usually carry. "Look, sandwiches." She holds up a paper bag. "Let's find a spot outside."

Her presence is another surprise. Because she knows the campus, she leads me to a half-shady, half-sunny spot where there's a single picnic table that is perhaps unknown to most attendees. I'm grateful that, again, I wore jeans and can straddle the bench easily, keeping my wounded arm lifted as I seat myself.

"I was afraid I was going to miss you," she says. "And the last day." Without taking another breath she continues, "Wouldn't have forgiven myself for not saying goodbye."

"How did you know we're leaving?"

"I ran into Jennifer yesterday in the thrift store and she told me about her plan. How great for the two of you to have an adventure together. You both deserve it after your week in the Minnesota deep freeze." She slings her badge over her shoulder and spreads open the paper bag. Inside are two sandwiches, potato chips, two waters, and a dark chocolate candy bar. "You choose," she said. "One is tuna, and the other is turkey and Swiss."

"As always, you're full of surprises," I say.

"I love hearing that," she says. "I never want to be called predictable."

"Never," I say, teasing her.

"Don't get too excited about seeing the last of me," she says. "I plan to pay you a visit when I need to get out of this state in the dead of winter."

"You're on," I say.

I can hear the change in my tone. "Are you coming to the seminar this afternoon?"

"Of course. I didn't go to all this trouble just to have lunch with you. Are you kidding?"

Since too much time has been taken up getting the food, we now gulp down the sandwiches and chips and split the chocolate bar. We follow others back to the lecture hall, once again going through the security lines with the two men who have become part of the routine.

"I won't miss that," I say to Audrey, nodding to security behind us. We hurry back toward our seats in the front row. It's already five after one o'clock. Knowing Gilbert, he's starting right on time.

We ease down the dark stairs to the two reserved front seats. Gilbert nods and smiles from the stage; we aren't the only ones late getting back. He then removes the microphone from his lapel and takes a stage mic in hand. He strolls to the middle of the stage where he might see everyone despite the overhead stage lights. I wonder if the lights even allow him to see the faces waiting to hear what he has to say.

"I know this is the last day." He pauses. "I also know that many of you will leave here disappointed that Roland was unable to finish the week with you." Again he waits for his words to settle in. "Let me assure you that while we are here, together and meditating, he is resting comfortably and meditating right along with us." Gilbert hesitates, then clears his throat. When he starts to speak again, he struggles with what appears to be emotion dislodging his usual poise. He clears his throat and begins again. "You in this seminar have been extraordinarily fortunate . . . to have Roland in his advanced years here with you." He pauses and allows that to sink in. "And I'm somewhat sad to tell you that Roland will not be returning." Quickly, he adds, "He is retiring due to health concerns."

The audience murmurs. A choked sob erupts from somewhere in the darkened room. "He and I both thank you for your participation; for some of you, it's been many years of involvement as we've moved around the country and to Hawaii." Again, he pauses.

"As of this afternoon we will be ending the meditation seminars with Roland." An uncomfortable silence ensues. Gilbert pauses before starting again. "For many years I have accompanied

Roland and served the seminar as best I can. But my time has come as well." His hesitation is brief. "As you experienced this week, I don't have the charisma and centeredness that Roland shares with you." When he laughs, a number of participants laugh as well, then become quiet in order to hear what he has to say. "What most of you don't know is that I have a daughter at home in California, a daughter who has been sorely neglected in order for me to do this work. I think it's now time for me to take on the most important job in a lifetime. I need to be her dad."

As I'm listening to Gilbert, my eyes mist. I notice Audrey glancing at me, but I stare straight ahead toward Gilbert. I suspect no one else realizes the price he's paid both in leaving his daughter Amy and now in letting go of his service to the seminars as well as Roland's life mission.

I take a couple of deep breaths and remind myself that this isn't the end of the story. That stories don't end until they do.

"This afternoon, at our final meeting, I'd like to hear what you want to do for closure rather than have me direct you."

Someone high in the elevated seats shouts, "Can we just sit and meditate where we are? This is a lot to take in."

Voices of assent are heard throughout the lecture hall. One person says, "I'd like to process this, what you said." Others agree with that voice.

Gilbert remains relaxed, the mic dropped by his knees. He waits for the voices to quiet. "Why don't we do some of both?" he says. "First we'll meditate for an hour. Then let's gather outside on the shaded lawn on this side of the building. We can bring chairs from the cafeteria or simply sit on the ground in a big circle where we can be more casual and comfortable."

Someone pipes up, "We won't be able to hear each other."

Others join the chorus in agreement. Gilbert raises the mic to his mouth. "Okay, I hear you," he says. "How about we turn up the lights and I'll sit on the edge of the stage. Then we can all see and hear each other."

Audrey squeezes my arm. "This is where I say goodbye," she says. "I need to type up the interview with you and write an article about the end of the seminars." She smiles. "But I know where to find you." She salutes, which seems somewhat strange yet perfect for Audrey.

I squeeze her hand resting on the arm of the chair. Nod. She has just enough time to scoot out before Gilbert begins. He's now back in Roland's chair, adjusting the mic on his sport coat in preparation for the closing meditation. While Audrey scoots toward the back, he nods toward me. He winks. Something he's never done before. Yet it seems like a signal that says, *We did it*, and, *I'm glad you stayed to see what's possible.*

Part II

Chapter Seventeen

Saturday, June 15

MIDAFTERNOON SUNLIGHT WASHES OVER FIELDS of sunflowers and alfalfa standing tall beside a highway that unravels from Bismarck heading west. The east/west highway remains quiet except for a tractor or hay baler inching its way along the road's shoulder from one field or farm to the next. The sun against the green fields and the sky the color of bluebells reminds me of my childhood. Cowslip grows abundantly along the road's shoulder or hides inside chokecherry bushes and Russian thistles. The road seems long, farther than I imagined once we leave the interstate; the sunflowers, like a field of yellow faces, are extraordinary to my San Diego sensibilities.

We've been driving for the better part of the day, taking our time, each inside our own thoughts with this shift away from Duluth and the cold wind blowing off Lake Superior. The time in the hotel and at the seminar begins to fade into memory as the miles speed by. Roland and Gilbert are likely on their way back to

California in Gilbert's Volvo. That last farewell with each of them, poignant in their own way, lingers in my memory and leaves a warmth inside my chest.

The meditation week emerged like a signpost on the road. A change point. While he time in Duluth provided navigation tools for the unexpected places where life's circumstances deliver new, often unpredictable events. I'm now seeing how they align, how they begin and end, frequently beginning and ending at the same time. The road, the land, the small farm towns. The bridge connecting Bismarck to Mandan where the Missouri River below once felt threatening. As a small child I feared my Mandan grandpa's car would fall off the long bridge, and we'd all drown in the cold, muddy water roiling below. Now, with the afternoon's drive on the other side of that bridge, the rolling fields lull us into a sense of ease I haven't known for as long as I can remember.

"How far off the main track is this town?" Jennifer asks.

"Farther than I thought."

Farmhouses here and there—all of them beautiful in an everyday, ordinary way—remind me of Norman Rockwell paintings. How we tend to romanticize the hard life of farmers and their families.

Jennifer, intent on a paper map, sits beside me. "All these towns are so small, Oma, really small. You can't even see half of them from the highway."

"Can you believe people are born and live and die in the same town, often the same house?"

She glances quizzically toward me. "Doesn't it seem to you like we're time-traveling into another century?"

Glancing over at her, I laugh. With her shoes on the dash and her pink hair, the heart-shaped sunglasses stare back at me. I haven't yet told her about discovering *heart travel* while she was standing in front of those engines at the train museum. Or that I would have made this trip with or without her. Definitely it's better with her.

"Does your cousin live on a real farm?"

"She's on the same farm my Great-granduncle Herman settled when he first came from Russia, the same farm where my oma's family lived after they arrived. The family story says that the land was barren before Uncle Herman came from Russia. Their efforts and faithfulness to the land and farming gave the farmers, and by extension us, wheat for over a century."

"That's almost half the life of this country, Oma."

A few more farmhouses sprinkle the green fields at a distance so far off the road that they appear deserted, though I suspect they're not. The massive barns dominate the houses nestled nearby. Green John Deere equipment sits idly in the yards outside barns. The road swoops up and down the rises, a distant cemetery waiting off to the side of the road. Cemeteries are often the sign-post that a town is close, maybe over the road's next swell.

The four o'clock sun glowers at us through the car's windows and sunroof. The short-sleeved shirts I couldn't wear in Duluth are welcome in the air-conditioned car. I'm already dreading the graveyards and churches, the prospect of no air-conditioning in my cousin's farmhouse. After the ongoing chill of Lake Superior, the heat likely won't be any easier.

WE DRIVE INTO MYRA ALONG what was once a gravel road. The houses sit widely apart, and the town seems so quiet. Not like California housing plots that practically butt up against each other. Jennifer's right: this is time travel. It's as though nothing has changed since I was a young girl along with that old déjà vu of knowing but not knowing a place. A newly painted two-story yellow house stands out against the tall chestnut trees. A church's spire, the steel cross almost majestic on its crown, sits in the immediate distance. We descend into what feels like a gentle valley but is really no more than a cleft in the road just five miles off Interstate 94.

Jennifer babbles about how beautiful it is. "But there's nothing here," she says, this girl who grew up in San Diego between the

Pacific Ocean and the irrigated desert of eastern San Diego County. She's used to the encumbrance of shopping malls and houses spreading like cornfields across the landscape with the ocean waiting at a distance, often too far away to see. "It's so green. Is it always like this?"

"I remember mostly snow and gravel roads." Mom spilling her bike with me and a dozen eggs in the basket. Snowsuits in photos with my sisters. Mom's pinup photos she sent Dad when he was overseas in World War II, her long leg poking out of a white chenille robe. A hay wagon pulled by a team of horses that Jennifer will never see on the town's streets. Today, there are few clothes-line poles. Gravel roads hide on side streets. Pickups replace the thirties and forties sedans. Still, there's only one grocery store on the main street. Two taverns. A single gas station. What's gone is the Kresge's Five & Dime where Uncle Ivan took us to buy pink ChapStick. When Oma saw us, girls of four and five, applying it, she grabbed the ChapSticks out of our small hands and scolded Uncle Ivan for encouraging the evil of lipstick. "Everything changes with time," I say, "except this."

"There's nothing but cemeteries here," Jennifer says. "Look, two right next to each other."

"And churches," I say. "I've counted three inside two blocks."

"But there are only three blocks to the entire town."

I laugh. "You're being generous."

WE'VE COME TO FIND THE graves. I know they're here. Yet Uncle Ivan, too debilitated with Parkinson's, couldn't give me specific instructions over the phone. He said the First Bible Church houses the records. I didn't think far enough ahead to contact the church, and now it's Saturday. While a pastor might be in their study preparing a sermon, those days may be gone as well. "We'll have to find our way around town on our own," I say.

"Let's find your oma's house first," Jennifer says. Her gray-and-white Adidas continue to rest on the dash of the car.

"We'll need luck," I say. "When I was here before, I couldn't find the house. Probably torn down years ago."

"What a shame. I was hoping to see it," she says. "At least let's find the house where you lived with Great-grandma Irene and Great-grandaunt Ada during the war."

I park in front of Hubner's Market on the main street, surprised but not surprised that it's still here. A fellow comes out carrying a six-pack of beer before he climbs into a new red pickup, nothing I would have seen in Oma's day, not in this town. Not the beer and not that fancy pickup. If Oma and her church had their way, anything to do with alcohol would have been outlawed. I glance at the Hubner's sign over the door and type the address into my phone. "Our house was down another block."

"We can walk."

There are no stop signs, let alone traffic lights. No one's in sight except the fellow who came out of the store. Trees block the late-afternoon sun but not the heat. We lock the car and walk in the direction my phone indicates is First Street. I'm wishing I could remember where Oma once lived. A Shell gas station occupies a downtown corner. I have an odd feeling that I know that corner, some inkling it's the old gas station where Uncle Ivan used to buy us sodas.

I'm slower than Jennifer, and I have trouble keeping pace with my eager granddaughter who prefers running to walking. She seems to forget or recall that exercise is not my strong suit. That I'm sixty-three years old. How would she know; we've never spent this much time together.

"C'mon, Oma. Shake it loose," she says, turning around and grinning at me. Her pink hair looks even darker in the shaded light. "This is what we came for."

I smile and pick up my pace, my sixty plus years lodged in stiffness from riding two-and-a-half hours in the car from Bismarck. Just to be safe, I told my cousin Donna we'd be at her place tomorrow around suppertime if not earlier. That will give us a day to acclimate to both the weather and the town.

The blocks are shorter than I remember, my once-young legs carrying me for what seemed like miles down the walkways. I keep trying to see the town through Jennifer's eyes, unclouded by memories and history. But the town seems foreign through that lens, like it belongs to someone else. I glance down at my tennis shoes, the sidewalk under my feet, the cement unevenly raised in enough places that I need to pay attention. Since cutting my arm, I'm no longer confident that I can trust my footing while my eyes roam the landscape.

"There aren't even that many houses, Oma. No movie theater or library," she says. "Just churches."

"I know. Churches and taverns. Not too different from over fifty years ago," I say. "Maybe the houses look smaller because the lots are bigger than we're used to." I'm thoughtful for a moment. "These towns keep shrinking. You can see why. All the young people move away."

"What do people do for fun?"

"They go to Dickinson or Bismarck. Hawaii in the winter and Alaska in the summer."

"Was it different during the war?"

"That gas station, the Shell on the corner? Might have been the Texaco I remember from when I was a girl. That's where Uncle Ivan took me and my sisters to buy Nehis, a brand of soda. The station garaged my uncle Ozzie's new car when he went overseas."

Unexpected sadness fills my chest. Except for Cousin Donna and Uncle Ivan, all the family who filled my memories have moved away or died. The same thing might be true of me, if and when Jennifer ever comes here again. In that moment I'm stunned by life's transience. What seemed important yesterday—an urgency to get the mail, to make sure the children got to school on time, preparation for an important trial—is a blip on today's horizon.

They're hardly a vague memory. Whatever worries or events populated the past have faded. I can't remember what I worried about a year ago. Besides, I can't trust that what I pull out of memory's well has any accuracy. It could be layered with a cloud of sentiment or the haze of forgetting.

The funerals. That's what I remember now as we walk the familiar but unfamiliar streets. I recall the dark and dour house where we went for Uncle Philip's funeral. Those old women in black lace. Men with black armbands arguing or singing as they sat against the living room wall. Oma across the room with Louisa on her lap. Her scarf around her neck and a blank look on her face behind the veil she wore to hide her scars. The same look whenever she was trying to figure something out. At Uncle Ozzie's funeral I sat beside her with my hand tucked inside her elbow. I think she hung on to my hand the entire afternoon when we went into the church basement afterward for what I called funeral food. I remember the smell of winter, wet wool, and mildew. The outside air so sweet and cold it felt like my lungs would freeze. That particular day Oma told me I could eat anything I wanted. Cookies, that's what I wanted. Especially the anise ones like Oma made at Christmas.

"We're crossing to First Street," Jennifer announces.

I look both ways, then wonder why. There's no evidence of cars except the one pickup that passed us on the main street. "Let's go slow," I say. "Haven't seen too much that I remember."

"How could you? There's no one here," she says.

"Not on the street anyhow." I attempt a joke: "Looks like the rest are in one cemetery or the other."

"That's spooky," Jennifer says.

"We'll probably have to call Uncle Ivan again."

"Let's see if we can find your house first."

We tromp along the sidewalk under the heavy shade trees, the day hot and alive with mosquitoes. They buzz around our faces and bare arms. Jennifer asks, "Is it this house, this one, or this one?"

I recognize nothing except that many of the older homes have been replaced by ranch-style houses that are already outdated. They appear crisp and clean in their white or pastel shades and have big lawns you don't see in Southern California and stoops rather than porches. Here and there a house from a bygone era spreads its wide porch across the front, the gingerbread trim marking it as being from the late nineteenth or early twentieth century.

"I don't see our house anywhere, Jennifer."

"You said small, one-bedroom, white with a front stoop, and back steps. Right?"

"Yes." I laugh. "By today's standards it was tiny. Back then, small meant one story on a single lot compared to the clapboard farmhouses and converted barns sitting on half an acre."

I stop and point back in the direction from which we came. "There used to be a water tower at the edge of town with a long staircase. Your great-grandma Irene pretended the stairs went into an airplane, an experience she never dreamed she'd have."

"Oh, look, Oma. Here's one like you described except it's painted yellow, and the stoop has an enclosed porch."

I glance at the side yard. No clothesline pole. Instead, a garden in raised beds. Behind the house on a berm some twenty feet above the yard, I spot railroad tracks I'd forgotten. "I'll be darned."

"You think this is it?"

I study the dirt side yard, the raised beds.

"Yes and no." I stare at the yellow house, still not believing that this is the place where my sisters and I sat on the back stoop with the pan of pudding, waiting for it to cool. The neighbor boy who played tricks on me and my sisters always lurked at that corner of the house. Evenings my sisters and I turned the pages of photo albums while Mom and Aunt Ada made divinity and fudge. There were no men except my grandfather, who was always sick. In many ways it was the best of times for my sisters and me, and for my mother and Aunt Ada.

"Makes me think about how I scared your great-grandma Irene

with my insistence on education," I say. "Then the way I trekked around the country with your mom and her sister, camping in godforsaken places like the Nevada desert and Utah's high timber. Grandma Irene was skittish about those things."

"Did Great-grandma Irene like living in a small town?"

I walk to the side of the house, careful not to intrude in case anyone's home. "I don't think so. Aunt Ada said Mom was afraid she'd live her mother's life, or worse, die of shame as an old maid in this town."

"Do you think they'll care if we walk around the house and see the back?"

"Hear that dog barking back there? We need to ask." I mount the few steps to the enclosed mudroom vestibule and open the outer door where a doorbell is mounted. I press the buzzer while a nervous jumble does somersaults in my stomach.

Jennifer stands on the steps behind me. I buzz a second time.

A man in his late sixties or early seventies appears. His red suspenders expand over his stomach, and he has a grizzled gray-and-white beard. Maybe I've just awakened him from a nap, though it's four in the afternoon.

"Sorry to disturb you," I say. I start to reach out my hand, then withdraw it. He stares at me and Jennifer as though we're aliens.

"You selling something?" he asks.

Strangers probably never come to town, least of all on a Saturday afternoon. "My mother and aunt lived here once," I say. "I'm Marta, granddaughter of Albert and Marta Gottlieb. And this is Jennifer, my granddaughter."

He looks first at me, then at Jennifer, suspicion heavy in his gaze. "Gottlieb," he says. "No one by that name around here now. I've been in this house for over thirty years and never heard of anyone by that name."

"Maybe you knew my uncle Ivan. Ivan Gottlieb. Lived here until he graduated high school."

"Was he that skinny kid that everyone said was queer?"

"I don't know what you mean." I can't give him the satisfaction of an answer. I feel Jennifer at my elbow. She's climbed the few stairs and stands beside me. Out of the corner of my eye I notice her clenched fists.

"His dad was a bricklayer, worked with my dad. His dad died of cancer. The old lady was always busy in the church, lived by herself. Think all the kids ran off including the queer one. That fellow?"

"Excuse me," Jennifer says. She takes a step closer to the man. "Queer is not a crime," she says.

She's ready to say more when I touch her elbow. I motion with my head that she come back down the stairs.

The man glares at her pink hair, her multiple earrings. "I can tell you're not from around here," he says. "Only someone like those Californians would say something like that. Must be where you're from."

Jennifer is not going to back down. She holds her ground and glares back at him.

I pull her arm until she has to step down another stair or two. "We only lived in this house for a couple of years," I say. "Sorry to bother you."

He strokes his chin. "Must be the same family where one of the girls got knocked up over in Horton after her husband died. Big scandal about an abortion."

Stories never die. They just get bigger.

My stomach feels hot and full of acid. I'm just not willing to give up and, obviously, neither is Jennifer. "Wonder if you'd mind us walking around the outside of the house," I say. "Want to show my granddaughter a few things."

"Stay away from the dog out back. None too friendly. He's fenced, but I can't guarantee a thing."

"Thanks for your time," I say. "What did you say your name is?"

"Heinrich," he says. "Better watch that young one. She'll get in a peck of trouble around here."

"Thanks," I say. "We'll be careful."

We barely clear the porch when Jennifer, about to explode, says, "What a nasty man. To say that about Uncle Ivan." She puts her hand over her mouth and whispers. "Was Uncle Ivan gay?"

I nod. "A gay man in the fifties could have been killed. Now you see why."

"No wonder he left. You all left."

We walk around the side of the house. I'm careful to note that none of the windows are open, so he can't hear us. "You grew up in California, Jennifer. You now live in Madison. Both places are considered liberal and overly open-minded by the conservative folks around here. You have no idea how lucky you are to have been raised in a climate of tolerance."

Jennifer gazes at the house, thoughtful for a moment. She points at the dog. "That pit bull must be the dog he was talking about."

"I just want to see the raised railroad tracks again," I say. "We spent a lot of time on railroad tracks when I was a kid. Looking for the gold glint of mica buried in stones. Walking the tracks to the Catholic cemetery."

Jennifer's face is a puzzle of questions. "Railroad tracks? Catholic cemetery? Why would you want to go there?"

"To look at the graves." I turn toward her. "Remember when I told you about the engineer who hit someone on the tracks? I was just a kid then, maybe nine or ten. It was out back of our house."

We walk beside the house but not too close. The shades are drawn, maybe to keep out the heat, maybe because he's suspicious. The closer we get to the berm from which the tracks rise, the more the dog barks. He bares his teeth, his multicolored camouflage matching his powerful legs as he chases us along the other side of a fence. I'm more than happy to snap a quick photo of the raised tracks and retreat, walking backward.

"Now you understand why our family hasn't rushed back to this country, even for memory's sake."

"That's sad. You should want to go back to where you came from," Jennifer says.

"That's not always true."

"I can't imagine thinking of San Diego that way . . . my high school friends, my family, the places where I went to school, the parks where I played. Swimming in the ocean."

I'm thoughtful for a moment. "We don't all get to have good memories."

We start back toward the front of the house. So much happened and didn't happen here and then later. Dreams that were just that, dreams. Those first inklings that I wanted more than this. To open doors I hadn't yet imagined. Now there's the proven history in the life I've lived. "Memories help me see if what I remember is valid or just the sediment behind a romantic overlay."

She stands away from the front porch, thoughtful for a moment. "Maybe someday I'll understand that too, Oma."

In front of the house, I snap another photo, then put my phone away in my small purse. "It takes as long as it takes," I say. I laugh to lighten the moment.

My phone had been buzzing on silent the entire time we talked to the old geezer who's probably younger than me. Of course the number is Stan's. He's likely ready to push for the house again. Well, he can damned well wait like I had to do for him all those years ago when I, too, wanted to be in law school. Once again, I need to contain my fury.

"I guess the cemetery's next," Jennifer says. "But the mosquitoes are getting worse."

We backtrack to the main street. The town seems smaller now. Our one encounter leaves me feeling less than welcome. More disappointed than anything.

"Do you want to stop in the store for anything?" I ask.

"Not really," she says.

She's not as eager as she was before. Our moods have so changed in a brief half-hour.

"Let's see if there are any local baked goods. I still miss Oma's kuchen," I say. "Funny how you can still taste things long after you've taken a bite."

Chapter Eighteen

Hubner's automatic sliding door seems out of place but not the smell of onions, garlic, and coffee. The store feels reminiscent of what it must have been over fifty years ago. Items are still housed in wooden barrels, fishing tackle and small tools sit on grocery shelves, and there are very few frozen goods. The commercial bread is past its sell-by date. Under the neon lighting, the shelves are mainly depleted of anything resembling groceries.

"Shipment hasn't come in," the clerk yells after us.

I leave Jennifer to wander the store. "Can't believe this store is still here," I say. It's thirty years since I've been here and twenty more before that."

The clerk laughs, her round cheeks a reminder of the Germans and Russians and Scandinavians living here. She leans back against the wall. "This town's not going anywhere, that's for sure."

"Any local baked goods?" I ask.

Her glasses slip down her nose and she eyes me over the tops of them. "If someone brought them in to sell, I'd be the first to buy them all and freeze them."

"Can't say I blame you," I say. "I was looking in particular for kuchen like my grandmother made."

"You won't find it in a store," she says. "Maybe five or so ladies in town still make it." She laughs again. "There used to be a woman who made and sold it before my time. She's legendary in this town. But that was a long time ago."

Jennifer, now standing beside me, touches my arm, eager to leave the store. "Know where I can get the recipe?" I ask. "Seems it died with my grandmother."

"Only place I know is Bismarck. State bookstore at the capital or the Germans from Russia research center might help you. Those recipes died with my grandmother too."

"Thanks," I say. Since there's no one else in the store, I step closer to the counter. "My grandparents, the Gottliebs, lived here after they came from Russia." I stretch my hand across the counter. "Never introduced myself," I say. I wince, having forgotten my arm, the bandage still in place. "I'm Marta, same as my grandmother. This is Jennifer."

"Knew you weren't from around here," she says. "No one ever asks about kuchen anymore. Think they've forgotten it ever existed."

"That's disappointing. Maybe just as well. We're headed for the cemetery. Hope to have better luck finding my long-dead family."

"Don't know the last time the mower came through. No one's left to tend the graves. Those who would are too old to get down on their knees." She stares at my arm. "What happened?" she asks. "Can't be good for digging around in the cemetery."

"An accident, you could say. A foolish accident."

"Hope you're going to be okay," she says. "Have to go to Dickinson to find a doctor around here." She leans forward against the counter. "Let me know if I can help. I'm here until closing at six."

Jennifer has an impish grin on her face. I should have never told her how I wounded my arm. She's probably looking for a way to get even after she got so shit-faced herself.

"Name's Gretta," she says. "It's really Jenny, but I can see that would be confusing."

I tell Gretta briefly that when we went to find the house where I lived those first years, the fellow who lives there snarled at us and made an accusation about my uncle.

Outside on the sidewalk, Jennifer says, "She was nice after that other fellow."

I smile. "*Welcoming*, that's the word." There was nothing welcoming about the man living in what could have been our old house.

We head in the direction of the two cemeteries. Jennifer's at the wheel of the car, and it's my turn to navigate. It's now nearly five in the afternoon, and the heat and mosquitoes have laid siege to the day.

"You know what we forgot to buy, Oma?"

"You mean wine?"

Jennifer nods and smiles at me.

"Can't imagine we'd find anything in that market that we'd want to drink," I say.

She laughs with her eyes on the rearview mirror as she backs into a parking place.

Not since we left Duluth has wine or booze of any kind seemed important. My arm is a constant reminder of the consequences of my too-long-indulged habit.

WHAT DISTINGUISHES THE FIRST CEMETERY are the wrought iron crosses, the distinctive designs of the scrolling unlike any I've seen before. Some crosses stand three to four feet tall, and others rise up five or six feet. Each cross is unique in design.

We park the car at the cemetery's outer edge. "Why don't you start at one corner, and I'll take the other," I say. "Maybe we'll get lucky since this is the smaller of the two cemeteries."

"How do you know this is the right one?"

"I don't. It's just where we'll start," I say. "Look for Gottlieb and

Schroeder. Only flat markers. Nobody had money before, during, or after World War II. See how the grass has grown up over the flat grave markers? This might be hands-and-knees work."

"The mosquitoes are terrible."

"We'll manage until we can't."

Names call up vague familiarity. Rolfs. Shively. Creed. Schimel. Names that were once attached to people Oma drank tea with or met in the grocery store or at church. Names that echo a past as foggy to me as the ability to attach them to people who lived and breathed. Mildred Rumford. Was she Oma's good friend Millie who lived next door? Agnes Fleischman. The one Oma declared was the church gossip? All these folks seem strangely familiar from stories I vaguely remember Oma telling me.

The mosquitoes buzz around my ears, nose, and eyes. One bites my leg where the cropped pants don't reach down far enough. The heat presses down and around us with the sun now at five o'clock in the sky, and we've just started our search. "Should we leave this for morning?" I ask. "Find a place to spend the night and come back?"

"We're here," Jennifer says. "Let's give it a go."

After a half-hour Jennifer says, "I can't read these markers."

I'm fighting the same complaint in addition to having the awkward dressing on my arm. "Maybe we should try the other cemetery. Closer to the church."

What was I thinking? That we could waltz in here and magically find gravestones I haven't seen for thirty years, which were hard to find even then? Grandpa Albert would have been in the ground the longest. Then Uncle Ozzie. Oma. That's the one I want to find.

I pull out my cell phone and am grateful to see three bars. Some farmer somewhere must have a cell tower in his pasture. At least now I can call Uncle Ivan.

When he picks up, Uncle Ivan sounds drugged, or maybe he's been sleeping. I can only imagine what he looks like, the group home always keeping him so combed and cleaned up.

"It's me, Marta. We're in Myra at the cemetery."

"What the heck," he says, a smile in his voice. "You went there alone?"

"Jennifer's with me. Kelsey's oldest. We're looking for Grandpa's and Uncle Ozzie's graves." I place my hand over the phone's speaker and whisper, "Start over there, Jennifer."

"Anybody living there?" Uncle Ivan asks.

"Not many. Nothing's changed, Uncle Ivan. Except they paved the gravel streets."

"Did you find the graves already?" He sounds winded, and we've only started talking.

"No. The headstones are sunk and buried beneath grass mowed over for so long you can't read the nameplates."

"The church would know," he says. His breathing remains heavy and loud. He takes a while to catch his breath between words. "You'll have to contact First Bible's pastor."

"But it's Saturday . . ." I start to say.

"Maybe tomorrow at church." I hear someone take his phone even as he yells, "I can't help you."

I sit back on my knees recalling how much I depended on him when I was a kid. He was the big brother I never had. I always felt safe with Uncle Ivan. He'd pull me in his Radio Flyer and let me pet his pigeons. He's just four years older than me, and I never stopped looking up to him. Now all these years later both of us are creeping up to Oma's age when she died. Both of us are helpless to reconstruct the past without those who came before us.

"Any help, Oma?"

"Afraid not." I swat at mosquitoes. "Let's give it another thirty minutes. I don't think we can stand it longer than that."

I turn to gaze at the tombstone I'm standing in front of. Gladys Reinhart. Her husband Kurt. Why do I know that name? My hand comes away bloody when I swat at a mosquito on my neck. *Damn, these bugs will drive us out of here.*

Gladys. Of course. One of Mom's best high school friends. She finally went to nursing school in Minot where Mom wanted to go but couldn't. There was no money in the family for such things, and I don't think Mom was motivated enough to work in the nursing home like Gladys did. That's probably how Mom ended up in the ice creamery where she met Dad. Gladys, dead at eighty-three just six months ago. If I'd come earlier I might have found her. Asked her questions about Mom, questions Mom would never answer. Now all that I might have wanted to know will remain a secret buried in this remote cemetery.

I no longer see most names on the flat, ground-level headstones. Instead I'm on my knees going from one nearly buried plate to the next, scraping away the long-dead leaves and overgrown grass with my one good hand, hoping to find any name I can recognize. Jennifer, downwind from me, swats at mosquitoes.

"Maybe we'll go back to the store. Gretta might be able to help us," she says.

We leave the car where it is and walk the two blocks to the store, slapping mosquitoes along the way. We've been searching for maybe an hour, and I'm ready to give up this craziness made worse by the nipping bugs.

"Thought I might see you again," Gretta says. "Mosquitoes are terrible this year." Shaking her head, she asks, "Did you have any luck?"

"None," I say. "I'm hoping the church has a record of the burial plots."

"Good luck with that," she says. "The new pastor is only here every other Sunday. Haven't had a regular pastor for ten years. Younger folks go to Dickinson."

I shake my head in frustration. "Guess it wouldn't have mattered if I had called ahead if there's no pastor to answer the questions."

"Someone would have answered," she says. "There are still a couple of old ladies from the guild who pick up messages and look in on shut-ins. There just aren't too many of those ladies left."

"How long have you been here?"

"Born here," she says. "Tried to leave a couple of times, but always came back for one reason or another."

"Your folks live here all their lives?" I ask.

"Yes and no. They farmed about ten miles north, though they did come to church here and bought whatever groceries they didn't grow. Like a lot of folks around here, we only ate meat our dad slaughtered." She sighs. "This town's been dead a long time. If it wasn't for farm subsidies, we'd look like Horton. Only thing there is the abbey and the health center, though don't ask me how either one of them exists."

"Any suggestions about how we might find these graves?" I ask.

"You'd have to find an old-timer," she says.

"Already met one who wasn't too friendly."

I turn around. Jennifer seems to have lost herself in the store. "Any place we can get a bite to eat?" I ask. "We aren't expected at my cousin's until tomorrow."

"You'll have to drive to Dickinson," she says. "Nothing between here and there unless you go home with me and eat my sloppy joes. Not too bad if I say so myself."

"We may take you up on that," I say. "Let me check with my granddaughter."

"All cooked up," she says. "Do that in the morning when it's cooler before I come to work. Just need to pick up some buns and a bag of potato chips. You guys like sauerkraut? Got a fresh batch of that too."

The sauerkraut sounds more North Dakota than the sloppy joes. "Let me buy the buns and chips," I say. "If you're sure we're not imposing."

"You're the only interesting people to come into the store in a month of Sundays. Of course you're welcome. Have to warn you, though, I live with a few critters." She grins and I'm left with the shine of gold crowns inside her open mouth. "Hope you're not allergic to cats."

I'm tempted to ask how many, but that would be rude. "I'll check with Jennifer."

Down the aisle near the fishing gear, Jennifer bends over what looks like fishing flies. "Can you believe they have all this fishing stuff, but I can't find Tom's toothpaste?"

"I believe it." I tell her about our dinner invitation. "Are you up for cats too?"

"Sure," she says. She fingers the packets of fishing flies, puts them back, and picks them up again. "All that digging around has made me hungry."

Jennifer follows me to the checkout stand. "Let's go have dinner," Gretta says. "If you wait outside, I'll be out front in five minutes."

We stand outside the automatic doors. Even five minutes of being prey to the bugs is more than I want to deal with. Jennifer doesn't hesitate. "I'll get the car at the cemetery. You coming?"

"Yes. We'll be eaten alive either way."

OUR HOSTESS WASN'T KIDDING ABOUT the cats. I count eight before we make it to the dining table in the kitchen. The table, its oilcloth peeking out from under piles of newspapers and unopened mail, has likely been stacked this way for some time. To her credit, the house is free of cat smell. Later she shows us the bedroom reserved for the cats where the litter boxes and pet beds crowd a Formica-topped dresser and card table as well as a large space under the only window left cracked for obvious reasons.

"Looks like you have your own animal shelter here," I say.

"Yes and no," Gretta says.

She begins to fuss with a Crock-Pot, stirring the contents until the odor of tomato and hamburger fills the kitchen. Grabbing a cardboard box, she moves to the table and sweeps everything off into the box. "Sorry about the mess," she says. "I never have company." Her raised arm takes in the whole house. "This was my folks' house for nearly a century before I inherited it. Leaves a lot to be desired, but the rent's right." She laughs and shoos a cat off one of the dining chairs. "They know they're not allowed in here, but days I work they get lonesome."

I can't help but wonder what lonesome has to do with taking over the kitchen. Oh, yes, there's a swamp cooler in one of the windows. Jennifer's already playing with the cats, petting one and rubbing another's belly. She seems right at home.

"This house reminds me of my oma's," I say. "Almost exactly. Bet if I look at the living room ceiling, I'll see the heating grate that lets heat rise to the upstairs."

"It's there," Greta says, pointing toward a room that looks like it was once a living room and is now more of an in-house storage unit.

"When I was a kid, we'd sit around the upstairs grate and listen to the adults down below us talk in the evening. We were spying, really," I say. "That's what we liked to call it. But most of the time it was boring. Yet every once in a while, we'd hear something juicy, or my dad and great-grandfather would get going about the world wars."

"Those are the stories I want to hear, Oma." Jennifer rolls a cat over while others tease at her arms, begging to play. "Is this like one of those old-fashioned farmhouses we saw along the road when we drove in?"

"That's what it is," Gretta says. "My brother moved the house into town from our family farm when we sold it ten years ago. He got tired of farming. But that's how we live, money from the farm. He's in California. I couldn't care less about this house, but it was a place to land, so I took it."

The aroma of the ground meat slow cooked in tomato sauce continues to invite my taste buds, unlike much of the food this past week. I lift the buns and chips out of the paper bag and set them on the table. With my good hand I take the plates Gretta hands me, some paper towels as napkins, and utensils for each place setting. The meat sauce has been in the Crock-Pot all day; it's hot and ready to be placed on the buns. Jennifer goes to wash her hands.

Having already washed mine when we arrived, I sit down at the table. Not unlike when I was a young kid waiting for Oma to set out the kuchen or cinnamon rolls. Lucky for me, Gretta brings me the first sloppy joe.

"Never heard of sloppy joes," Jennifer says. "Do you ever make these, Oma?"

"Not since your mom was a young girl and we needed a quick dinner before either your granddad or I ran out to an evening meeting."

"They smell delicious."

"Yes, these are nothing like the ones I made, quick and on the fly. All day in the Crock-Pot? What a difference that makes." I glance toward Gretta. "How lucky we stopped by the store. More ways than one," I say, holding up the bun filled with the tomato and hamburger mix.

"Sorry I can't help you more with the cemetery. Sounds like that fellow you talked to this morning wasn't too friendly and actually insulted your family."

"He did," I say. "I can see now why my gay uncle never stayed and was reluctant to come back."

Gretta gets up to fill the chrome pet bowl with dry food while the cats howl around her end of the table. She probably gives them nibbles while she eats.

"If I hadn't gone away to college, I might have had the same mindset. As it is, I simply watch and listen, write stuff down. Maybe I'll write a book someday," she says.

I'm far hungrier than I imagined. I'm already thinking about a second helping. Meanwhile, Gretta's window swamp cooler works hard to do its job. Once you leave the kitchen, the house is a sweatbox. "This is great, Gretta. A rest stop, you could say, before visiting my cousin tomorrow out on old Farmer's Road. I have her last name written down somewhere," I say. "North of town about five miles, she said."

"Don't think I know anyone out there," she says. "Does she go to church here?"

"I can't say. I haven't met her before. She's expecting us tomorrow. Tonight, we will drive into Dickinson and get a motel so we can get cleaned up and enjoy the air-conditioning before we tackle that cemetery again in the morning."

"Church will be open tomorrow, especially if you get here before noon. There's just a traveling pastor though—woman this time, I think—but the church ladies who know what's going on will be there." She pauses. "You'd be welcome to stay here but forget the air-conditioning. I actually pull a camping cot into the kitchen and sleep under that swamp cooler. A pile of cats on top of me." When she laughs, crow's feet gather around her eyes. She's probably older than I thought. Maybe fifty.

"Wow. Do they all sleep with you?" Jennifer asks.

"As many as can crowd onto the bed," she says. "One insists on laying on my head."

"That would make me itchy," Jennifer says.

"I'm used to it."

After supper I help Gretta clean up while Jennifer plays with the cats. "Hope the mosquitoes aren't as bad in the morning," I say.

"Not as bad," our host says. "Should have encouraged you to get some Cutters while you were in the store. I'll be there tomorrow. Think we still have a small bottle or two left. Darned supply man doesn't like to come to these small towns. Says there's no profit in it."

JENNIFER AND I ARE BACK on the road after supper. There's still plenty of light, enough to get us to Dickinson. We're so far north that the sky doesn't get dark until nearly ten o'clock. I have no idea what's available in terms of Dickinson motels, but this is North Dakota. I can't imagine all the rooms are full.

Satiated by two sloppy joes, Jennifer is content to watch the fields go by. A half hour passes before she says, "Gretta said she'd get run out of town if she did anything like my pink hair."

"She's probably right. If the remaining townsfolk are anything like Oma, they're bighearted until it comes to anything different. Pink hair might be at the top of the list. I noticed that restrictions must have eased if they're selling beer in the grocery. Oma would have never stood for that. Take home the devil's brew? Never. Your great-great-grandpa and my dad had to go to the local tavern if they wanted a drink."

"How did you grow up so . . . *okay* is the word, I guess."

"Your great-grandma and great-grandpa left Myra when I was five, almost six, and moved our family to South Dakota. The Black Hills. When I was about fifteen, we moved to California, the land of pop culture. That made the difference." I laugh. "Pink hair included."

"People sound pretty prejudiced if they're the way Gretta says they are. That man in your old house proved her right."

"Let's just say they have a different sense of tolerance. You have to remember they're what we call old country, mostly German and Russian immigrants. Scandinavians."

"Tolerance never comes up where I live." She turns to the window. "Can't believe all the sunflowers."

"Maybe the government pays farmers to grow them."

"Really?" she asks. "Why would they do that?"

"Too much wheat or corn surplus. I don't know. I'm not a farmer. It's my best guess."

Pulling into Dickinson, I spy a Vacancy sign at the Ramada Inn and another at the Holiday Express. I drive into the Express parking lot. "Let's pray for two good beds and a spa," I say. "We deserve it."

Chapter Nineteen

Sunday, June 16

My phone chimes at eight in the morning. "Come on, sleepy-head. If we're going to beat the heat, we need to get up and rolling toward breakfast."

"Really, Oma?"

"Yes, really."

"What are you doing?"

I shield the papers. "Just a settlement for a client."

"Working on vacation?"

"Sometimes you have to do what you have to do."

While she's in the bathroom, I reread what Stan sent me, my blood simmering over different parts of the document. The minute I see the house under his name, the out-of-control monkey bonanza starts again inside my chest. *Damn Stan. He hasn't listened to a thing I've said. Is this going to be a battle?*

Jennifer emerges fresh as a new baby, her skin only slightly pink from being in the sun yesterday. While toweling her hair, she says, "I still can't believe you brought work along. Don't you ever rest?"

I glance at her and close the folder. He just can't wait, can he? He'll get my answer with a fax before we leave this morning.

"Let's peruse the room service menu," I say. "Pack up and go to the dining room. That way we can get on the road by ten o'clock."

"Great, I'm starved."

I still haven't told Jennifer that Stan and I are divorcing, and that was part of the drama in Duluth. The fact that Stan has been in Reno for the better part of two months isn't something anyone in the family except me knows. Whether today is the right day or not, I need to tell her. I can't wait much longer.

We're back on the road by ten o'clock. Jennifer seems perkier now that we have food in our bellies, and the air-conditioning has restored our spirits. "Wow, I still can't get over all these green fields and the sunflowers," she says.

While I've considered telling her about the impending divorce on the drive, I decide that news can wait for a more appropriate time. When we're more relaxed and the day has ended. It's not exactly the way I want to start the day or have that be the over-riding discussion when we have important things ahead of us.

We arrive in front of Myra's Hubner Market about eleven fifteen, right in the middle of the Sunday service. Again I park near the store since it's central in the town. "Let's go in and see if Gretta's working," I say. "Pick up some Cutters."

Gretta isn't behind the counter. We're told she doesn't come in until later. I pick up the Cutters while Jennifer is once again drawn to the fishing flies. "I don't understand why people get so wound up about these flies," she says. "Or how the fish can be so stupid."

"Look at you," I say. "They've been a magnet since we entered the store yesterday."

"At least they're interesting," she says. Her defensive tone undercuts what I meant as a joke.

At the checkout counter the gentleman running the register is all business, not friendly like Gretta. He says, "She's at church. She'll be in at one o'clock."

I try to remember what I said to Gretta about the town's church women and if I implicated Oma. Once outside the store I gaze up and down the empty street. Again I'm amazed there's not one stop sign let alone a stoplight. But who would need to stop, and for what? We're now more or less stuck with fifteen minutes before the service ends, assuming it ends at noon. At least Gretta will be at the church and can introduce me to the pastor.

"Maybe we should list the names we're looking for," Jennifer suggests.

I pull a pen and a half-filled two-inch-by-three-inch notebook out of my purse, but my bandaged arm gets in the way and makes it difficult to juggle purse, pen, and notebook. "You'll have to write the names," I say.

It's not even noon and the heat's already pressing down, my armpits soaked in my sleeveless blouse and my feet too hot in tennis shoes. This part of the country contrasts with the West Coast in so many ways. There are not only no people on the street but the quiet feels almost ominous with the sense that we're being scrutinized by those who haven't befriended us like Gretta has. In California I'm used to the heat settling around four o'clock and am relieved when the Pacific's evening breeze drifts in around dinnertime. Here the plains heat descends early in the day and stays from midday on. There is no ocean breeze to blow away what feels like trapped air.

"We know Oma will be on the list," I say. "She's buried beside Uncle Ozzie. That's Oscar Gottlieb." No need to mention Uncle Philip; he's in Dickinson's Jewish cemetery. "Great-grandfather Jacob Schroeder will be in the same cemetery with Oma. And his wife, Katerina, will be there too. Oscar Schroeder, my granduncle. Albert Gottlieb, my grandfather. If we're lucky, maybe even Great-granduncle Herman Schroeder and his notorious wife, Tante Ketcha."

"I've never heard of half these people," Jennifer says.

"They're the true immigrants who came from Russia," I say. "Herman and Ketcha came first and built their first house. My Great-grandfather Jacob, Herman's brother, came a decade later with Oma and her two brothers, Oscar and Leo Schroeder. Great-grandfather Jacob was trying to save his sons from military service and the impending revolution in Russia."

"Wouldn't that be cool if we could find them?" she says.

"It would be a miracle."

The heat has already worked against Jennifer's fresh energy. She drops onto the grocery store bench beside me. She's either bored or ready to take a nap. "Look, Oma. There's that man who lives in the house on First Street. In a sport coat yet. What a bigot, saying that about Uncle Ivan, then turning around and going to church."

I let go of my impulse to modify her statement. I don't have the energy or desire at the moment. "Let's go," I say. "This is our chance."

We leave the car where it's parked and head across the street. I'm in a midthigh skort and Jennifer's in cutoff jeans; neither of us are in Sunday service attire. We wait for the First Street house's owner to turn and walk in the direction of his home. He glances at us briefly, maybe recognizing us, maybe not.

A woman in a long black robe stands on the church steps chatting with people. Her short silver hair shines in the morning sun. We wait until the others leave and she's about to turn back inside.

"Pastor?" I say. Jennifer and I hurry up the stairs. "We're from out of town," I explain. "Looking for deceased family in the local cemetery."

"Yes?" she asks. Is that a trace of annoyance, or is she just in a hurry to get to coffee or back on the road toward home?

"I was told there might be church records that would tell us where family members are buried and in which cemetery."

"Yes?" she asks, again impatient. "Come into the office and I'll check."

Now I'm the one who's torn. If the pastor doesn't know the church very well, she may not be able to find the records. In the meantime the ladies downstairs drinking coffee or tea and then cleaning up will likely be anxious to leave and go home to make Sunday supper. We could miss out all the way around.

"I'll have to go downstairs and check with the Ladies Guild," she says. "First, though, I need to change. Give me five minutes."

Five precious minutes. In the meantime Jennifer has wandered off into the church sanctuary, walking around looking at the stained glass windows and lingering by the altar. I don't want to lose her, for Pete's sake. I'm afraid time is running short with that crowd downstairs.

"There, now," the pastor says. "Much better."

She reappears in a pantsuit with a white blouse and open collar. Not the skirt or dress I expected. "Now let's go downstairs and see who or what we can find." She smiles for the first time.

"Jennifer?" I raise my voice as we pass the sanctuary, but Jennifer is nowhere to be found. Where could she have gone? There's no time to waste. I follow the pastor down the stairs and into the basement, aware that this would have been Oma's routine as well. I have every reason to suspect that the descendants of her old nemeses are serving coffee and tea at the same table where it was served years ago, probably with the same teacups.

Once inside the large room, the pastor is immediately swarmed by congregants who want to comment on her sermon or invite her to dinner or ask if they can have an appointment to discuss something that's troubling them. The room is cool compared to the upstairs sanctuary, more protected from the heat by the basement walls.

I'm impressed by how the pastor, while pleasant, accomplishes swift business with those who accost her. She heads toward the woman serving coffee at the head of a long table where congregants sit eating their doughnuts and drinking coffee. I note that the women no longer wear hats or gloves. Those fashion items disappeared decades ago, likely before the end of the last century. But the beauty parlor permanents and bifocals, the heavy paste jewelry around their necks, are reminiscent of the fifties and earlier. The woman at the head of the table—Mirabelle the pastor calls her—lifts her head from her duties pouring tea and coffee. She's who I would expect if I were here to see Oma. She's a hefty figure in a tight-fitting rayon dress with several strands of pearls layering her neck. I smile, remembering how much Oma abhorred jewelry. Mirabelle's short gray-and-white hair twists into tiny curls. She smiles at the pastor. She also observes my skort and Jennifer, who has suddenly appeared behind me in her pink hair and cutoff jeans. She lifts her nose and focuses on the pastor.

"Mirabelle," the pastor says. "This woman and her granddaughter are looking for family buried in First Bible's cemetery. However, they don't know where the graves are. Do you have the key to the church file cabinet so we can help them?"

"When I'm finished, Pastor. My purse is locked in one of the cupboards. As you can see, I'm pouring this morning."

While her tone is snappish, the pastor is undaunted. "Fine, fine. That will work." She bends closer to this Mirabelle person. "However," she says, "I'm due in Dickinson at one-thirty. It's already twelve-thirty. Is it possible someone else can serve in your absence?"

"Oh, no, I couldn't do that," Mirabelle says, shaking her head and momentarily avoiding eye contact.

Something in the pastor's demeanor shifts the conversation. Even without her robes, she's still the pastor. Her eyes never leave Mirabelle's.

"Maybe Gertrude Shakely can take over for a minute or two," Mirabelle says. Her tone betrays her reluctance. She folds her hands on the table, marking her place in the same way a cat sprays their territory.

"Lovely," the pastor says. "I'll meet you upstairs in the study. You might want to be available to these nice ladies if they have questions after I leave."

"Yes, Pastor," Mirabelle says. She lifts her chin and avoids eye contact with me and Jennifer. I doubt that once the pastor leaves, Miss Mirabelle will be as cooperative as the pastor suggests. Nonetheless, the pastor has accomplished what I might never have been able to do myself.

Gretta, our previous evening's host, appears behind Mirabelle. "You made it," she says.

I smile while remaining focused on the turtle-slow rise of Mirabelle from the table. The pastor has already turned in the direction of the stairs. I don't want to miss her lead to the study. "Do you want to come with us, Gretta?"

"Sure, I have a few minutes before I have to go to work." She stands in front of the elderly woman. "This is great, Mirabelle. Appreciate you taking us to the church records."

"I can if you'll get out of my way," Mirabelle says.

"Sure. I'm just along for the ride anyhow. Let's go."

"Not so fast. I have to get my purse and Gertrude to replace me. Stand here, Gretta, in case someone wants coffee or tea."

"Sure thing." Gretta winks at me and Jennifer. Once Mirabelle is out of earshot, Gretta says, "You have to kiss a lot of frogs, if you know what I mean."

"I like that. Kiss frogs," Jennifer says. "You're funny, Gretta."

"Not everyone sees it that way," she says. "Maybe you would like the privilege of pouring coffee or tea, Jennifer."

"No, not now," I say. "We don't want to rile the snakes."

Jennifer shakes her head. "Frogs and snakes. This is getting better all the time."

"What's this about snakes?" Mirabelle asks, coming from behind.

"Just a saying. We'll follow you," I say. "This is most kind of you. We had no luck yesterday."

"I'm not surprised," she says. She pulls a tatted handkerchief from inside her sleeve and wipes at her forehead. "Need to get this over fast," she says. "It's too hot upstairs."

Her tatted handkerchief and rayon dress remind me of Oma's style. Mirabelle's attitude takes me back to Oma's stories about the mean and gossipy women in her church, particularly one who had a precise recollection of events in Oma's house. She may have been keeping track for later reprisal. Ammunition, so to speak.

Mirabelle pulls on the handrail and takes one step at a time with her head bent toward her feet and the print rayon dress clinging to her blocky girth. We come behind, slowly, at a turtle's pace. Jennifer gestures that she wants to go around the elderly woman, but I shake my head no. Wiggle my fingers like snakes. Gretta disappears through another door and then appears waiting at the top of the stairs. She grins down at the rest of us.

Once we make our way to the study, Gretta excuses herself. "Did you get the Cutters?" she asks.

I respond with a thumbs-up. Jennifer says, "See you at the store later."

Mirabelle sits in the pastor's chair, out of breath. Sweat runs down her cheeks. I have no idea how old she is, but I'd bet money that she doesn't walk if she doesn't have to. She heaves what looks like a heavy purse onto her lap and begins to open zippers. "It's in here somewhere," she mutters. Jennifer and I stand at the edge of the desk. When she finally lifts a small, folded paper, she asks, "What was the family name?"

"The main name is Gottlieb," I say. "Albert Gottlieb. Also, if they're here, Katerina and Jacob Schroeder. They would have died in the early 1920s."

"I know Gottlieb," she says. "Marta Gottlieb anyhow. She had two sons. One died; I can't remember his name. The other . . . can't remember his name either. Two daughters who never graced the inside of the church."

"That sounds like them," I say. I try to keep my voice as casual as possible.

"Marta was acquainted with my mother. Could have been cousins for all I know."

"Was your mother's name Agnes?"

"How'd you know?"

She'll never hear from me the horror stories Oma told about the way Agnes denigrated the Gottlieb family. "I think they served tea together in the church like you did just now."

"I remember her now. She sold her pastries. They were a poor lot, that family."

She bends toward the two-drawer file cabinet with a small key. "Doggone," she says. "Can't see with these trifocals."

"Can I help?" Jennifer asks.

"I guess you're going to have to," Mirabelle says.

Jennifer walks around the desk until she's beside Mirabelle. She bends down toward the drawer and inserts the small key into the cabinet's lock.

"Does your mother allow you to have pink hair?" Mirabelle asks.

Jennifer glances up at me and smiles. "She's my oma, not my mother."

"What about your mother?"

"She lives in California. She hasn't . . ."

"Jennifer," I say. "Just focus on the lock. We can chat later."

"Yes, Oma."

Jennifer turns the lock and pulls the top drawer open.

Though it's dark in the study, Jennifer lifts out a big, official-looking book. She puts it on the desk in front of Mirabelle. "Is this it?"

"Suppose it is," Mirabelle says. She nods to me. "Would you turn on the overhead lights? Can't see a thing in here."

I find the wall switch and the overhead lights flood the once-dark room. Jennifer turns on a desk lamp that makes an even greater difference. "We don't want to leave them on too long," Mirabelle says. "They give off too much heat."

Sitting at the desk, Mirabelle opens the book to the center, perhaps knowing exactly where the information is kept. "Okay," she says. "Here's Albert Gottlieb. Do you have a pen to write down the plot?"

I quickly scramble with my fanny pack and pull out a pen and the small pad I loaned Jennifer earlier. "What's the number?"

"Row E, space twenty-nine," she says. "Now, understand that the spaces aren't numbered. Only the rows are marked. So you'll have to do some searching around."

"Can you repeat that?" I say. "My pen doesn't work quite right."

"Oh, for Pete's sake. I haven't got all day." She sighs and leans forward. "Row E, space twenty-nine. Do you have that?"

"Tell me if Oscar Gottlieb is in the grave beside him."

"Yes, same row, number twenty-eight. But there are two Oscars. One Oscar Schroeder in space 31 and an Oscar Gottlieb in number thirty-one."

"Marta Gottlieb?"

"Number thirty. Between the two Oscars."

"What about Jacob Schroeder and Katerina Schroeder? Those dates would be early twentieth century. I'm guessing around 1916 to 1920. Before Ketcha and Herman Schroeder."

"Slow down. That's too many names at once." Mirabelle gathers the massive pages and goes to the front of the record book. "The church was built in 1920. If they died before the church was built but the cemetery was designated, they'll be in the front of the registry."

Her finger traces the last name, but she seems to have trouble reading the names. Jennifer, who is leaning over her, blocks the light. "Jennifer, why don't you stand on the other side so Mirabelle can see better?" I wink at Jennifer, and she quickly moves.

"Would you like some help, Mirabelle?" I ask.

"Yes, most appreciated."

I remove a small flashlight that sits on my key ring. Walking around the desk, I stand where Jennifer just was. Flashing the light on the page, we can all see better.

"That's quite a gizmo," Mirabelle says. "Where'd you ever get such a small flashlight?"

"The auto store," I say.

"Must be a pretty fancy store."

"It seems to be a requirement in a larger town."

"That's what I hear," she says. "But I get tired of everyone saying that."

I stop scanning the page and look at her. She glances up at me.

"I bet you do," I say. "Especially if everybody says that."

For the first time a hint of a smile opens her lips. "You have to understand about small towns."

"I grew up here my first five years. During the war," I say.

"That would make us close to the same age," she says. She studies my face and my partly bare legs for a moment. "Is this what California does?" she asks. "Keeps you young?"

As soon as she says it, she seems sorry. Her head points at the book, and her finger runs up and down the columns. "Here," she says. "One of the early graves. Row B, grave number five. That's Jacob." She hesitates. "Looks like Katerina is in grave seven. There's someone named Leo in between."

That means they retrieved Granduncle Leo's body from the train wreck and brought it home. The accident was so bad, most of the bodies were burned. Not Uncle Leo's. One more piece of the puzzle.

"Do you see Herman and Ketcha Schroeder?"

"No. Probably a different cemetery. Maybe a different church."

I give her an extra moment to look again, but it's a lost cause. Sweat is pouring down her forehead and into her eyes. By now the tatted hanky is soaked.

"I think we have everything we need," I say. "I can't thank you enough."

"Most welcome," she says. She slams the big book closed, and dust motes dance in the overhead light.

"Would you like Jennifer to put it away?" I ask. "Might be easier."

"Thank you," she says. She studies her hand against the well-stained ink blotter curling at the edges. "Not easy dying or getting buried in this town," she says. "I've been here all my life. My day will come just like all the others."

I continue to stand beside the desk, and her, for a few moments while Jennifer replaces the book. It's not the fear or inevitability of dying that I hear in her words so much as a resigned loneliness. Loneliness that comes from living too long in too small a place. Watching all your family and friends die. While comfortable, the familiarity negates a wider life. I feel sad that her years have delivered this one bitter pill. At the same time I'm glad hers isn't my life. That I was spared what appears to be a narrow existence.

Chapter Twenty

JENNIFER AND I ENTER THE church restroom to apply the Cutters. The smell of baby powder permeates the small, two-stalled room. The baby powder along with the soap in a wall dispenser mixes with the Cutters and gives off an odor close to ammonia. I start coughing in the enclosed space, prompting me to hurry with the application.

We leave the church, and the heat is already a blast furnace. We begin our now-usual trek to the cemetery with the small notebook in my pocket.

"What's the story about Uncle Leo? I've never heard about him." Jennifer says.

"He died so young that it's easy to forget him. Leo was Oma's younger brother. Seems he never took to America. A quiet sort; he hated farming. Oma said he tended to be moody and not quite of this world. He longed to be where he could play the piano forte and daydream like he did in the early years in Russia. He somehow thought he would find his ideal life if he returned to the Russia he left when he was twelve. While traveling alone across America, he wrote to Oma that he was very ill. He even mentioned the Spanish flu and said there were passengers aboard the train who were put off at various stations because they were so ill. As luck would have it, his train hit a farmer's cart and left the tracks just west of New York City. The train caught on fire and most of the passengers and their baggage were burned. Oma's brother Oscar had to go and claim the body. When Oscar brought Leo's body home they buried him in the family plot, which is where he is now. This all happened long before my time or your great-grandmother Irene's."

"Why haven't I heard about the great-greats?"

"Except for granduncle Oscar and my grandfather Gottlieb, they had died by the time my mother, your great-grandmother Irene, was a young girl."

"They're all buried here?" Jennifer asks.

"Hopefully," I say.

"Sounds confusing. Oscar, Ozzie. Were others named after each other like that?"

"No, not that I know of except myself. Ozzie, Oma's son, was named after her brother Oscar. Ozzie was a way to distinguish the two of them. And the rest . . . the great-greats—that's what we'll call them—Oma, Granduncle Oscar, and Leo were the offspring of Great-grandfather Jacob Schroeder and Great-grandmother Katerina, who was half-Russian, half-German by birth."

"You told me the German greats were already outsiders when they settled in Russia," Jennifer says.

"From what little I know, they were evangelicals and perhaps persecuted for their religion in Germany. I don't know that for sure. Story goes that Great-grandfather Jacob's family went to Russia at Czarina Catherine's invitation. She couldn't get the Russians to farm what's called the Pale, today's Ukraine. Because Catherine was German-born, she knew that the Germans were good farmers. She promised them land as well as freedom of religion. She told them they wouldn't have to worry about their sons being conscripted into the military if they would just come and farm western Russia."

"Michael has told me a little about the draft. I didn't know that it happened so long ago." She sighs. "That's the kind of stuff Michael gets off on."

I can't say a word. Just hearing his name sets me fuming and, at the same time, fearful that all my buried resentment will erupt. We've managed the entire road trip without once tarnishing our time together with mention of Michael. I'd love nothing more than to scorch these green fields with the hide of that man.

"This story goes back a long ways," Jennifer says.

"Historically, it does," I say. "We're talking about the generation or two that first emigrated from Germany to Russia before my great-grandfather Jacob was born. Over time, Great-grandfather Jacob became a wealthy German landowner. Somehow he met Katerina's father, a prosperous Russian wine merchant. Since Katerina was his only child, her father may have felt she was better off with a German husband during a time when revolution was fermenting. As a consequence, the marriage was arranged by Jacob and Katerina's father."

"I wouldn't like that arranged marriage business."

"Those were different times. Marriages were often arranged for financial advantage," I say. "The turning point came when Oma and her brothers were in their teens. The family's Russian servants and the peasants who farmed and lived on their land rebelled against them. With the Cossacks' encouragement, the peasants burned Great-grandfather Jacob's barns and outbuildings and ran off the animals and livestock. That loss of loyalty and confidence in his workers proved to be the catalyst for his idea to follow his older brother, Granduncle Herman, to America."

The sun is mid-heaven by the time we get back to the cemetery where the heat hangs like a closed curtain around us and the small town. Though we're not in the same spot where we looked yesterday, there's relief that the mosquitoes aren't yet a nuisance this early in the afternoon, especially with the Cutters covering all exposed parts of our bodies. The notebook, a key to the designated graves, means that if we have to do the hands-and-knees business, we won't be searching blind.

"Should we dig together or separately?" Jennifer asks.

"How about side by side with my oma's husband—your great-grandpa Albert—and her son, Uncle Ozzie."

Dropping to our knees, we begin to clear the grass off the respective graves. My arm is sore after yesterday, and the bandage has become dirty from digging. The plates remain buried beneath vegetation and the infrequent mowing that has missed the grass lip altogether. Gardening gloves would make this easier. And trowels. Anything to dig away at the overgrowth, especially since I can only use one hand. At least I had the good sense to pick up sandwiches and a Styrofoam cooler with ice and drinks before we left Dickinson. Gracious as Gretta was last night, I can't do the cats again.

Since both men we're looking for were buried at approximately the same time, working together makes sense, though Jennifer is faster and stronger than I am. Also, she has two good hands. My bandage and the resulting ache slow me down. It takes a full half-hour with a water break before she clears the marked plate. Oscar Jacob Gottlieb. The brass plate's lettering, though completely tarnished, appears to be as intact as the day it was created.

We stop and lean back on our haunches. "Wow," Jennifer says, breaking the silence. "After yesterday I would have never believed we'd get even one grave marker unearthed."

"A lot more work than when I was here some thirty years ago. Oma probably paid someone to tend the graves for her."

"So who was Oscar Gottlieb?" Jennifer asks. "I'm still confused."

Her question takes me back to the edge of Oma's kitchen where, opposite her large counter by the mudroom door, on a shelf above a small sink, rested Uncle Ozzie's razor, eyecups, and hairbrush. We were forbidden to touch his things even before he was killed in the South Pacific during World War II. One day all his precious things disappeared. I never saw them again.

"You could say Ozzie was Oma's favorite son," I say. I snap a photo of the brass plate. "I didn't know him well. He had gone to war when I was young, but I remember the funeral. Sitting next to Oma. She never seemed the same after he died."

Jennifer nods. "How are you doing with your headstone?" she asks.

"Almost there," I say. "Maybe you can help me. My bad arm's aching."

Jennifer scoots closer to where I'm kneeling on the ground. She quickly clears away the grass overhang and accumulated vegetation. "Albert Heinrich Gottlieb," I say aloud. "The last time I saw him alive he was sitting at Oma's kitchen table over a bowl of soup with his mouth partly bandaged and his hair uncombed. The day after that he was in his upstairs bed, and no one ever saw him below the stairs again. Not even in his casket. Oma insisted it remain closed." I'm thoughtful for a moment. "The Great Depression, and then World War II, brought hard times for our family."

"You said your grandfather was an unhappy man."

"If happy means you smile once in a while, he was never happy."

"How awful," Jennifer says. "I can't accuse Grandpa of that."

"Right," I say. I lower my head toward the grave and continue digging with my free hand.

"By the way, has he tried to call? You haven't said," Jennifer asks.

I'd hoped to get through my cousin's visit and back on the road before having the conversation I both anticipated and dreaded. *When the trip is nearly over*, I kept telling myself, *I'll tell her*. It's not fair, but I dread the possible drama that might come with the news.

"I told him cell service was terrible here, which it is. He knows where we are." I reach into my fanny pack for my phone. Truth be told, I'm afraid Jennifer will blame me for the divorce. Why she might do that, I don't know. But it's the fear that has held me back. I can't bear the idea of Jennifer seeing me as the reason her grandfather and I are no longer together, no matter how irrational that justification for my silence might be.

"Let's look for the older graves of the original immigrants," I say. "Oma told me they dug them up from the farm and reburied them here."

"Oma," Jennifer hesitates. "Unless I ask, you haven't talked about Grandpa once since we left Duluth. Or in Duluth for that matter."

I sit back on my knees and wipe my forehead. "Let's take a break, Jennifer. Go sit under that tree and drink our water."

Once settled, I struggle to find my voice, the words. "The truth is that your grandfather and I have separated."

"What?" Her eyes fill with immediate tears. "But why? Whose idea? Were you unhappy? Both of you? Can't you fix it? You've been together forever. Does Mom know?"

"Slow down." We scooch together and lean against an oak tree.

"Why?" Jennifer asks again.

"Your grandfather retired a few years ago. You know that."

"Yes, but that doesn't explain anything. I don't understand what the problem is."

"I think he wanted me home," I say. "To be with him."

"But why? I thought he was proud of you and your work."

"He was. He is. Truth be told, I started quite a bit later, you know, just before your mother and Aunt Tara were going into junior high. When he retired, I was just hitting my prime."

"I think that's great. But what about Grandpa?"

"He got too lonely, I guess. He wanted someone there with him all the time, but he didn't know how to tell me. Please understand, Jennifer, I'm guessing all of this because he never talked to me about it." I hesitate for a few seconds. "Until he found someone else."

"Another woman?"

"Yes." I swat at a mosquito that lands on my arm. When I turn my head toward her, she's gazing at distant trees.

"Is that what you thought about me and Dr. Connolly? Why you thought we were wrong?"

"I didn't know what to think, Jennifer. I was stuck on the age difference, yes. And because he was your professor."

"Because he's so much older."

"Yes. And in a powerful position." I'm quiet for a few seconds. "Kind of what your grandfather has done."

"Someone my age?" Her face, a picture of exasperation, is almost comical.

"No, not your age, but significantly younger than me . . . by twenty-five or thirty years."

"Damn," she says. "That's why you don't talk about him."

I try to smile but realize I'm faking it. The frantic beating in my chest suddenly connects to my eyes and tongue. I'm hesitant, almost shy, when I say, "Yes, I haven't wanted to talk about him. Have in fact avoided the subject when you asked."

"And here I thought adults never made mistakes. That they had all the answers."

I reach across our cooler, take Jennifer's hand, and squeeze it. Her smooth skin and tender bones are precious in a way she can't know. "Adults make mistakes, kitten. And life changes people." I hesitate for a minute. "And I'm not completely innocent here either." I gaze at her until I catch her eye. "Because your grandfather became so needy for company, I began to avoid him. It was easy to stay busy with my work and the life I'd created around my work." A deep breath becomes a sigh. "In the end he found someone who adored him and his stories."

She doesn't seem to know what to say. Finally she says, "Thanks for being so honest, Oma." She smiles and her perfectly straight teeth peek through half-closed lips. "Though I'll still always think of you as near perfect."

"I'm anything but perfect, Jennifer. But at least you know the truth now. From my perspective anyhow."

Jennifer remains thoughtful and quiet for a few moments. She turns toward me and lays her hand on my arm. "I can see now why you reacted so strongly to Michael." She gazes down at her lap. "I wonder what I thought I was doing with him," she says. "You helped me see my affair—because that's what it was—with him differently than I did before." She raises her head and meets my eyes. "What was I thinking?"

I laugh. "You're young and beautiful," I say. "And a professor's attention is intoxicating. I can only imagine." I lay my hand over hers.

There's that moment of silence when the puzzle pieces begin to fit into place and the entire picture becomes clear for the first time. I see it in her eyes, in the way some visible tension releases in her face. That bittersweet moment when relief and a new awareness of life's mysteries and foibles lands on us. Always that question: *Why didn't I see this before?*

"I don't know what I was thinking, Oma," she says. Quietly, thoughtfully. "Guess I was just flattered by the attention." She's thoughtful again. "Maybe I was lonely." Tears crowd her eyes. "I didn't fit in. People accused me of being 'Californicated.' And I never received an invitation to a sorority during rush. So when Michael gave me so much attention, I lapped it up. Like I had one up on those other girls. Yes, I suspected that he was married, but you could say I didn't want to know. Then I got pregnant. Even the abortion didn't wake me up. At least he paid for it."

She gazes toward the car parked at the edge of the cemetery. "I'm afraid that if you hadn't come to Duluth, I'd have gone on deluding myself." She looks at me for the first time with tears glazing her eyes. "You knew all of that, didn't you?"

I nod. "Yes, I knew. But I figured you had to discover the truth for yourself if it was going to stick." I pull her close with my good arm. "Thank you," I say. "Now I think you understand." We sit like that for a few minutes, her head resting on my shoulder.

"I'm so ashamed, Oma."

"I know that feeling." We're close, our arms awkward around each other, for another few minutes. "At least the separation from your grandfather isn't a secret anymore." I sigh and begin to lean forward. "And you've realized the crucial lesson about being flattered by men like Michael."

She reaches over and kisses my cheek. Her broad smile assures me that she understands the whole mosaic of our lives now in a way she didn't an hour ago.

I lean on my knees and push forward toward standing. Jennifer, already on her feet, reaches down and grabs my good hand. "Come on, Oma, we've still got work to do."

Slowly I head toward the row where we were told we'd find the other graves. But there's a lightness in my gut that wasn't there before. I no longer fear that I've said too much or that I've somehow tarnished Stan's name. Whatever burden I was carrying is buried now, and the air is clear and clean in a way it wasn't before. Hopefully for both of us.

I scope out the other grave markers. It's easier now for some reason. We have a job to do.

"Where did you go?" I holler over my shoulder.

"I'm coming," she shouts behind me after returning the cooler to the car. Her voice echoes throughout the small cemetery.

Looking over my shoulder, the town has the same emptiness we experienced yesterday driving into town now that the church hour has ended and the streets have cleared, the same sense of vacancy. There's still the one-car bridge, the yellow house, the sign above Hubner's Market, the street devoid of vehicles. As though the town has slept since I was five, or even thirty years ago when I last came here. I take the notebook from my pocket and go to Row B. About five graves in, the other two graves with their flat and sunken stones lay at crooked angles as though the earth beneath and around them has both sunk and shifted over time. That must be Granduncle Leo in the middle between my grandparents' headstones.

I bend in front of what I think is Leo's grave. I feel Jennifer beside me, her arm stretching around my shoulders, her hug tight. "I'm so sorry," she says. "For you, for Grandpa."

I'm afraid to look at her for fear the emotion I've held on to so tightly will leak through. "Thank you," is all I say, my fingers already clearing the vegetation off the flat headstone. My chest feels full and there's that familiar rush just before emotion finds its way to the surface. I focus on the headstone, buried so deep in the ground that I have to bend closer to read it.

I glance over at Jennifer and see the shine of tears. "What's this?"

"Divorce changes everything."

I take her hand, still innocent and barely touched by the life waiting for her, and I lift her fingers to kiss the soft skin. "It *will* change everything. No doubt about it." This is no longer just my grief; it's the ripple effect. "Your grandfather is about the best man your mother and Aunt Tara ever knew until your own dad."

Jennifer wipes away a tear. She gives me a sheepish nod. "As long as you're okay, Oma. You can always live with me."

My throat swells. "That's sweet, Jennifer. But I hope we're a long way from that."

"Just so you know."

Without another word, Jennifer bends toward the grave in front of her. It doesn't matter whether it's her Great-grandmother Marta or her Great-uncle Leo. She now knows that even supposedly mature adults change direction or lose their way when they least expect it to happen.

Chapter Twenty-One

As I dig around the graves I'm again astonished by the parallel between Stan and his soon-to-be-wife and Jennifer's recent liaison with Michael Connolly. Though younger than Stan and older than Gilbert, Michael has no business cavorting with college students even when they throw themselves at him. He most likely has a wife and children. Impregnating someone as young and innocent as Jennifer is unforgivable. Worse, he blamed her for getting pregnant.

"Do you think we should go back to see Gretta and buy some trowels? At least gardening gloves? Look at our hands," I say.

"Let's take a break," Jennifer says. She removes two more cold bottles of water from our cooler, and we sit back under the tree. Using the handy wipes I keep in my purse, we clean our hands as well as we can. Within minutes we're eating sandwiches. "Figure we have another hour before the mosquitoes run us out of here," I say. "Too bad the motel is so far away. Would have been worth paying for another day just to shower before we show up at Cousin Donna's."

"She probably won't mind if she knows what we've been up to," Jennifer says. She crumples the paper wrapper from the sandwich. "These folks we're looking for were the immigrants, right?"

"The ones I know about." I pull myself up off the ground. "We'll save more stories for the ride to Donna's. What do you think about the gloves and trowels?"

"It's going on three o'clock. We don't have much time left, Oma. The mosquitoes are already buzzing, just not biting thanks to the Cutters. Besides, it's getting super hot."

"Let's give it another half-hour or forty-five minutes. Looks like we're coming back tomorrow."

An hour later we're back in the store; there's no one else there. Gretta sits behind the counter reading a magazine. "How'd you do?"

"Can't you tell? We're pooped," I say. "Do you have any gardening gloves or trowels?"

"Probably not," she says. "Around here, the ladies' hands are so calloused from everyday work and digging in the garden that they'd scoff at needing to protect them."

"I'll ask my cousin for work gloves," I say. "By the way, do you know Donna Grebes? She lives just out of town?"

"Sure. Angus and I went to high school together. Is that where you're going?"

"She's my third cousin. Seems to be the only one left. I've never met her."

"You'll like her. She's a card and a darned good cook too."

"Good. We'll be hungry when we get there."

"How long are you staying?"

"Maybe a night or two. We want to come back and finish what we started."

"Stop in at my place when you come back. I'll see what I've got in terms of work gloves and weed diggers. Don't bother to take hers."

"You've been a big help, Gretta."

"Who knows, I might show up on your doorstep one day, and you can give me a tour of San Diego."

Jennifer comes from behind me with a couple of fishing flies. "They're so pretty I can't leave them alone. How much?"

"They're ten bucks apiece," Gretta says. "Kinda steep."

"No problem," Jennifer says. She pulls the Velcro on her canvas wallet and hands Gretta a twenty-dollar bill. "This should cover it."

Gretta keeps her hand extended. "Sales tax is 6.5 percent. I'll need another dollar and give you the change."

"Wow," Jennifer says. "This place is as bad as California."

Gretta and I smile at each other. "Not quite as bad."

We drive down another gravel road, the car kicking up dust in the rearview mirror and the sound of gravel spitting against the tires and underbody of the car. As far as we can see, there's no one else on the road. The air conditioner is working overtime while a combination of heat and dust leak in through the ventilation system until I close the vents. I'm thirsty, but we've run out of water. I neglected to ask Gretta if we could buy more there. It's likely not available if the meager stock on the shelves is any evidence.

Tractors with air-conditioned cabs traverse the fields. The farmers are likely listening to their radios. Jennifer's driving and I have to remind her to slow down because the gravel's not always trustworthy. This isn't a freeway where the pavement can be forgiving. Jennifer hums to herself, and I close my eyes. Having talked to my cousin a couple of times on the phone, I know the yakking will start soon enough and only end when I close the door to wherever we're sleeping tonight.

It strikes me as strange to be in touch with Donna, Uncle Herman's great-great-granddaughter by his youngest and my third cousin once removed. She must be my age. How I found her address is a miracle. It was in an address book I unearthed when sorting Uncle Ivan's things before he went into the group home. I doubted that she'd still be on the family farm, or that anyone would be there. She said on the phone that she was there and she'd like to sell off their land and move to the city with a pile of cash. When I wrote to Donna, she wrote back, "You have to come. Just my son Angus and I live here now." During a second phone call when I told her that I was bringing my granddaughter, she said, "Good. Maybe you'll share her with me. I'll never have grandkids."

What a shame I've never been to the farmhouse my great-granduncle Herman first built over a century ago. Once, when I was a girl about four years old, Uncle Ozzie took us for a ride in his new Buick. He wanted Mom to see the old place. I remember Mom told us to keep our shoes off the car's back seat, which was nearly impossible. Our legs were too short; that was especially true of my two younger sisters.

Sunflowers bloom everywhere. Alfalfa blossoms lift their sweet scent into the air and through the air conditioner. "We're five miles out of town," I say to Jennifer. "Donna says we can't miss the red silo. And to save our appetite. We're going to have a real old-fashioned Sunday dinner."

Between the sound of Sunday dinner and the gravel dust trailing the car, there's that strange sensation again that we're stepping back in time. I've had it ever since we left Duluth and entered farm country. Nothing has really changed over the years. The towns remain small, the farms seem forever vast, and the fields stretch toward the horizon. What I hadn't expected were the sunflowers that keep amazing both Jennifer and me. Fields and fields of blooms, their petals faced toward the sun. They're taller than I would have expected.

When we pull into Donna's yard, I'm not surprised when the stout woman who could be Oma comes out through the back screen door. Unlike my grandmother, Donna wears tennis shoes beneath her print dress. Beside her appears Cousin Angus, a heavy-set man of indefinable age in overalls and a straw hat I later learn hides his bald spot. Two spaniels run ahead of them. Maybe if we're lucky there are no cats here.

I smile toward my distant and unknown cousin. This whole scene resembles a tableau that Norman Rockwell might have painted. A time reversal. The screen door slams behind them and the dogs run to greet us. This bulky woman in her rayon dress and her son in his farmer's straw hat remind me that some things never change with time. Decades evaporate even as we stand there.

"My land, you made it," Donna says. When she wraps her heavy arms around me, I tear up. An immediate recollection from my childhood with that feeling of being cushioned against a soft, massive body like Oma's. To be held like I once was adored by Oma. But her welcoming hug scrunches my wounded arm, which now hurts like hell. I wince and pull away.

When she steps back, she holds me at arm's length and eyes me up and down. "What the heck did you do to your arm?"

"Accident," I say. "No big deal."

"Here," she says to me and Jennifer. "Meet your cousin, Angus."

He nods but doesn't remove his hat. "Howdy," he says. I note his momentary reticence when he lumbers toward Jennifer. "Are we cousins too?" he asks.

On her face, Jennifer's surprise betrays her reluctance at this sudden change in her sense of family. This farm isn't like the university campus or the family she grew up with or anyone she knew in California. This entire trip has been new territory for her, and it's now written on her face. "Guess we are," she finally says, even as she backs away from the anticipated hug.

"You better come in the house so we can get some food in you. How the heck do you stay so skinny?" Donna asks. "Must not eat enough." She laughs the deep laugh I'd expect from a man. "We'll change that."

She stops in the gravel driveway and turns toward Jennifer. "Who's this young lady with pink hair?" she asks. "Better not go into Myra. They might tie you up."

"This is my granddaughter, Jennifer. Kelsey's youngest."

"Great-granddaughter of Irene?" she asks. "Looks something like her. She leans closer to Jennifer. "It's in the eyes." She puts her hands on her hips. "Good old Irene. Running off with that handsome railroad bum. Guess she did alright in the end though."

"Great-grandad was a railroad bum?" Jennifer asks. "How come you never told me, Oma?"

"That was a long time ago," I say. "Things changed."

"For some folks," Donna says. "Just not for us."

"I can see that," I say.

"You must be starved," she says. "What the heck were you doing all that time in Myra?"

Now it's my turn to laugh. "Looking for the graves."

"Whatever for?" she asks. "Dead is dead. I say leave them alone."

I wasn't going to respond to that until she asks, "Who'd you find?"

"The greats and the great-greats," I say. "I was educating Jennifer about family history."

"Some stories shouldn't be repeated."

She opens the screen door to a wide porch. Two old sofas sit at an angle to each other. There are TV trays covered with plastic placemats and what look like half-empty coffee cups sitting on the mats. Magazines and newspapers lay strewn on the couches.

"You farm here alone, Cousin Angus?" Jennifer asks.

"Some," he says. "Though mostly not. We rent the land to a fellow down the road."

"Any animals?" Jennifer asks.

"Not really. A milk cow, some chickens. Mom sold the goats—too much work. It's just us, happy to take it easy," he says.

Cousin Angus is the same size as his mother, the red suspenders curving over his belly. Once we enter the house, his hat comes off. "Mom says you guys were in Duluth?" he says. "What's it like there?"

"Cold," I say. "Too cold, even in the heart of summer."

"I hear they have big lakes," Cousin Angus says. "Really big lakes. Never gone there to check 'em out."

As I recall, Angus is Donna's only child. *Developmentally delayed,* she said in a handwritten note to me. He's always lived at home with her. The father died in a farm accident when Angus was ten. Donna refused to leave the land, and she never married again. She hired men to work the farm for a long time. Over the phone she said she did as well by renting the land and letting someone else do the hard work.

We follow Donna into the kitchen. "Wow, look at this spread," Jennifer says. "Good thing we're hungry, Oma."

"Not often we have company, especially kinfolk," Donna says. "Here, let me take your things into the bedroom. Hope you're okay with sleeping together. We only have one bed apiece."

"We can always drive to Dickenson," I say.

"Wouldn't hear of it," she says. "Long as you can live without fancy air conditioners."

I'm now sorry I said a night or two. If this is anything like Gretta's place, we're in for a sleepless night, especially together. We were lucky to escape Gretta's for Dickinson's Holiday Express. No chance of that here.

"We'll do great," Jennifer says, better with her manners than I am. "We're just here for one night anyhow."

Thank you, Jennifer. You're learning how to be an ally.

"If you want to wash up, the bathroom is near the back of the house," Donna says. "You probably don't remember what a big deal that was when Great-great-grandpa Herman added that bathroom. Unfortunately, Mom said he couldn't be talked into adding another. We've learned to live with it."

At least it's not an outhouse. That means toilet paper and not the Sears catalog I learned to live with at Oma's house. For Jennifer, an outhouse might sound novel until she has to pee in the middle of the night.

The kitchen table, big enough to feed twelve, is loaded with cut ham, cold green beans, corn on the cob, and a turkey breast sliced and ready to eat. Mashed potatoes center the spread with huge lumps of butter on top. A heavily dressed tossed green salad sits beside orange Jell-O with what looks like fruit cocktail folded in. An apple pie and a chocolate cake, both uncut, wait on one end of the table. All the food looks cold. I have no idea how long it's been sitting out on the table. Donna has set four places with paper napkins beneath the tableware. If we were camels, we could load up for a week with this meal.

I wash my hands at the kitchen sink and Jennifer follows suit. When I reach for a hand towel, I'm stunned to see what looks like a yesteryear flour sack, hemmed and faded on a rack beside the sink.

Donna directs us to two chairs opposite Angus; she takes the chair at the head of the table. "Dig in," she says. Jennifer and I both sit like the polite guests we were raised to be. But Donna and Angus don't pass the food around. Instead, they stand in front of their chairs and reach across the table toward the open bowls. Large portions plop down onto their dinner plates. Jennifer and I hesitate, waiting until the two of them sit down.

After I've taken a slice of turkey and another of ham, a scoop of green beans and a small portion of Jello salad for old times' sake, Donna points at my food. "That's not enough to keep a bird alive. Have some potatoes. Sorry I don't have rolls. It's too hot to heat up the oven and bake them."

"I think I'll be fine." I smile to reassure her. "Saving myself for the pie."

"You can have it all," she says. Her arms spread wide to include the entire banquet spread before us.

Jennifer loads her plate, including a big mound of mashed potatoes. We've been working hard at the cemetery and eating pretty sporadically, not always the best food either. She's young. She can afford mashed potatoes and the heavily dressed salad. Even a piece of both pie and cake wouldn't make an appearance on her still-young body.

"Tell me what you discovered at the cemetery, Jenny," Donna says.

"It's Jennifer," Jennifer says. She smiles when she says it, but I can see the sting of her correction when Donna jerks ever so slightly.

"Okay, Jennifer," Donna says too loudly. "So you found the grands."

"We did," Jennifer says. "The graves have been mowed over so long that we couldn't finish clearing them in order to read the headstones."

"I don't think I've ever been to the cemetery," Angus says. "We just go to the store to buy fishing bait."

"You don't have worms here?" Jennifer asks.

"Don't use worms, and I get tired of tying flies. I like to pick up a couple of handmade flies when we go to the store," he says. His grin gives away his crooked front teeth and an overbite.

"I'll have to show you mine when we're finished with dinner," Jennifer says. "I've never fly-fished, but I sure love the flies I saw in the store."

"They've got great flies," Angus says. "I treat myself sometimes."

He glances at his mother, who ignores him.

Angus must be Kelsey's age, mid-forties to fifty. Because he's delayed, I doubt he's ever had a girlfriend, much less spent time off the farm. He takes me back to a time when farmers like Great-granduncle Herman had all those kids in order to work the farm.

An era when folks abided by faithfulness to farm, family, and God. All decisions were based on what was best for the crops, the farm, and the overall good of the family. When young people fell in love and married, they were expected to adhere to the same rules. Oma told me that's the way it was on Great-granduncle Herman's farm. His sons-in-law were expected to work his farm and their parents' farms, too, especially if they were first in line to inherit. The way I've lived my life and Jennifer is living hers—taking off with her grandmother on what could be seen as a harebrained adventure— stands outside their code of conduct. College and living away from the family home is likely contrary to what's acceptable. Angus, however, is a century past due in terms of picking up the plow and hitching the harrow, in continuing to live on the property where he was born, and he's following a long succession of family who worked this land, living and dying here.

"Where do you fly-fish around here?" I ask Angus.

"He goes to the nearby river with one of the neighbors," Donna says. "Gets out a couple of times a year."

"Yeah, what Mom says," he replies, giving her words a dull punctuation.

Though I'm careful to eat slowly, I'm finished before the others. Donna and even Jennifer have reached for seconds on the potatoes and ham. Angus reaches his arm right behind them. "C'mon, chow down," Donna says. "Can't have you leaving here as skinny as when you came."

I stand behind my plate and take another small scoop of Jell-O, the table and food pulling me back in time. While Oma would have never served both ham and turkey—how could anyone be that extravagant—the rest of the table resembles something she would have put together. Not the lukewarm mashed potatoes but everything else, including the pie and cake.

"Where do you go after you leave here?" Donna asks.

"Jennifer returns to her studies in Madison, Wisconsin. I go back to San Diego to finish my work before I retire," I say.

"You work?" Angus asks.

"She's a lawyer," Donna says.

"Wow," Angus says. "Never knew a woman could do that."

"For the last thirty years," I say.

"Don't you have a husband?" he asks.

I smile, unsure if it's the incongruity of what's happening right now or a certain bitterness, maybe even resignation. "I do. He's a lawyer, too, but he's retired already."

Angus shakes his head and glances toward Jennifer. "You going to be a lawyer too?"

"Not sure," Jennifer says. "Need to get through college first."

Angus turns to his mother. "Did you ever want to do something like that, Mama?"

Donna lets out a snort. "Never," she says. She lifts another fork filled with mashed potatoes.

Her single word ends the conversation, and we finish the meal in silence. Finally Donna rises with her empty plate and comes around the table to get mine. While she clears the plates away, I turn toward Angus.

"What do you do for fun, Angus?"

"Fly-fish some." He grins at Jennifer. "Play with the dogs. Do puzzles. Read comic books."

The weight of our differences hangs over the room. We haven't even edged toward politics, which I'm sure would be a firebrand. However long the rest of the visit lasts, it will be both polite and superficial. In fact, I can't recall the last time I was blamed for being who I am.

There's a moment after Donna moves toward the kitchen's crowded sink that Jennifer catches my eye. Just that. A look between the two of us. I sense that she, too, is feeling the cloak of some ancient disloyalty heavy on her shoulders. We are marked now. College. Professions. The big city. Whatever hope this visit held, whatever eagerness we brought with us that we'd be able to put together the family's puzzle seems lost in this moment. More likely buried the same way Oma's glass Ball jars were secreted to the family cellar. We only dared lift out one at a time then, and the heavy cellar door would slam back into place once we surfaced with whatever small jar we'd been given permission to retrieve.

Chapter Twenty-Two

JENNIFER AND I ALLOW DONNA to shoo us onto the front porch where the two large sofas wait. Jennifer picks up a comic book. Maybe she's thinking what I'm thinking: Gretta back in Myra has been our best hope for getting close to family history.

Angus sits down beside Jennifer on the couch and glances over her shoulder at the comic book. *"Tom and Jerry*'s my favorite."

Jennifer nods and smiles.

I don't need to be a psychologist to see that this nearly fifty-year-old man has probably never been far from the farm or to understand why his mother seems incredibly protective. It also explains their isolation. This was an incredible stretch for Donna to invite us to stay. She was probably relieved when Jennifer said we'd only be here for one night.

The sliced cake and pie return on a tray along with a pitcher of iced tea and floating lemon slices. "My specialty," Donna says. Her broad grin erases whatever pall hung over the dining table.

"Your sweets remind me of Oma's kuchen . . . I mean Marta's . . . when I was a girl."

"I only bake those on holidays. These things were in the deep freeze. Always stock up in winter when it's too cold and turning on the oven takes the chill out of the house."

"I'm going to pass," Jennifer says. "I have a stomachache." She puts her hand on her belly and leans back against a pillow. Her smile is weak when she says, "Think I ate too much."

"You can have your dessert later," Donna says.

While Donna shows Jennifer to the bathroom, Angus busies himself with the *Tom and Jerry* comic book that Jennifer left on the sofa. I pull my phone out of my purse and check my emails. I've been so wound up in searching for the graves that I've only checked my phone a couple of times a day. There are four bars here, which is better than we had in Myra. Maybe we're closer to a cell tower on a nearby farm.

Two new phone messages from Stan. One that the divorce papers arrived unsigned. *What was the blood about?* However, the second one came a half-hour ago. Seems his intended lies in a Reno hospital, cramping and bleeding so badly it looks as though she may lose the child. I sit back against the couch like I've been punched in the stomach. This was the justification for the divorce. They could have their child and start a new life. If the child goes away, what then? Stan is now two weeks past the six-week waiting period, except I haven't signed the papers yet. Even if everything turns upside down, would I ever take him back?

Jennifer returns before Donna. She sits next to me and whispers close to my ear, "I don't want to stay here, Oma. This place is spooky."

"Not what we're used to," I say.

"Can we go back to the motel?"

"Of course. But what's the problem?"

"Thank you, Oma." She puts her hand on my good arm. "I'd just feel better if it was the two of us. Air-conditioning will help too." She hesitates and leans closer to whisper, "Have you been in the bathroom?"

"Is something wrong?"

"A board in the floor is missing. You're looking right down at the ground."

I bend over and kiss her cheek. "For sure, we'll have to leave." I laugh. "Would be just like me to get up in the middle of the night and fall through that hole in the floor."

Donna returns and refills my iced tea. The cold glass against my hand feels like a miniature air conditioner. For the first time I notice the untouched plate with a generous piece of pie and a piece of cake that sits in front of me. "Quite a combination," I say before recalling that my sense of humor can be a little sarcastic. "Looks delicious."

I start with the apple pie. Its homemade lattice crust is like Oma's. Angus sits on the couch eating his dessert from a dinner plate, as does Donna. "Hard to believe this is the house that Great-granduncle Herman built," I say.

"You can see that the bathroom floor has nearly rotted through. Just haven't had a chance to get it fixed. Angus and I make do, but it's not the safest when you have company."

"Does that mean the basement doesn't go all the way under the house?" I ask.

"Right. I think they left it that way thinking they'd keep the chicken coops under there in the winter. Easier to feed the chickens and get the eggs."

"Do you live in Duluth?" Angus asks.

I laugh when I say, "No, not ever. I live in California."

"That's a long ways away," Angus says.

"Probably why I don't get back here more often than every thirty years."

Angus looks at his mother. "Can I have more pie?"

"There won't be any left for breakfast," she says. "Besides, what if Jennifer wants a slice?"

"Okay," he says.

"Isn't it time to feed the chickens?" Donna asks.

He pulls himself up from the couch by leaning against the armrest. He has to be at least two-hundred-seventy-five pounds, which explains why the armrest sits at an angle. "You'll still be here when I get back, won't you?"

"Of course," I say.

"I'm going with you," Jennifer says.

Donna and I remain silent while they leave the front porch. She turns to glance down the hall toward the mudroom and stays turned until she hears the screen door slam behind them. "Can't really take him off the place. He's slow, as you can tell."

"Must be hard for you to get away."

"It is. I have to take him with me. But folks around here know him and accept him the way he is."

"That's good," I say, not knowing what else to say. "Do you ever get lonely out here?"

"Not really," she says. "I have Angus and the place. We're kind of lazy, as you can see. But things could be worse. They were when my husband was alive."

My forehead must be a question mark.

"He couldn't accept Angus the way he is, and he used to beat him pretty bad."

"I'm sorry," I say. "That's awful."

"Was," she says. "We're happier, just the two of us."

"Did something happen when Angus was younger?" I ask.

"Actually, before he was born." She hesitates and looks down at her large hands. She rubs her coarse knuckles. "Probably shouldn't tell you this, but it was a late abortion gone wrong."

"I'm really sorry." I sit up taller, straighter.

"It's okay," she says. "Remember my oldest sister, Rena?"

"Vaguely."

"She tried giving me an abortion with a knitting needle. We got caught just after she started. Mama beat the living tar out of both of us."

It takes a moment for me to realize I'm holding my breath.

"Seems we did just enough damage." She continues to work her knuckles. "The sad part is I knew his father was a bad man. I was just trying to get free of him." She meets my eyes. "Didn't work."

Her suddenly sad eyes and her revelation are so unexpected that I'm frozen where I sit. When I finally find my voice, I say, "I'm so very sorry, Donna."

There's nothing else to say.

The pie sits on the end table, half-eaten, with the chocolate cake untouched. There is no freedom here unless death carries it into the house. I have no words to convey the sadness I feel in my stomach. It could have been me. Or Jennifer. Whatever judgment I held against Donna a half-hour ago has disappeared inside her brief revelation while Angus is out dealing with the chickens and Jennifer's likely looking on or helping. How, then, do we make a graceful exit after she just opened her wounded heart to me? Not that she's looking for pity, just the grace of one woman understanding another.

I scoot to the edge of the sofa and reach across the coffee table where my dessert waits. I lift her hands off her lap. I take them in mine. They are rough and chapped and tell a whole different story than my hands ever will. She starts to take them back, but I hold tight. "It's okay," I say. My eyes on hers; hers on mine. This is my cousin. My blood. She's suffered in ways that neither Jennifer nor I can ever imagine, though we've all three been in the same room when the lights went out on our youthful innocence.

I hold her hands in mine, gently as I can, and look into her gray eyes. There's a hint of tears behind her glasses. She finally withdraws her hands and sits back against the couch, her hands now in her lap like two ill-adapted fish figuring out how they got where they are and how they'll ever find their way back into the water.

"Seems to run in the family," I say, not knowing what else to say. The words fly out of my mouth before I know it.

"What runs in the family?" she asks.

An embarrassing heat climbs my neck. "Never mind," I say. Donna begins to pick up the plates but leaves mine when she sees my dessert remains unfinished. She carries off Angus's plate and her own to the kitchen. She returns with a glass full of ice.

We're suddenly quiet. Embarrassed from saying too much and not enough. Knowing each other but not knowing each other. Both of us so different and not. Just two women in a world of women with our common stories.

"Don't know what's wrong with Jennifer. Probably just her period," I say. "Said she's cramping. I didn't bring any supplies and now the store in town is closed."

Donna picks up the comic books and straightens them into a pile. "Can find a way to make do," she says. "One of you could sleep out here on the other couch along with Angus, but his snoring would wake the dead."

Thank you, Donna, for that little gift. "Probably best to take her back to Dickinson tonight," I say. "I hope you won't be offended. Seems we're just getting started with our visit."

"You have to do what you have to do," she says. She pulls the newspapers into a pile.

"How long do you think you'll hang on to this place, Donna? Not that I know where you'd go from here."

"I'll probably die here," she says. She looks up from the newspapers piled on her lap. "Thing is, I don't know what will happen to Angus. He doesn't really have any place to go but here. He'd never be able to stay on the place alone."

"What about the rest of your family? Have they moved away?"

"Rena's kids have a place near Myra. But they're older than Angus, and they've got their own kids to care for them."

"If you sold the place to one of them, would it bring enough income that you could arrange a place for Angus?"

"Can't even think about selling the place," she says. "It's been in the family forever."

I lean forward from where I'm sitting, my hand on the sofa's arm, my bandaged arm cradled on my lap. "I know you said on the phone before we came that you'd like to sell and use the money differently. So, this is a big dilemma, isn't it?"

She nods. "It's that time of life."

She stares at the newspapers piled on her lap. For a moment she seems to have drifted away. Then she asks, "Does your arm hurt?"

"Only when we were digging in the cemetery," I say. I lift the arm. I'm sheepish and for a moment don't know what to say. "Truth is, I cut it on a wineglass."

"How the heck did you ever do that?" she asks. "I could see a finger or a hand, but an arm?"

"I was in the bathtub. Drinking wine when I shouldn't have been."

Donna shakes her head, her eyes closed. She makes the same clucking noise Oma often did with her tongue against the roof of her mouth. That gesture alone tells me that this is way outside of her experience. I blush and wish I hadn't been so honest.

"Good thing you have another driver," she says.

It seems we've fallen into a deep valley between two mountain peaks and don't quite know how to get out of it. The silence remains uncomfortable as she shuffles the newspapers in her lap, looking at them but not looking at them. "Did you find my great-great-grandad's grave? Herman's?"

I'm relieved when she breaks the silence. "Not yet, but a woman at the church told us that he's probably buried in another cemetery. Mirabelle is her name. Do you know her?"

"Busybody, that woman is, and trouble. Don't know what you told her, but whatever it is, it will be all over town."

"It's true she wasn't very pleasant," I say. "Do you ever go to church in town?"

"Not for years . . . since Angus left high school when he was sixteen. Wasn't any point of him continuing. We only go to town once in a while. We go to Dickinson about once a month for groceries and whatever else we need. There's nothing in Myra except those fishing flies."

"Whatever happened to your sister Rena?"

"Died five years ago from a heart attack. She had diabetes too. Dr. James is after all of us to eat some ridiculous diet none of us will ever eat. Heart attack is what usually gets us in the end," she says. "From the looks of it, that's not something you'll ever have to worry about."

"Do you remember if that's what killed Uncle Herman?"

"Cancer got him. Stomach cancer. Barely fifty when he died. Great-great-grandmother Ketcha carried on for another twenty years. She was a tough one."

"That's what I've heard."

My stomach rumbles with a kind of panic. It seems there should be other questions I need to ask, but I can't think of a thing. They'll all come flooding back to me the minute Jennifer and I drive down the road on our way back to Dickinson, the minute I see the sunflowers rise up from the fields. Truth be told, I'll likely never see this woman again. There will be nothing from me beyond a thank-you note I'll write when I get home. The sadness of connections lost across generations and, likewise, the geography that once anchored our family fills my chest. Behind the loss, there's an urgency to get back to where we were when she revealed her attempted abortion. The rawness and truth of that moment. The intimacy of shared secrets held for one's entire history.

This awkward silence seems such an unfinished way to close the history book on our family. I'm disappointed in myself for not thinking ahead and for being so distracted by the divorce business. Without funerals or weddings, there's no natural way to meet and pick up the threads of what feels like an unfinished afghan Mom crocheted. Yet I'm sitting here across from my cousin, whom I'll likely never see again, and in the silence, a moment so fleeting, she has finally picked up one of the newspapers in her lap and started to read it. She probably doesn't see or even care about these vague possibilities that are slipping away. An urgency inside me betrays my sudden need to find the right question. Any question.

"Did you ever know my Uncle Ivan?" I ask.

"Vaguely," she says. "He came back to the farm once to see Mom. His cousin he called her though how removed they were I can't say." She says nothing for a while, her eyes back on the newspaper. "Seems he left quite an impression when he moved away. Can't say the town welcomed him back with open arms."

Though I know exactly why that happened, I ask, "Any idea why?"

"It's a bad thing in a small town when you step out of line," she says. "If you know what I mean."

"No, I don't know what you mean."

"Folks said he was kind of a . . . pansy."

"That he was gay?"

"Ho-mo-sexual," she says, stretching each vowel as far as it will go.

"Guess that would have been a scandal."

"No kidding," she says. "When Cousin Walter turned out the same, the town blamed your uncle Ivan. Said that he was turning all the young boys in the wrong direction."

"Guess I never heard about that," I say.

"Not surprised. It was hush-hush."

I'm silent for a minute. It doesn't feel right to leave homosexuality sitting on the table like a bad batch of sauerkraut. "Being gay isn't a crime," I say.

Donna stares at me like I've just blasphemed. "That must be a California thing," she says. She stands, the newspapers overflowing her arms. She starts to step toward the main entry. "For sure, a California thing."

We gaze at each other for what feels like a long minute, neither one of us saying anything until the back screen door slams.

Angus lumbers down the hallway, his straw hat back on his head. "Chickens got out," he says. "Took me forever to get those doggone hens back in their cage. Can't find the rooster."

"He'll come back if the coyotes don't get him first," Donna says.

"Will serve him right," Angus says. "Jennifer was a big help."

"Her grandma's taking her back to town," Donna says.

"Doggone," Angus says. "Thought we could go fly-fishing."

"Maybe another time," I say.

"Will you come back tomorrow?" he asks.

"Let's see how we do at the cemetery."

"Wow, just when we started having fun."

"It's okay, Angus," Donna says. "Maybe you and I will watch a movie tonight. Would you like that?"

"*Tom and Jerry*?"

"No, something even better than *Tom and Jerry*."

Why I choose this moment to rise from the sofa, I'll never know. "Sorry, I need to excuse myself," I say. "A phone call I need to return."

I walk to the back of the house in search of the back door. When I pass the bathroom, I can see what Jennifer pointed out. A huge plank is missing in the middle of the bathroom floor. *How in the world do they manage? Are there no men around to help them?*

Then, I register my automatic thought. My own sexist statement.

On the other side of the chicken coop where I'm away from the house, I dial Stan. "Sorry I didn't text first," I say. "I'm at my cousin's and had to come outside to talk to you."

"Glad you called," he says.

From the tone of his voice things aren't going the way he planned. Depression isn't new to Stan. It's been an ongoing occurance ever since he retired. Now, with the impending death of an unborn child, his new life could pop like a giant balloon.

"I'm sorry to hear your friend isn't doing well," I say, wondering what I call this woman who's not yet his wife, who's too old to be a girlfriend, who is the identified interloper in our marriage. Why do I even call her his friend?

"She's already miscarried," he says. The reluctance in his voice resists admitting the painful fact.

"I don't know what to say, Stan, except that I'm sorry for her. For you."

Even as I say the words, I realize I couldn't have said these things two weeks ago. Instead, I would have been raging at him, glad he had cause to be miserable, glad his dreams were smashing to bits around him. That he was getting what I thought he deserved after destroying the life I thought we had.

"Is she going to be okay?"

"Other than a tremendous loss of blood, the doctor says she'll be fine."

"Good," I say.

Silence follows. What more is there to say? Neither one of us is who we thought we were before this event. Before Duluth and all that's happened here. "I am very sorry, Stan. I know you were counting on this." I can't say *to begin your new life.*

"Thanks, Marta. I'm glad you can say that."

More silence. Then I say, "I'm afraid this doesn't change my feeling about the house."

"I didn't really think you were going to change."

"Not about the house," I say.

"We'll have to talk about this," he says. In that moment I'm aware that the *we* no longer includes *me.*

I let that sink in. "Call me when the two of you have had time to talk. No hurry."

"Appreciate your calling back," he says. He seems unable to ask about where I am, about Jennifer, least of all the original family farm. His new life completely absorbs him now. My stomach roils just thinking about that. I'm no longer part of his story; every-thing's now about their story. If nothing else, the tragedy will either hold them together tighter or pull them apart. But it's not my concern today or tomorrow either.

My watch says seven-thirty when we wave out the window to Angus and Donna. We leave so much unsaid or unwelcome behind us, but not the heat or the dust. Jennifer drives while I sit in the passenger seat with a Ball jar of ice water in my hands while the air conditioner cools the car's interior. "Sorry about leaving, Oma."

I glance over at her as we swing back onto the gravel road. The car thermometer records ninety-nine degrees outside. "If you hadn't said something, I would have found an excuse," I say. "They're very sweet people, and I'm glad we had a chance to meet them and see their farm, that part of our family history. But I'd surely have fallen through the floor in that bathroom."

We both laugh. Jennifer turns toward me. "Angus was sweet. Do you know what happened to him?"

I don't say anything for a minute. "Things happen sometimes," I say. "Always sad when they do."

"Think we'll ever see them again?"

"Probably not."

"That makes leaving even sadder," Jennifer says.

"How's that?" I ask.

"Staying connected," she says. "Being family."

"I thought you wanted to be as far away from family as you could get."

She says nothing for a while. "From my family . . . at least for a while," she says. "Except you."

The slanted light across the sunflowers turns their faces black on the underside where the sun has passed over. We still have a few more hours before the sun goes down but, for the blackbirds, the day is close to finished as they swarm into the few trees along the road. We'll return to Myra tomorrow and finish what we came to do, then check in with Gretta at the store to say our goodbyes. This time, though, we'll bring trowels and gardening gloves from Dickinson. We can't depend on other folks to give us what we need.

Chapter Twenty-Three

Monday, June 17

WE DIG DEEP AROUND THE Schroeder graves where the embedded grass stubbornly clings to the ground, the clumps having held tight for longer than I want to think. Likely since Oma was alive. This time I have a blanket under my knees. Though I handed another to Jennifer, she insists she doesn't need it.

She sits back on her legs. "What will happen to the graves after we leave?"

I sit back as well and wipe perspiration from my forehead. My right arm aches. "I'm not sure, Jennifer. Maybe we can make a deal with Gretta. I'd be happy to pay her to keep them cleaned up. We have a better chance with her than the elders at the church."

"She'll outlive them is what you mean."

It feels good to laugh after both of us have been so serious lately, especially since we came to Myra. That man the first day who repeated gossip about Uncle Ivan set the tone. He simply preceded Mirabelle at the church. Going to Donna's and recalling that last conversation remains sad and unfinished in the way loose ends sometimes remain that way forever. The cats—let's not forget the cats—and gracious Gretta. She's been like the sunflowers, a ray of humor and welcome. "Yes, she'll outlive them. That's a more direct way of saying it."

"What then, Oma? This town looks like it's dying. Gretta's the only person we've seen who's under sixty, and I can't see her staying here forever."

"As long as she has those cats, she'll be here."

Now we're both laughing. "Let's take a break."

We sit under the oak tree that's become our rest stop. Jennifer opens the cooler and takes out a Coke. "I'll have one of those," I say.

There's surprise on her face. "You sure? I've never seen you drink the sugary stuff."

"Blame it on the heat."

We lean against the tree, drinking our sodas. "We have at least three generations here, Oma. Maybe more we don't know about."

"True," I say. "My generation is missing and so is yours, thank heaven."

"What are graveyards good for anyhow?" she asks.

"Good question." I reach into the cooler and take out one of the sandwiches, handing half to Jennifer. "In previous times cemeteries were the place where people paid their respects. Remembered those who came before them. An honoring, you could say. But as we became a mobile society, families moved away from where their ancestors had put down roots, and graveyards often became what this one has become . . . overgrown and neglected, never visited and, basically, forgotten. You heard Cousin Donna. Close as she lives, she never comes here. In fact, she said, 'Dead is dead.' Unless you're into genealogy, which is usually just one or two people in a generation, no one even knows where the grave sites are. I have an aunt on my dad's side buried in a large cemetery in Orange County, California. The last time I looked for her grave, I gave up. I also have two uncles who belonged to my dad buried in the same cemetery. I've never even seen their graves. And when I think of all the land and all the miles of cemeteries that exist in this country, I'm amazed. Except for special holidays, I don't know that people visit them anymore."

"Why don't you tell me again how each one of these relatives died? Seems like just remembering them will make our work worthwhile."

I have to think back to the stories I heard from Oma and what I know from my own history. When I think of the eldest great, Great-grandfather Schroeder, I hesitate for a minute, instinctively putting my hand around the bulge in my pocket. "Your great-great-grand-father Schroeder shot himself."

"Wow," Jennifer says.

"According to Oma, he couldn't live with the shame of having gambled away the family gold he'd been entrusted to bring from Russia to America. He wasn't yet fifty."

I fold the wrapper from our sandwich and toss it back into the sack, replacing the sack in the cooler. "As a consequence Oma said that Katerina, my great-grandmother, Oma's mother, died of a broken heart. That's what they called severe depression then. Probably closer to the truth than a fancy diagnosis."

"Sounds romantic and tragic at the same time." Jennifer's thoughtful for a moment. "I can see why someone would die of heartbreak. You know, the same shame and disappointment that killed Great-great-grandfather."

"You're probably right," I say. "I already told you that Uncle Leo, who's buried between them, was Oma's younger brother. She said he'd always had bad lungs. Seems he was on his way by train to a sanitorium in New York State before his hoped-for return to Russia. It was during the Spanish flu epidemic, and Uncle Leo was already vulnerable."

"Really, Oma. I should be taking notes."

"You are, after all, the history buff," I say. "We could at least photograph the graves in case you ever want to write something or even come back."

She's thoughtful for a few minutes. "You hardly have to go outside of your own family to know what the world was like at any particular time. The 1918 flu epidemic, two world wars, and the Great Depression."

I nod in agreement. I never thought of it that way, but she's absolutely right. "Let's finish cleaning up these graves, then find someplace where we don't have to sit in the heat."

Jennifer cocks her head and gives me a strange look. "Oma, are you showing your privileged self?"

I laugh. "Guess I am."

"First, though, tell me about your oma."

"Oma's real name was Marta. I'm her namesake. She lived until she was about eighty-two, a long time considering she ate so much pastry and whipped cream and butter. She died of a heart attack just like Cousin Donna talked about with the rest of the family. I think I've told you why I couldn't come to her funeral, and why Uncle Ivan couldn't come. But she was here with her church and friends, people she had known all her life. She told me when I was a young girl that she wasn't afraid of death. She always had the Lord with her."

"What do you mean by that?"

"She was a woman of faith. I'd rather say that than religious, which is what the rest of the family said. But they didn't know her the way I knew her. This town and its people were her life. She lived here from the time she was fourteen until she died. I can't be in this town without feeling her spirit walking the streets, sitting in the church we visited, and at the church basement table drinking tea and eating donuts with the ladies. She's still here with her dead family. Someone needed to tend the graves she always said. Everybody else, your Great-Grandmother Irene and Aunt Ada, left. They were some of the first to go shortly after the war. They hated it here." I'm thoughtful for a moment, gazing off into the sun beyond the shade trees. "Maybe Myra reminded them of everything they wanted to forget. The poverty and family discord. My grandmother clucking her tongue at them. They simply wanted a larger life and World War II opened that up for them."

Jennifer pivots on the ground, her arms around her knees, her long jeans covering the mosquito bites of the last few days. "Why would they hate it . . . such a strong word."

"Remember Mirabelle yesterday in the church?"

"Yes. But, what about her?"

"It's an attitude, I guess. You could see it in Cousin Donna or maybe you didn't since you were with Angus. Why fuss with the world when everything you need is right here. The world is a dangerous and sinful place. Those beliefs are pretty old and popular in many agricultural parts of the country. Maybe they go back to the reasons the immigrants left their native country. Your Great-Grandother Irene would absolutely cringe at the idea of coming back here to live. So would you."

"At least San Diego doesn't have mosquitoes," she says slapping at her arm. She's thoughtful for a moment. "I honestly don't know what I'd do here. I guess you could say that I've grown up living in another world. Liking the excitement, the opportunities, the utter freedom to be myself."

"True," I say. "Here, your DNA would tell you to carry on the way generations before you did. Change is often an unwelcome word in places like this."

"That's a tough one, Oma." She rocks on her butt, her hands still clasped around her knees.

"Did you notice how people reacted to your pink hair?"

"I just thought they were being funny."

"They were dead serious."

She gazes off into the distance, past the cemetery where we sit and an adjacent one, toward the only highway in and out of town. The amassing mosquitoes bring her back into today. "I can't imagine who you would be if you'd stayed."

I laugh, but there's an edge of sadness in my chest. A tightening. "I think I knew I couldn't stay here once my father took us away, especially after we moved to California. Here, you only do things one way and there's no deviation. It was a very big deal when Oma started baking her pastries for a restaurant ten miles away. She'd learned to drive Uncle Ozzie's big Buick to take the pastries to the café. You heard Mirabelle mention her yesterday although you didn't know that's who she was talking about. You can imagine what it was like for Aunt Ada to get an abortion in this country."

"Bet she had to go out of town."

"She did. Your Grandmother Irene took her to Dickinson. It was a big secret and then it was a scandal when people began to make up stories about whether or not she was pregnant after her husband died flying over Germany during the war."

I shift my hip until I'm able to reach into my pocket and pull out the uncomfortable bulge that's been bothering me, the prongs around the jewels poking through the bunting and purple silk bag. "I have something for you," I say. "I've been waiting for the right moment."

"A surprise?"

"More than a surprise," I say. "Something precious."

I begin to untie the silk bag's strings and then to lift out the white bunting. What's inside weighs down my hand. I shouldn't be surprised when unexpected emotion works its way into my throat. My chest suddenly feels heavy.

"I was waiting until I came to Madison to give this to you. But this seems like the best place of all."

"I love surprises," she says, her smile eager and her one dimple showing inside the tree's shade. "What is it, Oma?"

"My oma gave this to me just before I married your grandfather. She called it a special gift across the generations." I pull away the bunting that sticks to the jeweled prongs. Jennifer moves closer and sits on her knees in front of me.

"It's an Easter egg," I say. "But not an ordinary Easter egg."

When the egg is finally revealed in all its brilliance, the jewels gleam in the afternoon light. The diamond bands glitter and the sapphires seem bluer than blue. I stretch my hand toward her. "This is for you."

She takes the egg into her cupped hands and holds it in front of her, allowing the glimmer of diamonds and sapphires to shine under the midday sun, her smile one of delight. Exactly what I'd hoped for. "Oma," she says. "I don't know what to say."

"There's a story that goes with it," I say. "It seems that one of the greats, Grandfather Grozinski, gave it to his granddaughter, my grandmother Marta, on her fourteenth birthday before her family left Russia. She carried it with her during their long and difficult journey across the Atlantic to Ellis Island. Despite the desperately poor times during the Great Depression and World War II, Oma and my Great-Grandpa Albert never hocked it to help with their desperate needs. When she gave it to me on my wedding day, I knew that someday I would pass it on to you, my granddaughter. This feels like the right place to do that, partly in celebration of this trip to Myra but, mostly, because of our precious friendship . . . yes, our friendship."

Jennifer finds my eyes, now blurry with emotion. "Thank you, Oma," she says. She holds the egg in one hand and reaches with her other hand for my free hand. "I love it, I . . . don't quite know what else to say." She smiles at me in a way that allows me to imagine an older, more mature Jennifer. "What do I do with it?"

I take her hands in my one hand, dirt under our fingernails. I feel along the callous on her right index finger. "You can't wear it," I say, laughing. "Maybe you do what I've done all these years. You find a special place where you keep it until you have a daughter or granddaughter of your own." I lower my head and gaze closer at her. "Not even your grandfather knows about this egg. It's always been my special secret. Something that belonged only to me, no matter what."

"Wow," she says. "Where did your oma keep it? Where did you keep it?"

"Oma had a special shelf hidden in the house . . . that's what she told me. Except for Grandpa Albert, who I barely remember, and my Uncle Ozzie who was killed in World War II, no one else knew about the egg or where it was. I had a special safe deposit box that only my legal assistant knew about. She had instructions to give it to you if anything happened to me."

Jennifer is silent, her eyes on the egg with a quick glance toward me from time to time. "I'm so grateful, Oma." Her fingers explore the rough surface where the prongs lift the jewels. She hesitates. "But I confess, I'm afraid that Madison isn't the right place for it."

"I can take it back and keep it where it was," I say. "Just know that it's there waiting for you when you're ready." *When you're ready.* The words release the tension that I've been holding onto and keeping silent deep inside my belly. What emerges aren't tears, but a deep sigh. I can finally let go. "You now have the stories that go with the egg."

She glances at the headstones behind us. "My Oma, your oma and your oma's mother. All together in the same place." She's shy for a moment. "Almost like to was meant to be."

I smile at her youth, her innocence, a larger life already knocking on her door. My heart feels too big for my chest. Heart travel. This is what it means.

She stretches forward and hugs me. It's an awkward hug considering she's still on her knees and my legs are stretched in front of me. Her sweaty arms surround my neck, until she's close but not too close, the egg still tight inside her fist.

GUARDING THE ONE-WAY BRIDGE OUT of town, blackbirds—a seeming flock of them—hang onto a branch that sways over the bridge. Like they've been waiting for us these last few days.

Waiting while we pass the city limits. I can't help but wonder if they or their predecessors were here the day my family left town. Three little girls in the back seat. Past the Texaco where the night lights had come on not long before, down the main street with Jake's Tavern and Hubner's Market. First Bible Church across the street. The Lutheran Cemetery with its wrought iron crosses. The corner where Mom spilled the bike and the eggs broke over me. Somehow, the blackbirds bring some humor to the stuck place I've had in my throat. My chest so swollen with what? Happiness? Sadness? The bittersweet of things ending and beginning? Eyes straight ahead toward I-95, Jennifer's feet rest once again on the dash. Her pink hair and ear studs. We've rolled the windows down despite the heat. This moment will live on just like the silence that guides the car down the road.

Once on the freeway, we're quiet. The fields spread wide and peacefully into the distance. All the tractors seem at rest and parked beside the barns. Suppertime is likely happening in the lighted kitchens. The houses stand back from the road like sentinels in a green desert. There's a kind of quiet that sinks into the belly, a quiet that lets you know your roots are fastened tight and still holding on. That you're always safe on the land. The roots in the land. An inheritance that goes as deep as blood.

ALSO BY DIAN GREENWOOD

Double Fire Burning (Press 22, 1979)

About the Carleton Sisters (She Writes, 2023)

Forever Blackbirds (Travelers Moon, 2024)

ABOUT THE AUTHOR

Dian Greenwood has been writing poetry since age fourteen. She studied writing at San Francisco State University (BA and MA), then did further studies in counseling psychology. The early focus on poetry led her to fiction. She is the author of *About the Carleton Sisters* (She Writes Press, 2023), *Forever Blackbirds* (Travelers Moon Press, 2024) and the sequel, *Blackbird Whistling* (Travelers Moon Press, September 2025). Dian's essays have appeared in *The Big Smoke,* an online magazine. She publishes a monthly Substack, *It's Never Too Late*. Dian writes and works as a life coach in Portland, Oregon.

ACKNOWLEDGMENTS

This novel began in Duluth, Minnesota, where I studied for a week with Robert Olen Butler and had the good fortune to meet Chin-Sun Lee (*Upcountry*, the Unnamed Press). What started in Duluth as a short story grounded in a particularly bad travel experience through Denver became *Blackbird Whistling*. Proof that, for a writer, even negative experiences are fodder for the written page.

During the years in which this novel was written, we lost two significant figures in the Portland writing community. Our dear friend, Robert Hill (*The Remnants*, Forest Avenue Press), passed first. This last year, we lost Dangerous Writing teacher/mentor Tom Spanbauer (*Now Is the Hour*, Houghton Mifflin), whose teaching and novels spanned decades. Both writers influenced my stories, my writing and my sensibilities.

My thanks to the Henry Writers—Liz Scott, Robert Hill, Gigi Little, Laura Stanfill, Steve Arndt, Kathleen Lane, David Ciminello and Sara Guest—who were first readers along with my sister, Peggy McMillen. As happens, the short-story-turned-novel became part of the *Blackbird* duology begun with *Forever Blackbirds*, a tribute to my grandmother and all immigrants who land on these sometimes unwelcoming shores. *Blackbird Whistling* concludes the original generational story. Special thanks to Suzy Vitello and Gina Walters, the editors. Again, to Laura Stanfill and Gigi Little for shepherding the book into publication. To Mary Desch and Nancy Townsley, also early readers, for their moral support. To Elise LeSage for her steady hand with marketing. Always, thanks to my family for quietly supporting my obsession with writing. Thanks also to the Oregon bookstores, San Diego Writer's Ink, Seattle's Third Place Books and book clubs for hosting me. Most of all, my heartfelt thanks to you, the readers.

BOOK CLUB QUESTIONS

1. Marta Bufford, granddaughter of Marta Gottlieb, enters the novel as protagonist. What is your initial reaction to her?

2. Is this a geographic part of the United States that you're familiar with? How? If not, did you understand enough from the landscape descriptions to satisfy your curiosity?

3. When Marta is first introduced to the leaders at the university president's home, were you drawn to the two men who lead the meditation seminar? Did you have reason to doubt them?

4. What were your thoughts about the role alcohol use played in the novel? Was that surprising?

5. When Jennifer confides her abortion, were you sympathetic? Did her somewhat casual attitude surprise you? What was different about Marta's experience? Her cousin Donna's?

6. What kinds of things did Marta Bufford learn from her Oma

Marta Gottlieb? How did Marta's remembrances of her grandmother enhance your sense of who Marta the second is as a
person?

7. What were some of the underlying themes that *Blackbird
    Whistling* was meant to convey? Did those themes dovetail
    with those in *Forever Blackbirds?*

8. Could you enjoy *Blackbird Whistling* without having read
    Forever Blackbirds?